THE KEY OF AMATAHNS

ELISABETH WHEATLEY

www.argetallam.com
www.facebook.com/Argetallam

Copyright 2011 by Elisabeth Wheatley
Published by Chengalera Press

ISBN-10   0-615-49902-3
ISBN-13   9780615499024

PROLOGUE

Janir didn't move. She remained absolutely still, staring down at the white, polished marble. If she moved it would only make Lucan angrier and then he would strike her again. Her tormenter stood over her like a glowering tower of disdain. She bit back her tears and tried to maintain a stoic pose. Janir was sure her life could not become any more horrid.

"Weakling," Lucan hissed. "Are you certain that you are indeed the Lord Argetallam's daughter? Or perhaps it is merely that the Brevian half of you is greater?"

Contempt and unchecked scorn were unmistakable in his voice.

"Ah, yes. Your mother is that Brevian wench. Isn't she?" he continued.

"Stop," Janir quietly pleaded. Her lip was bleeding where her face had hit the marble floor when he shoved her down.

"Stop?' Is that all she says?" She could almost see her half-brother shrugging in a gesture of help-lessness toward the other children gathered around the white pillars to watch. Tensing, she heard him walk around her before the toe of his small boot was driven maliciously into her back.

She shouted with the sting when his blow landed, but quickly hushed her scream.

"You are unworthy to be our next leader. You will lead us to ruin. Would you have us endure the abuses of our enemies, as you endure mine?"

Though he was barely eight, Lucan spoke with the tongue of a great orator. It often sent chills down Janir's spine to hear her brother talk like their father.

With desperation Janir groaned and looked helplessly toward her older cousin, Emilla, and her father's other child, Kestrell. But they both just stood gazing transfixed at Lucan, Janir's half-brother. He shrugged.

"You see?" Lucan pointed down at Janir's hair, it shone like spun gold when brushed and in the light. "Even this seeks to remind us of her Brevian heritage."

Maliciously, he seized a fistful of Janir's hair and jerked her forward before releasing her. Janir screamed again and resumed her motionless pose. "You have more than just the fair coloring of a Brevian woman, you have the heart of one!"

"Our father had a Brevian mother too," Janir weakly pointed out. Lucan ignored her and went on.

"What say you, my half-sister?" he sneered.

"I think," Janir moaned, repositioning herself so that she could look Lucan in the eye. "I think that my master will not be happy when he hears about this."

"*Our* master, you little vixen." Lucan would have struck her again, had not the massive mesquite double doors at the end of the foyer opened without

2

the slightest creaking and the Lord Argetallam himself entered.

He was a tall and dark man. A dark beard concealed whatever expression he might be making. His black cloak with chain mail beneath it showed that he had just returned from riding about his outposts. Boots covered with dust that was almost white, signified he had been to the western front. Again. Upon his entry, the Lord Argetallam surveyed the scene with eyes that reminded Janir of fog--gray, cold, and concealing.

The other children, who were standing around the thick white pillars which lined the hall, quickly scurried out of the room through the huge double doors at the other end. Lucan had been about to follow when the Lord Argetallam called to him.

"Lucan, my son." Without taking his eyes off the boy, the Lord Argetallam handed his cloak to an attendant. "Ernic," the Lord Argetallam barked to a by-standing page. "Fetch the girl's mother."

Lucan turned to face his father in the manner of a puppet fighting the strings of his puppeteer. "Yes, Master?" The boy's tone and face held defiance, fear, and submission at once. But even in his terror, his voice still held that eerie adult-like tone.

"While I am away, making business transactions to assure you and your sister's future, you are here preparing for that future. It would appear that you have been fighting your sister for practice. But, judging by her many bruises and the blood on her face, she is not your equal. Come; let us spar for a moment so that you may face a true challenge."

Janir's mother entered after the young page and went immediately to her daughter. She knelt beside the girl, gently brushed away tears, and comfortingly caressed Janir's forehead.

The Lord Argetallam caught Lucan in an iron grasp and brutally struck him, sending the boy rolling across the floor. Lucan was struggling to stop weeping, but couldn't help himself.

"Forgive me, Master," Lucan sobbed.

Janir noted her mother rising from her knees. "Mother, please, no!" Janir frantically whispered. Too late.

"My lord." Her mother interrupted strongly, but with a quaver of fear. The attendants who had accompanied Janir's father to the outposts stirred with agitation.

The Lord Argetallam paused, roughly gripping the collar of Lucan's tunic. Deliberately turning his head, Janir's father icily replied.

"You know I will punish my offspring as I see fit, Aryana," he hissed.

"Yes." Janir's mother was clearly afraid, but she kept the air of an empress about her as she replied. "But...I implore of you..."

"And you know that I allow for no insubordination. Either between future heir and future subject, or myself and those in my possession." The Lord Argetallam's chillingly even tone made Janir want to become invisible.

Aryana faltered. "The boy's mother instigates his actions. This is more her doing than his."

In a cold, emotionless voice, Janir's father replied.

"Your point is?"

Lucan whimpered quietly, staring up fearfully, yet with a controlled manner at the Lord Argetallam.

"You should not punish…" Aryana was cut off when the Lord Argetallam nearly threw Lucan down to whirl around and clamp an iron hand on her throat.

Janir wanted to be anywhere but in that room. When both parents were in the same place with her, she was unceasingly worried for her mother's sake. Janir's heart raced as she stared at her father with trepidation.

Aryana didn't look the Lord Argetallam in his face. He pulled her closer to him. She offered no resistance as he glared bitterly toward her downcast eyes. Janir's mother trembled slightly, not knowing what his next move would be. Those few moments seemed to drag on forever.

Lifting her face to meet his gaze, the Lord Argetallam surveyed Aryana with a coldly contemplative air. "Continue," Janir's father emotionlessly stated.

Aryana hesitated half a space. "The child is obeying his mother. It is she who should be reprimanded." Janir thought the suspense would kill her as her father observed her mother with an unreadable expression.

"Regardless, he should not direct such actions toward his future ruler. What say you to that?" the Lord Argetallam mused.

Aryana cautiously continued. "Yes, Master."

"What if I deem it suiting that you be punished for your rebellion?" Janir's father mildly inquired.

"You know I shall accept your will, my master. I always have," Aryana quietly replied. It was true. Janir could not recall a single instance in which her mother had defied her father. But by Aryana's even tone, it was clear that she stood by her earlier words. Janir felt like trembling, but fought to stay motionless.

"He beats our daughter, yet you risk my wrath to spare him pain," the Lord Argetallam murmured.

No one said anything. Aryana obediently stared up at Janir's father with a wearied fear.

"Strength such as you have is rare," he deliberately remarked. Janir breathed a little easier. "I chose the mother of my eldest child well." He drew her even closer and whispered something in her ear. Aryana's expression changed from one of fear to one of acceptance.

Pushing her back several steps before relinquishing his grasp on her throat, the Lord Argetallam surveyed Aryana silently. Janir thought she saw the slightest trace of admiration in his eye, but couldn't be sure.

"Summon Bricen to tend my son," the Lord Argetallam commanded one of his servants. "See to our daughter," he added dismissively to Aryana.

Aryana nodded stiffly and watched him file out of the room with his retinue. Within moments, Bricen came to shuffle away with Lucan. She glared bitterly at Janir and Aryana as she always did.

Shortly thereafter, in her mother's chambers, Janir sat on the soft bed with a poultice over her eye while her mother bathed a bruise on her arm. This chamber was the place Janir felt safest, the place she always came when afraid or upset. Even though the girl was supposed to have her own chambers now, she spent more time here than anywhere else. The silk curtains over the balcony were blowing freely in the wind behind them, while Janir traced patterns on the soft carpet with her bare foot. Although it seemed a happy, homey place to Janir, the girl had always thought her mother more regarded the sparkling walls and colorful tapestries as a prison.

All children think their mothers pretty, but Janir knew hers to be striking. With wavy and rich golden hair that fell below her shoulders, rose-red lips, fair skin with long, dark eyelashes, and a slender, feminine figure, there were not many women to compare with her. She was a fair lily amongst the darker roses of the palace. They had their own kind of beauty, but Janir still considered her mother to be without equal. She knelt before her daughter, staring up at Janir with pity.

"My poor child," Aryana sighed. "That little imp has given you another lashing."

"He's not so little, Mother, we're practically the same age, but he's been taller than me since we were two," Janir mumbled, glancing at her battered reflection in the smooth mirror which hung on the wall.

"Oh, but he is little, Janir," her mother contradicted. "Or at least, that is how he feels. He feels small and insignificant. That is why he lashes you. It

7

makes him feel big and important."

"I hate Lucan," Janir pouted.

"Never say that," Aryana scolded.

With confusion, Janir protested. "But he has done nothing but torment me. Our whole lives. Why shouldn't I hate him?"

Her mother sighed. "The child has an Argetallam for a father. And his Stlavish mother sees him only as a way to extend the legacy of her family into the Argetallam bloodline. No one cares for him the same way I care for you. You should pity him."

Glancing down at the bruises on her arms, Janir appealed her mother's statement. "Mother, he hates me. So why shouldn't I hate him?"

"Oh, my child," her mother sighed. "Do not hate him. When the day comes, favor me and show him what compassion is."

"What day?" Janir wondered.

"The day he is at your mercy."

Janir didn't ask for an explanation, shrugged, and glanced up nervously as her father swept into her mother's chambers.

"Master." Her mother bowed deeply, with submission, as she always did when he entered a room. Janir, his eldest child, was not required to bow. Though at that moment she would have done it just to escape those piercing eyes, had she not been holding the poultice to her face.

"You are leaving," the Lord Argetallam stated simply.

"What? Why Master?" Janir asked, confused. Then wished fervently that she had kept her mouth shut.

"Never question me, Janir!" he shouted angrily, his temper suddenly flaring up like a fire fed oil. "You may be my firstborn, and heir to my kingdom by our laws, but you have the weakest powers of any of my children, and are therefore rendered potentially dispensable," he added the last detail in a dangerously cold voice. Forcing herself to keep a straight face, Janir held eye contact with her father, she remembered all too well what had happened the last time she had looked away from him. As his head had snapped around to her, the collar of his tunic had become mussed, showing a spiral seashell, dappled with brown spots and hanging from a thin strip of leather. The girl tried to think about that as she stared submissively up at her father. Tried to remember the happy times.

Intervening, Janir's mother rose to her feet and stood beside her daughter, placing a protective hand on the girl's shoulder. Janir didn't look up at her mother, but she was certain that if she had she would have seen a pleading and beseeching look in the woman's eyes.

The Lord Argetallam's anger seemed to become restrained, as if he didn't wish to cause Janir's mother any more harm than he already had.

"You and your mother are going to the winter residence of Sanreal. Adasha is not safe for you as long as Lucan holds this loathing for you and his mother encourages it.

"I have made the arrangements. You will depart in ten days and go through the Norwin Pass, through Brevia, and from there on to Sanreal." Her father glanced to her mother. "Do you foresee any ill coming about?" he demanded.

Aryana turned and gracefully strode across her bedchamber to a chest of drawers against the wall. Opening a small drawer, she reached inside and gently raised a glowing golden orb. Janir's mother turned and faced the Lord Argetallam, glancing at him briefly before staring down into the depths of the sphere. Cradled in her mother's hands like a small bird, the orb made soft warbling sounds. Like a sphere of liquid sunlight, it swirled and throbbed with an illuminating glow. Janir's mother was silent for several moments. Her gaze seemed to shift beyond what she could see with her eyes. Accustomed to that look, Janir watched her mother tolerantly, knowing that she would be back to normal in a moment.

"Answer me, woman," the Lord Argetallam impatiently snapped.

Almost reluctantly drawing her gaze away from the orb, Janir's mother replied firmly, but with a hint of some indecipherable emotion. "Our child will be safe," Aryana announced.

"Then you will depart as planned." Her father spoke efficiently, hardly pausing for breath. And without another word, he moved to sweep out of the room.

But Janir's mother stopped him. "Master," she called. The Lord Argetallam stopped and looked impatiently back at Janir's mother. "I just wanted to tell you, thank you."

"For what?" the Lord Argetallam raised one

eyebrow in suspicion.

"For giving me that which I love most in the world," her mother gently stroked Janir's hair.

"I will miss you, Aryana," the Lord Argetallam brusquely stated.

As if his own words were insignificant, the Lord Argetallam swirled around on one heel in a practiced motion and marched out of the room. Janir's mother knelt down and whispered in her daughter's ear.

"Your father is what he is, my child."

Nothing in all the land is quite as mind-numbing as the Norwin Pass. It is not beautiful enough to be soothing, nor ugly enough to be stimulating. It is so normal that it is unearthly. During the monotonous time, when she was riding through that place, beside her mother and surrounded by their retinue, she was musing on what her father had given her before she left. He had handed her a mahogany box that had been polished to a shine. The Lord Argetallam told her to open it when she reached Sanreal and now it was tucked safely in her horse's saddlebags. Before they left, he had come up to her when she was playing, or rather hiding, in the gardens the day after Lucan had beaten her. The Lord Argetallam cut the back of her hand with a slick, clean, and razor sharp blade. It sliced through her skin like a hot iron through butter, causing bright red blood to well instantly to the surface. After slapping her pitilessly for crying, the Lord Argetallam twisted her hand around and let several very large drops of blood soak a frayed and rough patch of cloth. Then he had stormed off as if enraged, leaving her there.

"I love you, Janir. Very much," her mother had interrupted her thoughts spontaneously, leaned across from her own horse and squeezed Janir's small hand. "Never forget that, my child."

"I love you too, Mother," Janir's soft and child-like voice replied.

No sooner had Janir spoken than an arrow zipped past her head and buried itself in the neck of one of their guards. Janir never remembered much of what happened that day, just blood and screaming, voices shouting orders and other voices calling for help. She was sure that she had fallen off her horse, but beyond that she only remembered still images and sounds. Later she decided that she must have opened the mahogany box at some point and clenched the objects inside. Janir did recall feeling something painfully slicing the side of her neck, screaming, and falling to the ground in a heap.

She opened her eyes to the brutal glare of the afternoon sun. Slowly her vision began to focus and she saw clearly that she was in a camp, a busy camp with men and dogs, horses and swine, sweat and dirt. She could smell the scent of smoke from cook fires that were already burning. Dogs barked pointlessly at whinnying horses. Through two rows of tents, a pair of horsemen rode by with their clanking armor.

The shouts of captains as they instructed their new troops came from all sides.

It occurred to her that she wasn't breathing. As soon as she thought about it she was gasping for air, her lungs wouldn't fill. Terrified, she couldn't catch her breath for what seemed like an eternity. It was like some invisible hand was crushing her from the inside, trying to suffocate her from within. As she began to breath easier, she realized that the left side of her neck was bandaged where she had been cut in the skirmish and a strange smelling substance was held against the wound by a white linen bandage. With panic she realized that her hands were behind her back and bound together.

There was a sound like a tent flap opening, then a young male voice shouted, but in a muffled tone, as if the tent dulled the sound. Someone was shushing the lad to be quiet, then the same voice speaking in a low tone behind her. She tried to twist around to see, but couldn't. Then a strong hand gripped the collar of her dress and dragged her backwards into the tent. It was dark inside and took a moment for her eyes to adjust to the near-night darkness.

The strange hand untied her only to bind her hands around a brace in the middle of the tent. The person was rough, but not in a necessarily malicious way. Janir panicked, realizing that she could neither speak, nor move her arms to resist.

With effort she could move her head and she thrashed it about wildly in spite of how much it smarted the cut on her neck, trying to catch a glimpse of something, anything that might give even the smallest explanation for all of this.

Standing to her right was a man who was tall, like her father. He was fair and in the dim light his long straight hair seemed to give off a silvery glow. One thing that surprised her more than almost anything thus far were his ears. Like lilies they tapered to delicate and subtle points that would have been hard to notice if she hadn't been surveying him so closely. Of course her mother had told her stories of elves and their magic; but she had never expected to actually meet one, certainly not like this, staring at her icily, as if she and he were ancient enemies. She thought that strange, in all the stories, the elves were good. Finally, she was able to speak and her voice was raspier than she had ever heard it. The actual sounds were not what she had intended, still the meaning was the same.

"Where's my mother?"

Just like a hummingbird, Janir's heart raced. Her gaze darted quickly from one side of the tent to another, taking in the glowering face of the man the others addressed simply as "Elf" and the several soldiers standing by. She made a careful procedure of looking deeply into the eyes of each and every one of them, as the grown-up Argetallams at home always wanted her to. As the elf spoke, Janir snapped her gaze around to him and maintained a hard stare into his eyes. Her father had always shouted and become angrier with her when she hadn't looked him in the eye. Still, this man seemed to be angry about something she was doing.

"What is an Argetallam with full retinue doing

on this side of the Pass, in Brevia? Why did you leave the designated Argetallam realm of Staspin?" the elf demanded, his slight accent adding flourish to the interrogative rants. He asked all sorts of questions for twenty minutes. She did not know the answer to any of them. For some reason, he seemed to regard her with a brutal eye, as if he considered her a being incapable of feeling and undeserving of mercy.

Janir was confused. "Master was sending me and Mother to Sanreal." She forced herself to speak levelly without stammering. Voicing the words in even, emotionless tones and keeping a steady and hard eye contact with the elf. Anything less enraged her father and other adult relatives, why should this elf not be the same?

"And why would you go there?" he incredulously pressed.

Without warning or reason, Janir felt a wave of agony sweep over her. It was as if her heart had been ripped out of her chest by a bear's claw. The sensation burned, stung, and chilled at once. Her sight blurred and sweat beaded on her forehead. Suddenly it became clear to her that she was screaming. When it was finally over, Janir coughed and let her small head hang.

The elf looked about to say something when a stately man stepped in from outside. He looked to be around forty with dark, sad eyes; his entire appearance spoke of nobility even though he was dressed much as her father had been when he had announced to her that she would leave the Staspin Waste. At first glance, Janir thought that he looked similar to her father. Like some children, she tended to compare all men she met with her father. But his eyes were different. They held a kinder and more forgiving glow, nothing like the cold and bitter fire that she saw in her father's eyes. This man held himself with an air of dignity, not of controlled hostility as her father seemed to.

"Unbind the child, Daric," the stately one commanded. He wasn't looking at her, so didn't even notice that she was trying to achieve the hard eye contact that was demanded back at Adasha. It seemed to Janir's child-intuition that he had been crying, not too long ago, but no one else seemed to have noticed. Immediately the soldier who had been standing behind her stepped forward.

"But Armandius..." the elf protested. "She is the daughter of the Lord Argetallam. She herself admitted it."

The stately one stood stock still for several seconds with a pain-filled expression, as if those blunt words had pierced his very soul. But again, no one else seemed to notice.

"Unbind her, Daric," the stately one numbly repeated. He stared at the soldier and didn't even look at the elf.

Turning his brutal glare back to her, the elf added: "Look how she stares into my face and shows no respect. Typical Argetallam behavior."

That wasn't acceptable here? she wondered.

Torn between the elf and the overall superior, the soldier hesitated for half a moment and then obeyed. Janir hadn't realized that her wrists had gone numb until the ropes fell away.

This was too much. She had been beaten and cursed countless times in Adasha and Sanreal, by her father and other Argetallam relatives. But she had always known what would set them off and what would abate their rage. Here, she had no concept of what these men wanted her to do. It was impossible for her to predict their reactions. Taking advantage of the situation, Janir clumsily leapt up, scrambled into the shadows, and ducked under a rough wooden table at the back of the tent, covered in papers and pens. No sooner had she scrunched up in a ball between two large trunks, tucking her legs as close to her chin as they would go, that the ringing of half a dozen swords echoed in the air. She couldn't help the whimper of fear that escaped her lips. Watching from where she was, Janir had only a view of their boots under the cloth that had been draped over the table.

"Put those away!" the stately one hissed with irritation.

"But…" the elf began to protest.

"Can't you see she's afraid?" he demanded, trying to keep his voice down.

The elf made an annoyed sound that signified the start of another protest, when the stately one continued.

"If she were capable of killing us, why would she need to hide in the first place?"

There was a reluctant scraping of swords being replaced in their scabbards. Deliberately, a pair of large and weathered boots neared where Janir had sought refuge. She could see him kneeling before her, his silhouette blocking the light. Carefully, one of his hands reached under the rugged tablecloth and grasped the frayed edge. Slowly he lifted it so that he could see her and she could see him. He had a nice face, kind, but with very sad eyes, like a deerhound's. He reached a hand toward her. Janir knew what that meant. When a man reached toward her, that could mean only one thing. He must have been angry about her running away. It had always made her father angry when she had fled from him. Now that she considered it, she should have stood and looked up at him the way her father and other, older, relations always wanted her to. She hunched her shoulders in expectation of the blow and let her eyes close for a moment. Then she realized he would strike her for that too, so she should have kept steady. To her surprise, he retracted his hand instead of striking her with it.

"Come here, little one," Aramandius gently coaxed.

Janir tried to squeeze further between the chests, but there was no more room to do that. The canvas of the tent was pressing against her back. Straightening her face, and staring squarely at him, she struggled to keep her eyes from wandering away from his.

"Come, Janir," the stately one encouraged. "That is your name, isn't it?"

Janir stared with terror, not speaking, barely moving except for her rapid breathing and trembling shoulders.

"No one will harm you," Aramandius assured her

with a cursory and threatening glance at the guards and the elf who seemed to have faded into the background.

He extended his hand again, with a kindly but forced smile that boded no harm. Hesitant as a young fawn, Janir cautiously reached out her small fingers toward his. When his fingers started to close around hers, Janir jerked back and curled herself into the smallest ball she could manage.

"It's alright," the stately one crooned. "I won't hurt you."

Hurt? Her father had never called it hurting. He had always told her that she had earned punishment. Prompting, the stately one held out his hand to her again. With as much caution as a hunted animal, Janir let him circle his fingers around her hand. Gingerly, he tried to guide Janir back into the open space. Still uncertain, she let him lead her out from under the table. Glancing at the hateful expressions on the guards' faces, Janir was suddenly even more afraid. She sprang from under the table and entwined her little arms around the stately one's neck, knotting her fingers together in a solid clasp. Janir liked him; he felt safe, solid and warm. He seemed surprised, like this hadn't been what he had planned. But still, after half a second's hesitation, he wrapped his arms around her back and rose to his feet, letting her cling to him for protection. Still, her sudden movement had caused the guards to flick out their swords again.

"Stop it!" he hissed, as if he found their relentless pugnacity unbearable. "Leave us," the stately one dismissively commanded. Like a toddler just denied a whim, the elf looked about to protest, but when the guards began obediently filing out of the tent, he clamped his mouth shut and stalked out like a cat that has been offended.

Janir buried her face in the stately one's shoulder. He smelled of horses, dust, pine trees and worn leather.

"Did they hurt you?" he gently inquired. He seemed concerned, carefully touching the bandage on the side of her neck.

"No," Janir replied. It seemed rude not to address him by his title, but she didn't know what his was, so she said the first thing that came to mind, "Master."

"You needn't call me 'Master,'" he corrected.

Janir's brow wrinkled. "What then?" she hesitantly ventured.

There was a scraping sound as he pulled a chair away from one of the tables to himself ease down into it. He sat with Janir in his lap, while she continued clutching his neck as if it was a solid place in a storm. Blindly, she released her grip with one hand and tried to rub the cloudiness out of her eyes.

"Who are you?" she mumbled, having forgotten her earlier predicament. "Why are you being so nice to me?"

"Because I promised your mother that I would look after you." The stately one seemed to be fighting himself almost, as he placed a comforting hand on her shoulder and gently brushed her wet hair behind one of her ears. "You're safe now," he half-heartedly added, as if he despised her but couldn't help show compassion to her.

Worn out by the pain that had swept over her, Janir was too tired to ask any more questions. Being in so much pain was exhausting.

"Is Mother alright?" Janir moaned, hardly able to keep her words from blending into a single noise.

Uncertain of how to respond, the stately one paused for a moment. "I am sorry Janir." His voice became strained, as if he were on the brink of tears. "I too, loved her very much."

 Banished

Janir stared blankly at herself in the smooth glass mirror that hung above her chest of drawers. The evening fire had already been lit, though the sun was still well above the horizon. Brushing back a stray strand of her hair, she glanced briefly across her spacious personal chamber. It had been nearly seven years since she had first met Armandius. Though at times she couldn't remember what Adasha had been like at all, sometimes it seemed she had been born in this castle. Janir glanced over her shoulder to survey the four-poster bed, the two upholstered chairs gathered by a bearskin rug near the fire, and the tall windows that reached to the vaulted ceiling.

A smallish, round woman of around fifty years peered over her shoulder. "Don't you dare move yet," she snapped. "There you go, sweetheart," the woman crooned, affectionately patting Janir's head. Setting down the boar's hair brush, she stood back and admired her work.

"Thank you, Dame Selila," Janir smiled, reaching up to finger her locks.

"No charge of mine shall go about looking as if you play in the fields all day," the old lady proudly declared. "See? I told you getting dressed up for these kinds of guests wouldn't be so horrible."

"Would you mind telling the lord that I will be down soon?" Janir requested.

Dame Selila nodded and scurried away to inform Armandius. With a sigh, Janir turned back to her reflection. Thankfully, the usual tan complexion of an Argetallam had not been bestowed on her. She could easily be taken for Brevian. Reaching across the top of the dresser, she clasped a slender silver chain. As her hand passed over a mahogany box, she felt a tremor in the air, a pull toward the box. As she often had before, she let her hand release the chain. Janir, captivated, stroked the sleek box with her finger tips.

Open me.

It was hardly there, a hazy concept of thought that her mind translated into whispered words. The moment the familiar beckoning voice was heard inside her head, Janir jerked her hand away from the box as if it were poisonous.

"No," she firmly snapped out loud to the inanimate object. It was a constant reminder of her Argetallam blood. Janir hated the very sight of the gleaming thing, yet something deep within her, some innate instinct perhaps, was loath to throw it out. Therefore, it had remained in its current location for nearly seven years.

Snatching up the silver chain, Janir fastened it around her neck. A silver medallion hung several inches below her throat. It was a seven point star, with a solid emerald in the center and each of the points crafted into the graceful shape of a sword. This last detail was due to an ancient pact made among the seven of Brevia's ruling families.

Armandius had given her the medallion on the day he had brought her here to his castle from the Norwin Pass. She had been frightened and timid, a motherless and defenseless child. Armandius had hung the chain around her neck and told her: "You are a part of my family now."

Janir bit her lip. She knew she was not Armandius' daughter. But how she wished she was! On second thought, she removed the medallion from around her neck. She wanted to avoid any questions about her parentage as Armandius was the last of his house and everyone knew he had no children.

Smoothing the front of her unadorned blue satin dress, Janir realized that she could no longer stall. The man she called "Master" had guests tonight, and it would be unseemly to delay any longer. Turning on her heel, Janir strode to the oaken door and slipped into the long corridor that was lit by flickering torches.

She made her way along the hall, her shoes clacking against the stone. Knowing the way quite well, it was not long before Janir arrived at a pair of large double doors at the end of one corridor. Sighing again before entering the banquet hall, she placed a hand on the door and swung it open.

The interior scene was unusual for this castle, though it might have been considered normal in any other. Janir's master stood with a polite but strained expression as a thin, powdered, and perfumed young woman stood giggling and chattering. The woman had enough lace around her neck to have been a milk weed and a large enough skirt to house a family of goblins. Beside her stood a bored-looking man only slightly older. The man appeared to be unremarkable in every way, except for his thin mouth. He kept contorting and pursing his lips as if he were waiting for something that was taking forever to arrive.

Janir did not spend an excessive amount of time surveying at the two mortal guests. Her gaze was immediately drawn to a tall elf, standing slightly to one side and staring at her. Janir almost sighed with disappointment when she spotted Velaskas. The maiden suspected that his frequent visits which, according to the older staff, previously occurred only every six years or so, were planned to be certain that she was not a credible threat.

The servants know and tell all, was a proverb that Armandius had once said to her. Janir could only hope and pray that none of them suspected her of being an Argetallam.

Velaskas' arrivals were occasionally enjoyable when he would bring his son Saoven with him. Saoven was pleasant company. But she always felt that she was on trial when Velaskas came, like there was some forgotten evil she had committed and he was just waiting for the perfect moment to punish her for her crime. However, it had been several months since she had last seen him and she had begun to hope that he had decided to trust her.

The elf did not so much as nod when their gazes met, he stared at her with a blank expression that spoke more than a thousand words could have. Janir was well aware that if it were not for Armandius' devout protection of her, Velaskas would have killed her at the Norwin Pass. Janir's hand conscientiously went up to the left side her neck where all that remained of the wound was a faint pale scar. She admitted to herself that Velaskas had saved her life that day when he had dressed it. Still, he had only done so to keep her alive long enough to interrogate her.

Armandius heard the doors swing open and whirled around swiftly, visibly elated by having an excuse not to look at the young woman chittering away behind him.

"Jenny," Armandius smiled, using his pet name for her. "You're late, my child." His tone was chastising, but Janir knew that it was more for abandoning him with the giggling little doxy than for her tardiness.

"Forgive me, Master." Janir tried to block the girlish grin that threatened to spread across her face.

Armandius clasped her hands, drew her toward him and kissed her forehead lovingly. "Duke Ronan, Lady Rowella," Armandius addressed his guests. "I would like to introduce you to my ward, Janir."

Janir's master presented her to the man and the woman.

The woman, Lady Rowella, smiled her artificial smile and curtsied in the most sumptuous fashion. Duke Ronan made a bored gesture.

"Why do you not curtsy, child?" Lady Rowella inquired in her high-pitched squeak of a voice.

"I never learned, milady," Janir stammered awkwardly.

"But you have been raised by Sir Armandius Caersynn, one of the finest knights in all Brevia! Surely he taught you manners," Lady Rowella trilled.

"Does my master strike you as the kind of man who knows how to curtsy?" Janir demanded, already thoroughly annoyed with their guest. She had never found it irritating in the least when her master had called her "child." When he used the term, it had always been one of endearment. But when Lady Rowella had uttered it, Janir had sensed an underlying intent of belittlement.

Armandius allowed a strangled smile before assuming a rebuking frown. Duke Ronan remained unbearably expressionless, while Lady Rowella stood looking baffled at Janir's retort.

"Forgive Janir," Armandius apologized, "it is not often that we have guests."

From the wall behind Armandius, a door creaked open and a demure boy of about ten peered out into the small foyer. "Excuse me," the page interrupted. "Dinner is served."

Armandius turned to acknowledge the boy. "Thank you."

The five of them filed into Armandius' banquet hall. It was well-lit and spacious. Simple tapestries adorned the walls and the table was of a rather plain design. Janir knew that theirs was not the most ornate banquet hall, but she treasured it along with the rest of the castle's furnishings for one reason.

"Oh, my." Lady Rowella was quite obviously displeased with the adornment of the hall. "How quaint." She feigned a smile. "But, uh, when was the last time you redecorated?"

"Twenty-two years ago," Armandius replied simply.

Janir seethed with possessive jealousy when Lady Rowella took Janir's usual place next to her master. She found herself seated directly across from Velaskas. She stared down at her plate to avoid his unnervingly emotionless gaze.

From the head of the table, Armandius tried to engage Duke Ronan in conversation out of courtesy. Nonetheless, the duke's sister talked enough for the both of them and Armandius soon realized that the duke wished to remain silent.

"Really, Sir Armandius," Lady Rowella stated, "This place looks rather dreary, if you don't mind my saying so."

"What's wrong with it?" Janir demanded. Was this woman trying to get Armandius to let her help with the castle decoration? If so, Janir wouldn't stand for such a thing. But everyone ignored her.

"Are you certain that the castle isn't lacking..." Janir noticed Lady Rowella's hand moving over Armandius' hand. "...a feminine touch, perhaps?" Lady Rowella completed in a breathy voice, laying her hands over his in a very disconcerting gesture. Janir nearly gagged on her piece of wild boar.

"There are females all around me," Armandius deftly replied. "Janir, Dame Selila, Willowyn the milkmaid…"

"Servants and children," Lady Rowella countered. "Not at all the companionship a man, such as yourself…" Rowella leaned closer to Armandius. Armandius leaned away from Rowella.

"Tell me, Sir Armandius…" Rowella was speaking in a tone Janir had never heard a noblewoman use before, not that she had met many of those.

Velaskas looked almost bemused, while Duke Ronan seemed to be thoroughly absorbed in his slice of venison. Armandius stared at Rowella with a displeased expression he had sometimes used when chastising Janir for something she had done. Without a word, he pulled his hand from beneath Rowella's and returned to his plate.

Janir stared at the gold band with an intricate weave pattern he always wore on his left hand. Nearly seventeen years of living as a widower and he still wore it.

"You say you last decorated twenty-two years ago?" Rowella tried to strike up a conversation she could follow. "What was the occasion?"

Armandius turned a stiff gaze to Rowella. "Aryana Meliard was brought here as my newlywed wife," he blandly stated.

Janir grew even more uncomfortable, if that was possible. Her mother was a nearly forbidden subject with her. What would Armandius make of a relative stranger causing her to be brought up, so frivolously too?

"Well," Rowella seemed to take no notice, "that was quite awhile ago. Have you ever considered…

remarrying?"

Janir felt sick. Was this actually happening? At dinner of all places? The maiden whispered a prayer, pleading that this was just a nightmare and that she would wake up.

"I admit that I have," Armandius quietly replied, speaking more to himself than to the chattering little twit to his left. He glanced at Janir for a moment before continuing. "But all of the women interested in me for nuptial purposes would be either too old to bear heirs to the house of Caersynn, or too young to be tolerable." Armandius stared hard at Rowella as he uttered the last phrase.

While Janir nervously wondered if he found all young women to be as abrasive as Rowella, the noblewoman herself had not recognized his remark as directed at her.

"But perhaps there could be one...who you would find tolerable, maybe even enjoyable." Rowella had taken on that same disturbing tone in her last sentence.

Armandius was clearly not allured by Rowella's advances. Still, the wench seemed not to notice.

That night's dinner proved to be one of the most awkward meals Janir would have in her life-time, listening to Rowella's nauseating talk while pretending to still hold an interest for food.

By the second course, Janir was longing for Rowella to choke on something, maybe the piece of lamb she was sliding around her plate. But no, Rowella took such small bites that a rat couldn't have choked on it if it tried.

"Carrots, cabbage, and peas?" Rowella incredulously balked as the third course was delivered. "Vegetables are peasant food!" she protested.

"Not anymore," Janir mumbled. Part of this dish's presence could be attributed to her. Shortly after she had first come here, she had asked Armandius why it was that the nobles refused to consume anything even remotely associated with the commoners. It was as if the elite class considered themselves too lofty to feed on the same sustenance. When she had put it that way, he had ordered that vegetables be served regularly.

After dinner, Janir and Armandius would normally go up to his study and play a game of chess. Armandius always won indisputably, but Janir still enjoyed vainly trying to defeat the veteran knight.

That would not be happening this evening because *they had guests.* Instead, Janir found herself in Armandius' study beside the fireplace, seated on the floor with a pair of deerhounds. Being with the dogs was not a problem itself. What had driven her off the couch was. Rowella still seemed clueless as to Armandius' rejection of her. Better to be in the company of a four-legged brachet than a two-legged one.

Janir stroked the head of one, Rani. The maiden had named her when she was a puppy. Rani yawned and placed her head wearily between her front paws.

Velaskas leaned against one side of the fireplace, staring down into the flames with contemplative eyes. Armandius seemed to be struggling to maintain a gracious outer appearance. Duke Ronan still held that impatient air. Words drizzled into silence. If just Velaskas had been there, they would have found something to talk about. But Janir disliked strangers and it had been many years since Armandius had entertained noble guests...about seven years, actually.

"Would anyone like some wine?" Armandius cast about for something to say.

"That would be lovely," Rowella trilled.

"Yes," Duke Ronan blankly added.

"And I think I will be needing some," Armandius muttered to himself.

"Call the servants to get it," Rowella suggested.

"No," Armandius protested. "I can manage myself."

"Well, are you not sweet," she giggled.

Rolling his eyes, Armandius rose to his feet and made his way to a cabinet across the room. Once his back was turned, Duke Ronan seemed to spring to life. The duke's eyes stopped staring off into space and snapped around to Armandius. Duke Ronan silently stood.

Janir's back straightened. What was happening?

Rowella was talking about something. Ronan moved to follow Armandius. Janir clambered to her feet. What happened next haunted the girl often enough in her dreams, but she still wondered *how* it happened.

From behind Armandius, Ronan drew a gleaming dagger from the folds of his doublet and raised it above her master's head. Velaskas didn't see.

Janir shouted "No!"

That distracted the duke from plunging the dagger into Armandius' back just long enough for Janir to cross the room and fling herself at Ronan. Why she did it, she couldn't be sure. Janir lunged for the duke's upraised hand, foolishly trying to wrest a blade from a grown man's fist.

Duke Ronan made his last mistake in dealing with the girl. Instead of using the dagger on Janir, he struck her with the back of his hand and tried to stab Armandius.

Janir felt something shake her body. A force commandeered her actions. She was no longer in control. A bright green light went over her eyes and her efforts to fight it were useless. It happened in barely the time it takes for a heart to beat.

When the sheen covered her vision, Janir felt anger. Rage such as she had never felt before. Untainted and uncontrollable fury. Letting out a mad cry, Janir sprang at Duke Ronan with an inhuman hatred.

Snatching his head with both hands, the girl snapped his head to one side easily. She felt his spine twist and then crack like dried twigs. The dagger fell to the ground and his limp body soon followed.

The dominating power settled back into inaction and the green light left her eyes. Feeling suddenly weak, Janir staggered backward. Armandius caught her and she leaned helplessly into his arms.

Rani and the other dog who had been barking madly with confusion, trotted up to Duke Ronan's motionless body and sniffed it.

Popping up like a frightened pigeon, Rowella

fled from the room screaming. "Magic! Witchcraft! Sorcery! Enchantments! Help!"

The woman's voice receded down the hall while Janir leaned feebly against her master and Velaskas stood with a bearing of mild surprise. The elf was still standing by the fireplace, staring with an unidentifiable expression.

"That gave me quite a turn," Velaskas remarked. "It would seem your powers are more manifested than we thought." He seemed concerned.

"Stop Rowella!" Armandius snapped to the elf.

"What am I to do?" Velaskas wondered. "Chase her down and drive a knife into her heart?"

"Just stop her!" Armandius repeated.

There came a clatter of hooves from below the window, in the courtyard and a flurry of excitement as Lady Rowella's horse galloped away without consideration for any of her normal traveling arrangements, which were extensive.

"Too late," Janir gasped. She would have slid to the ground had not Armandius pulled her up. "What was that?" she whispered. "What did I just do?" Her master stroked her head and said nothing.

The sight of Ronan's sightless eyes gazing into space was more harrowing than she could have expected. She had killed a man with her bare hands and it hadn't even been her choice to do so. Why had she done that? Were her Argetallam powers awakening? Was it possible to control it? Of course it could be controlled, she realized. Her father didn't go about killing everyone who drew a knife. But then, nearly everyone with a weapon in the Staspin Waste, was an Argetallam. Could that affect it? Janir turned and buried her face against Armandius' chest. Tears sprang to her eyes.

"What have I done?" she shuddered. "I'm sorry," Janir whimpered. She was becoming like any other Argetallam. Like her father. What had she done?

"You saved my life. What is there to forgive?" Armandius gently stroked her back. "I should have been more wary."

He didn't rebuke her for being weak. Janir knew that he had killed people in wars, and it was nothing new to him. But still, she felt that he understood the horror she experienced at ending another's life, no matter how much that life may have deserved it.

"Armandius, son of Aragol and friend of the Elves," Velaskas took on a very formal tone, "I must again beseech you to reconsider..."

"Not here," Armandius interrupted. He summoned his chief steward, Broffy. Leaving Janir lying on the couch beside the fireplace, he commanded the man to take Duke Ronan's body somewhere until he could think of what to do. The faithful old steward had served Armandius' family since the days of his father, and he could be trusted to keep quiet.

Janir was relieved when the duke's body was moved to where she could no longer see it. The image of it kept memory of the anger and the rage frighteningly alive. Recollections of the power that had possessed her and held her in an iron grasp tormented her mind.

Armandius seemed distressed. His face held a

weary, exhausted look and his brow was troubled. Rani went to Janir and licked the girl's hand comfortingly.

"My lord," Broffy began humbly, "with all due respect, I believe that now is the time to discuss the rather pressing issue of the…"

"Not now, Broffy." Armandius cut him off, but not angrily. "Tell me in my office."

Janir watched weakly as Armandius and Broffy hefted Duke Ronan's mortal remains out of the room and into another part of the castle. Velaskas opened the doors.

For several minutes she was alone. The sound of men lugging a limp corpse faded down the hall. Why had the duke tried to kill her master? Why had he waited until now? Wouldn't dinner have done just as well? The duke was seated beside Armandius at that time. Then she realized, this was the first instance she could recall when Velaskas and all the servants loyal to Armandius had been too far away to intervene and her master's back had been turned. Once the body was moved, Broffy and Velaskas went into Armandius' private office, where his letters and correspondences with the other six lords of Brevia were kept.

"Stay here, my child," Armandius commanded.

"But Master," Janir sat up, "I feel better now, really."

"Stay." His voice was firm and unrelenting.

"Yes, Master." Janir leaned back against the cushion of the couch.

Armandius laid a hand on her head for a moment

before striding off to his office. No sooner had the door closed than the heated sounds of argument could be heard.

Velaskas and Broffy were trying to persuade Armandius, judging by the tones of the voices. Her master was being resolute in his decision. The word "pig-headed" was shouted by Velaskas. Armandius snapped something in reply. The confrontation grew louder, Janir began to discern more and more words with each passing sentence. Broffy shouted "Argetallam" furiously and Armandius shouted back a phrase with "Janir" in it.

She had been taught that eavesdropping is not polite. Armandius had scolded her for that several times, but not for years. She hated disobeying him. But they were talking about *her*. *Her* future, *her* fate. After a moment's hesitation, Janir clambered up from the couch and tip-toed to the door. The conversation had become so passionate that none of them heard her make her way across the room. Pressing her ear against the oaken door, Janir could hear every word clearly as if they had been standing in the room with her.

"She is an Argetallam, you *imbecillus!*" Velaskas could be heard slamming his fist down on something, using the Elvish word for "idiot."

· "She is like a daughter to me…" Armandius was cut off by Broffy's remarks.

"Aryana's child should have been your daughter, my lord. Why do you pretend with this foul creature of the Staspin Waste?"

"A child has no choice in their origins, only in

their actions and Janir's actions demonstrate that she rejects the Argetallam way," Armandius countered.

"Why don't you kill her?" Velaskas demanded. "If your place were reversed with the Lord Argetallam, it is what he would do!"

"I am not him!" Armandius exclaimed. "Do not *ever* compare me with *him,* either of you!"

"Be calm, my lord," Broffy placated. "Still, you must admit, over the years you have surely questioned yourself? Have you ever doubted that sparing her was the correct decision?"

Janir felt fear prickling her spine. Would Armandius turn on her? No. Never.

"Yes," Armandius sighed, his anger simmering into emptiness.

Confusion, doubt and consternation filled Janir's heart.

"Yes, I confess that over the past seven years, I have had my doubts," admitted Armandius. "Several times I even sought her out in the castle, to kill her."

Overflowing with a jumble of emotions, the girl forced herself to listen. Armandius, the man she trusted like no one else in the world, had come close to killing her?

"I told myself that Aryana must have been broken by the Lord Argetallam and that sparing his child may not have been what she would truly want. I would then usually resolve to destroy Janir."

"Why did you not?" Velaskas' tone was cautious, trying not to ignite another storm of rage in the room.

"I knew Aryana. I know she would never ask

a child be punished for her father's actions. I also know she was not broken by what she said to me before her death," Armandius coldly stated. "That and..." he paused mid-sentence for a moment before continuing. "That and every time Janir looked at me," he hesitated. "I could see how much she trusted me. In time I saw that she had come to love me."

Velaskas was obviously trying to think of something to counter this blow, since there was silence.

"It's an intoxicating feeling," Armandius murmured.

"What is?" Broffy inquired, also practicing caution in his tone and word choice.

"To be loved," her master calmly replied. "As you know, I have no kin left."

Janir began to relax.

"Then along came Janir. She was a child, she needed me. And now I realize that I needed her just as much."

Neither Broffy nor Velaskas could think of a retort to transpose his words.

"She is everything to me. She the only person on this earth whom I hold so dear and I would die for her in a second if it came to that," Armandius concluded.

The elf and steward seemed to be searching for something to say in reply. It was a long space of silence before either could answer his statements.

"I understand, my lord," Broffy carefully started. "But surely, there are things more important than this Argetallam..."

"Nothing is more important!" Armandius bitterly

snarled. "Not to me!"

"I understand that, sir," Broffy conciliated. "But what about Green Haven? What about the people here you swore to protect? Are they safe?"

"Janir couldn't bring herself to kill a deer before this and you ask if they are safe?" Armandius retorted.

"Not just from her my lord." Broffy's voice was calm, like an adult reasoning with a child.

"Where do you think Rowella has gone?" Velaskas demanded. "To Virida, no doubt. And how long do you think it will take your steward there, when he hears her story, to realize that there is an Argetallam in your midst?"

No reply from Armandius.

"He will alert Lord Meliard and Lord Kecim and they will come here with swords drawn and blades sharpened. Then what will you do?" Velaskas let those words hang for an agonizing moment. "Will you fight them for the girl? While among you I have seen mortals commit much sacrilege, but I pray that I never see any of the Seven Swords cross."

"I swore to protect her," Armandius coldly stated.

"You took another oath, son of dust," Velaskas reminded him, "an oath to protect the people of Green Haven. If you continue to harbor this creature, you are endangering them."

Janir was beginning to feel afraid again. Velaskas was using the one argument that her master might heed.

"Would you ask them to shed their blood for her?" the elf concluded.

"My lord, the elf speaks true. Something must

be done about her. There must not be a breathing Argetallam here when they arrive or else there will be bloodshed. And if they do not kill you outright, you will certainly be arrested for treason!"

Armandius said nothing. Janir wondered if she was trembling.

"As Broffy said, Armandius," Velaskas added, "something must be done. For the sake of Green Haven, for the sake of your people…something must be done."

In the ensuing pause, Armandius silently considered their statements. "You're right," he agreed. "Something must be done."

Janir heard him turn and with heavy bootsteps cross the room. The next thing she knew, Armandius had flung the door open and she was staring up into his surprised face.

For the first time in years, she was afraid of him. Stepping back a pace, Janir eyed him with a suspicious gaze before whirling around and running as fast as she could out of the study.

"Janir! Wait!" her master called. But she ignored him.

Fleeing down the poorly lit corridors, Janir raced through halls that she had explored thoroughly in her time here. Hardly needing light to show her the way, the girl whipped through the castle by backways and unused passages.

Sobbing uncontrollably, Janir found her way to a secret side-door she had once discovered. She slammed her weight into it several times before it gave and swung open on creaky hinges. The door opened into a bramble thicket, sharp and prickly. After beating the door shut and wiping her tears away, she charged through the scratching thorns. With a backward glance at the castle, she spotted no one stirring on the battlements. No one had seen her leave.

Slowing to catch her breath, Janir made her way through the knee-high grasses toward her destination.

Slumped on a low rock wall, Janir stared in the moonlight at the large stone monument before her. She was on a small hill overlooking the valley below the castle, a lush and green vale. Behind the hill, far in the distance were the mountains. Their powerful silhouettes blocked the stars behind them.

Mounds and stone pillars lined the side of the hill to mark the generations of Caersynns and their wives who had lived and died over the years. Each one of them was a relative of Armandius' in some way or another.

Some might have considered the hill a frightening place, particularly at night. More superstitious people believed it to be haunted. Even if it was haunted, Armandius had guaranteed her that the ghosts would be friendly. He once asked her, if there was nothing but trust and love in life, why should that change just because a person was dead? If there were any of his deceased family members lurking about the mounds, they wouldn't harm her because she was precious to Armandius and they would respect his judgment. Though Janir had often wondered if her being an Argetallam would make a difference to them.

It took her at least two hours to trudge her way through the brambles and briars of the woods that lie around the cultivated and tilled fields of crops. Janir was crying again, tears streaming down her face. Her skin had been scratched and abraised in many places and she was sore from branches hitting her so many times. Rocking silently back and forth, Janir felt very alone.

"I wish you were still here," she whispered to the wind.

The sound of a horse's hoofbeats came softly from behind her. Janir recognized the murmured command from the rider. Not turning her head, she heard the horse ease to a halt and the rider swing off the steed and habitually pat the beast's neck.

Tensing, Janir covered her head with her arms and remained still. She didn't actually believe that her master would kill her, but she was afraid nonetheless. Not once had she suspected that he felt confliction over his choice to rear her. Now she learned that he had come very close to destroying her several times. He hadn't though, she reminded herself.

Janir felt Armandius wrapping his arms around her shoulders. Pressing against his chest, Janir flung her arms around his neck like she used to do as a child. Neither of them said anything, as words seemed inadequate.

"You ran quite far," Armandius remarked,

releasing her from his embrace and glancing back to the castle. "Nearly a mile. No one saw you go."

"Then how did you know where to find me?" Janir sniffled.

Armandius shrugged. "You have always come here after you and I had an argument or when you were upset. Always."

Janir nodded and turned her gaze back to the monument. "I know she's not really there, but sometimes...sometimes I feel like she's standing there, listening to me," Janir vaguely commented.

Armandius stared absently at the stone pillar. "It's almost as if you can see her looking at you from beyond the other side," he mildly remarked.

Janir often thought common loss had been part of what had drawn herself and Armandius so closely together. "What am I to do?" she asked, quavering. "I know I can't be here at dawn."

Armandius did not answer straight away. He continued gazing vacantly at the monument. "Velaskas and Broffy want me to kill you."

Janir shuddered. But she was nearly an adult; she should be able to endure such talk. "I heard," she replied, since he seemed to be waiting for a response. Straightening her face, Janir stared up at him expectantly.

"You must leave," Armandius deliberately announced.

Janir was dumbstruck. *Leave?* Where would she go? She had never left Green Haven since arriving there. Where could she possibly go? The world seemed to begin spinning beneath her, whirling wildly without any apparent direction.

"But Master…what will I…how will I…." she stammered.

"Only for awhile," Armandius assured her. "Until I can work some things out."

"Where will I go?" Janir managed to mumble.

"To the mountains. Higher up they are relatively uninhabited and rather nice this time of year."

"What? With the werewargs and the griffins and the snow?" Janir hesitated.

"My girl," Armandius lifted her chin to stare into her eyes, "you know I would come with you if I could, but I cannot. I must be here when the other lords arrive, if for nothing else, to convince them that we are not under attack."

Janir said nothing. The utter shock of this revelation left her feeling dizzy and disoriented. Attempting to pull herself together, she covered her face with her hands and tried to think of something, anything except what was happening.

"Now, Jenny," Armandius prompted.

"Right." Janir was stunned, but rose to her feet and looked up at him. "Do we go back to Green Haven Castle so I can grab a few things?"

"No," her master replied. "I have everything you will need here."

Glancing past his shoulder to where he had motioned, Janir beheld her tall bay stallion Kalbo standing beside Armandius' dappled gray steed.

Kalbo looked confused and uncertain, but ready. Sadly, she noticed that his saddlebags had been fully packed for a long stay in the mountains. Kalbo's dark coat gleamed in the moonlight and his intelligent eyes watched her with expectation. Sensing the impending departure, he snorted eagerly and pawed the ground.

"But how will I know when to come back?" Janir asked, gathering her wits enough to think of that question.

"I will send either Velaskas or Saoven for you," Armandius elaborated. Taking her hand in a firm grasp, he commandingly lead her to stand beside Kalbo. "Good-bye, my child," he tenderly, but resolutely stated.

"Don't say that." Janir was crying again.

"It's not forever," he assured her. "Just for now."

Guiding her hands up to the front and back of Kalbo's saddle, he boosted her onto the stallion's back. Seated astride her horse, Janir began to wonder if she would ever return.

"There most likely aren't enough provisions in those saddlebags, so you'll have to hunt at some point," he warned her.

"Fine." Janir was only half-listening.

Armandius stared up at her for half a moment. "I love you as if you were my own daughter, Janir Caersynn."

"Master…"

"You need to go," he interrupted. "Now!"

There were at least a dozen things she wanted to ask him before she left, but in that instant Janir was too dazed and distressed to think of them. "What about wild animals?" Janir numbly asked.

"You can deal with them," he replied. "You are a

fine huntress, my child. They are in greater danger than you."

"You say that in spite of my previous hunting record?" Janir remarked.

"If it came to Kalbo's or your life against the beast's, I believe you would not hesitate to destroy the creature." Armandius paused. "Farewell." Slapping Kalbo's hindquarter just hard enough to frighten the stallion, Armandius stood back as the horse charged past the mounds and up the hill.

Doing her best to guide Kalbo through the dense brush of Green Haven, Janir tried to keep tears from clouding her vision. But it was no use and soon Kalbo's mane was moist with the drops of sorrow that fell from her eyes.

The world was still. No sound but the gentle thumping of Kalbo's hooves on the grass. Restlessly, Janir shifted in the saddle and looked down at her new clothes. Armandius had sent them with her to replace the blue satin dress she had been wearing. Her new clothes were forest green, to blend with the countryside. Necessarily, the long sleeve tunic would keep her warm in the chilly mountains and her black leggings underneath her split skirt would as well. The skilled seamstresses who worked for Armandius knew how to make something both comfortable and functional. In Kalbo's saddlebags were a blanket for the horse and the girl's arrows and disassembled bow, as well the mahogany box.

Dread and despair filled her heart, for her father had sent her away, too. And she had never seen him since. Though she wouldn't mind horribly if she died never seeing the Lord Argetallam again, she couldn't fathom never again seeing Armandius.

She and Kalbo had been moving all night, since her brief stop to change clothes and hide the blue satin dress in some prickly shrubs. The distant mountains were drawing nearer with each step of the bay stallion. Her eyelids felt heavy, but she forced herself to stay awake.

Before she knew it, they were making their way through the winding path of a narrow mountain gorge. Like curtains, the clouds hung in a gray sheet against the sky, spreading the sun's rays evenly.

The foothills of the mountains were cold and uninviting. The harsher wind was blocked by the mountains, but soon could be heard wailing at their peaks. Once or twice the stallion balked at an unusually loud cry from above their heads. But always he settled, trusting Janir that it was nothing to concern himself with.

Kalbo's ears twitched intently and soon Janir heard a moaning voice being carried on the steady breeze. Curious, she turned Kalbo and continued in a southeasterly direction up the mountain side through the blossoming trees. As she drew closer, she could hear the rushing of a river and words from formerly indistinct moaning.

Kalbo emerged from the trees quietly. Cautiously, Janir reined in Kalbo to behold a rather odd little person. He looked to be about two years her junior, with spiky red hair that stood on end. His freckled face was contorted into a look of self-pity. A pair of pale eyes stared off blankly into the distance, too busy daydreaming to notice the bay stallion and his incredulous rider.

The complainer was shorter than Janir, with a body built like a stick. He had no muscles to speak of and was skinnier than a willow branch. He was wearing a long, shapeless robe of indistinguishable color. Janir couldn't tell if it was a faded brown, or a dirty gray. The odd garment was much too big for him and resembled a huge sea creature that was swallowing him alive. He was suspended by the back of the shapeless garment from a tree branch that hung loosely from a leaning tree.

"Woe to me, I am out here all alone, away from the warm kitchens and bright banquet halls of home," he moaned pathetically.

Kalbo snorted and the boy snapped to attention. Like a deer spotting a wolf, he surveyed the girl and horse for a moment, then asked, "Have you any rolls or cheese?"

Janir shook her head negatively. "What are you doing here?" she demanded.

"Have you any food at all?"

"I believe you have larger problems than food," Janir pointed out.

"Yes, but at the moment I am rather hungry," the boy replied.

"What are you doing here?" she repeated.

"Hmm? How do you mean?"

"Here. In the mountains. What are you doing?"

"At the moment, I have been strung up by my robe and am dangling suspended from a tree branch, so I'm not doing much of anything," he explained, pointing up to where his robe was caught on the oak.

"Why are you here?" She tried to make the question easier.

"Because I can't move," he replied honestly.

Taking a deep breath, Janir attempted a different angle. "Why are you here instead of wherever it is you came from?"

"I left," the boy bluntly stated, staring at her with a gaze that said he considered her to be stupid.

"Why did you leave?" Janir demanded.

"I wanted to be somewhere else." He blinked disgustedly at her lack of understanding.

Before he could explain himself any further, the tree branch spontaneously snapped and the boy landed in a jumbled heap of robe and white legs. Kalbo shied and Janir gently held his reins until he steadied. The boy shuffled and clambered to his feet like a duck that has been dropped on its head.

"Karile Kerwyn, Enchanter of the Ninth Degree," the boy declared, with a sweeping bow made less impressive than intended by the leaves in his hair.

"Ninth Degree?" Janir scoffed. "You couldn't even save yourself up there. And you expect me to believe that you are an enchanter of the second most powerful degree?"

"Well, I am very close to the Ninth Degree," Karile protested.

"How close?" Janir pressed.

"Well, I do have a few Degrees to go before I am

of the Ninth," he sheepishly admitted.

"How many?"

"Eight," Karile confessed.

Blinking incredulously, Janir deemed that this boy was harmless whoever or whatever he was. Swinging down from the saddle, she lightly grasped Kalbo's reins and politely announced her own name.

"Janir Caersynn." No sooner had the words crossed her lips than she realized she should have at least withheld the anomalous last name. But hopefully the lad wouldn't notice.

"Caersynn?" he repeated. "But that is the name of one of the Seven ruling Brevian houses."

"So?" Janir shrugged, wishing to brush it off as irrelevant.

"You should be careful about revealing your appellation, the power of a name is a powerful thing," he chided, even though he had disclosed his own without a second's hesitation.

"Your point is?" Janir asked in a surly tone, shifting her weight as she discovered what long hours in the saddle had done to her muscles.

Even this dense enchanter seemed to take her reply as a hint that she did not wish to share the details of her life. "Do you have any food?" he inquired.

Janir sat by the fire Karile had made. Even an Enchanter of the First Degree could start a fire and for that Janir was thankful. She caught a rabbit with a snare like the ones Armandius had taught her to make. While she still had qualms about killing things, she found using snares mostly bearable.

Of course she had to clean the rabbit. Karile was apparently terrified of blood.

He whined the entire time she was skinning and cooking the rabbit, then ate more than his share. Janir stared in disbelief as the skinny boy consumed more than half the animal. He would have eaten the whole thing, bones, hair and all, had she not stood her ground.

"I caught it. I cleaned it. I cooked it. I eat it!" she shouted angrily, tearing off a back leg.

"No need to be selfish," Karile protested.

Janir was beginning to loathe this annoying little troublemaker. She suddenly understood why someone would leave him hanging from a tree.

"Who put you up in the tree, Karile?" Janir demanded.

"Very unpleasant people," the enchanter mumbled through a mouthful of rabbit.

"I'm not so sure," Janir murmured.

"I was out here riding to the next Enchanter Temple. You see, I get moved around a lot. No teacher seems able to handle me," Karile explained, seemingly proud of this fact.

"I don't think a legion of knights with war-dogs could handle you," Janir muttered.

"Anyway, I was out here riding when I met this group of goblins who were camped not far from here. Well, we start chatting and the whole time we're talking the leader keeps sort of narrowing his eyes at me. Like this." Karile narrowed his eyes into little slits. "Then, next thing you know, the little green fellows have strung me up on the tree." Karile then jammed a piece of rabbit in his mouth. "My pony's probably halfway home by now, the little traitor," he mumbled.

"Do you actually expect me to believe that?" Janir snapped.

"Well, yes! Do you call me a liar?" Karile righteously exclaimed through a mouthful of rabbit's flesh.

"I think you have more of an explanation there," Janir remarked.

"Well, I don't, and it's too bad for you!" Karile exclaimed.

Janir rolled her eyes. This young wizard was too mad to be believed.

"You know," Karile remarked between mouthfuls of Janir's rabbit, "I really wasn't going to go to the temple to be trained."

"That's probably a good idea. They might just turn you into a frog and all jump on you," commented Janir. Now that she had mentioned it, it sounded like an attractive option.

Karile didn't seem to hear her. "I only said that to see how you'd react. I was really going to go after the Key of Amatahns."

Janir closed her eyes and leaned against the trunk of a tree. Two days without sleep had taken their toll and she was exhausted. As she was drifting off into slumber, she heard "…..infinite power to the one who holds it…" At that her eyes opened. If there was one person in creation who shouldn't have infinite power, it just might be Karile.

"What? What gives infinite power?"

"Haven't you been listening?" Karile demanded.

"No, I haven't," Janir snapped back, now wide awake.

"Why are you so irritable?" Karile complained.

"I'll tell you why I am so irritable you little thistle thorn," she whispered in a dangerously quiet voice. "I am alone in this wretched wasteland with an Enchanter of the First Degree who..." Karile began swimming out of focus. Janir whipped a hand up to her face to wipe away the tears before he could see. The other things that were wrong, she couldn't tell him.

"Well, if that's all that's wrong with you, why are you complaining like a child?" he inquired.

Janir hissed wordlessly and leaned against the tree again.

"Do you have any idea what the Key is?"

"No." She wanted to sink into the dream world where anything is possible and she might escape the nightmare her life had become, even if only for a few hours. But with his selfishness, Karile was forcing her to keep a grip on cruel reality.

"We've got to get that Key before they do," Karile resolutely announced. "Look, one reason I decided to go to the temple was that I was finding out things. Putting the pieces together." His voice had dropped to a whisper.

Janir might have been interested if he had explained what exactly this key was. But he had, she reminded herself, and she didn't care.

"And my father told me to stop looking for clues to the Key, that the crypt should stay sealed and lost as it is. But of course I wouldn't listen."

Janir yawned and would have just rolled over had not Karile said something else to peak her interest.

"This power I was telling you about, well, it is so powerful, it can control entire races. Can you imagine?"

CHAPTER 2

Saoven

It was morning of the second day after she had met Karile, three days after she had last seen Armandius. Karile made a habit of sleeping late, so Janir rose as early as she could to avoid him for as long as possible. It was not at all difficult to rise before the enchanter because he snored like a drunken sailor with asthma. Janir had moved their little camp near the river to be closer to water.

She had dreamt about killing Duke Ronan the night before. The appalled feeling still haunted her. Even though she had done it to save her master, she abhorred her own actions. She had been so furious, so mad with rage when she had killed. The sheer *anger* Janir had felt in her heart frightened her to the core.

Janir lifted the lightweight, collapsible leather bucket that had been included in her pack. Birds were singing even though sunrise was still an hour away. The water was a short walk through the woods. Janir glanced around their meager campsite to make sure everything was in order. Kalbo was hobbled in the trees, Karile was a nondescript mound of grunting robe.

Satisfied, she turned and entered the dense trees. The previous year's leaves lay on the forest floor like a crunching blanket under her feet, crackling with each step. The sound of the river grew louder as she drew nearer. She stopped. She thought she had heard an echo to her foot steps. Janir swirled around but saw no one in the dim light.

"Hello? Is anyone there?" She surveyed the trees around her suspiciously. "Karile, if that is you, I'll break your nose," she threatened.

Not a sound. Deciding it was nothing, Janir went on to the river bank. The river was flowing gently here, placidly strolling instead of racing to where ever it is that water usually can't wait to go. Janir knelt by the riverside to fill the bucket. She heard a twig snap in the trees behind her. Setting the bucket down quickly, Janir stood erect, searching for the one who was following her. When she spotted nothing in the trees behind her, Janir scanned the treeline of the opposite bank. There was a flicker of motion, but it could have been only a bird. Janir listened intently, trying to hear over the constant murmur of the river.

Janir could not see or hear anything. She stooped down again to fill the bucket. Chills shot up and down her spine as she felt a hand noiselessly touch her shoulder. She was already tense and her reaction was quick as a viper's. She swung around to club the intruder in the head with the sloshing bucket. Water splashed over both of them. Without it the bucket was little more than a flopping boot. She threw it at his head and landed a right-cross in the middle of the intruder's face. In the dim light she could see his hand go to his face and he made a noise that sounded like a surprised protest.

She threw herself at him and hit him in the nose again. The stranger shoved her backward. Janir grasped a branch that was lying near the base of a tree and used it as a club. She struck him on the arms several times while he blocked. The intruder was backing up when she tripped on an exposed root and lost her balance. Seizing the opportunity, he tackled her to the ground, holding her wrists against a tree to keep her from hitting him again.

"Janir, it is I!" he snapped, irritated.

"Oh. Hello." She embarrassedly greeted him, stopped struggling and stared up at him. "I'm sorry about that, Saoven. But, what is an elf doing here? And how did you find me?" she wondered, a little surprised.

"I was passing through in my search for you and heard someone wandering by," he explained. "Armandius asked me to protect you, though I wonder if you need it," Saoven remarked. "I followed you here and you know the rest."

"How nice. You can let me go now," Janir added.

"Yes. I suppose I can."

A tree branch hit the elf in the side of the head before he knew it was there. Like a skinny, freckled-faced demon, Karile flew out of the shadows, springing on Saoven and hitting him in the face with bony fists.

"Wizard, leave him alone!" the maiden commanded.

"What is this thing?!?" Saoven shouted to Janir.

"I will tear your liver out through your eyeballs!" Karile shrieked in a wild and deranged tone.

"For the fourth time, I know Saoven very well and he isn't a goblin. My master and he are familiar acquaintances," Janir impatiently explained.

"I still say he looks like a goblin," Karile argued stubbornly.

"He and I are old friends," she snapped. It seemed odd for so young a girl to claim the friendship of an elf, but Saoven did not correct her.

"Really, then why did he attack you?" Karile refuted.

"It was a misunderstanding!" Frustrated to the point of anger, Janir made an irritated noise. The sun had long since retired over the western horizon and the young enchanter was still suspicious of their new companion. After Karile had so enthusiastically attacked the elf in spite of Janir's very vocal protest, she had finally talked the pair into a truce and then caught a pair of grouse for them all to eat.

The bones of that night's meal had long been tossed into the flames and now Janir was trying to convince Karile into accepting her friend. Already acting like old rivals, Karile and Saoven were seated across from one another around the fire on logs, glowering bitterly at one another. Saoven was holding a poultice over the side of his head and over one eye, while Karile sat with his left wrist cradled in a tight bandage, his narrowed eyes surveying this newcomer. Playing the role of arbiter, Janir was sitting on one side between them, with Saoven on her right, Karile on her left.

"If he isn't a goblin, why is he scowling at me?" Karile demanded.

"Perhaps it has something to do with the fact you bashed him over the head with a very large rock," Janir suggested.

"A very hard rock," added Saoven.

"You sprained my wrist and were attacking my friend," Karile countered.

Saoven mumbled something in Elvish to the effect of "I should have broken it."

"Who said we were friends?" Janir demanded.

"I said we're friends and that means you are my friend whether you like it or not!" he shrieked.

Janir rolled her eyes and turned to Saoven "He's insane," she whispered.

"I *have* noticed," Saoven replied.

"I am not vain!" screamed Karile.

With resignation, Janir rolled her eyes. "I feel like I'm talking to a stump."

"Well, that's not surprising. Goblins aren't known for being smart," Karile pointed out.

Janir closed her eyes in frustration. "You are the…..oh, never mind," she sighed.

"What will we do with the stump while we are looking for the Key of Amatahns?" Karile persisted.

"I don't know. What *will* we do with him?" Janir growled.

Saoven balked. "*The* Key?"

"Yes, *the* Key," Karile tried mimicking the elf's

refined accent.

"Why exactly are you seeking it?" Saoven demanded.

"To keep the Argetallams from getting it, of course," Karile replied.

At the mention of her original family name, Janir felt like she had been frozen. It was as if she was outside of time, her thoughts racing like rapids while everything else stood still, trying to comprehend what this meant. She had fervently hoped so many times over the years that she would never have to see her father ever again. If the other Argetallams were searching for the Key, then meeting him and other members of her huge and horrid extended family might be inevitable. As Saoven began interrogating Karile, his words sliced through her inner musings like a knife through paper.

"Why do the Argetallams want it? Can they even use the power it would unlock?"

"No one knows, but they don't want it for themselves." Karile could be rather loose-tongued, even when talking with a man he believed to be a goblin.

"Then why?" Saoven pressed.

"Apparently they have a client with some very deep pockets," Karile shrugged.

"Why sell the Key? It is a way to almost unlimited power," Saoven pointed out.

"The Lord Argetallam never has put much faith in magic," Janir murmured, almost to herself. "He would go through the trouble of having his kin track it down only if someone was willing to pay enough."

"Even if it would give his client that kind of

magic?" Saoven wondered.

"He probably thinks that the magic won't apply to him or his kin, on account of us…." Janir stopped abruptly and cleared her throat, "on account of *them* being Argetallams and all," she corrected.

"I often wonder if the world would be any more peaceful if we elves had wiped out the Argetallams when they were weak," muttered Saoven. Janir felt her skin prickling and the color draining from her face. Saoven didn't know what she was. Had Velaskas kept that secret from him to minimize the number of people who knew? She had known Saoven for years; her master trusted him enough to call him a friend. Still, not enough to let him know her secret?

"Yes, you should have," Karile passionately agreed. "Why didn't you?"

"The Oracle told us that we should show them mercy." Saoven seemed to consider that an idea of debatable soundness.

"Why show mercy to a clan whose main vocations have been mercenaries and assassins since there have been mercenaries and assassins?" Karile demanded.

"I have not the slightest inkling as to why," Saoven admitted, "only that that is what he said, and that is what we did," he explained.

"So instead of ridding the world of a blasted nuisance, you just drove them into the Staspin Waste and left them there." Karile shook his head and made an exasperated sound.

"Well, you are rather biased," Saoven noted. "Enchanters have no reason to befriend the Argetallams."

Seeming to consider it a fact of life, Karile shrugged.

"Are you well, Janir?" Saoven inquired. Janir was staring into the fire with a blank expression, not certain what to think or do.

"What? Yes, I am fine." She dismissed his concerns.

"You spoke earlier with assurance, as if you know the Lord Argetallam well," Saoven mentioned. "Have Armandius' conquests ever created a situation for your acquaintance?"

"No." Janir shook her head and tried to brush off the question. "I never left my master's estate. I used to know someone who was one of his courtesans."

"Who?" Karile pressed.

Janir felt shivers of panic shooting up and down her back. That stupid little enchanter never shut up, let alone when she wanted him to. Like children, Karile and Saoven were both staring at her expectantly.

"I…I would rather not talk about it," Janir stalled.

"Why not?" Karile cluelessly inquired.

"Because….because the person in question was very dear to me and I am still grieving that loss," Janir stammered.

Karile opened his mouth to say something else, but Saoven spoke first.

"We understand. We will not insist that you tell us," he interjected.

Janir smiled thankfully at Saoven. He was a good friend, protecting her without knowing it, even though Saoven was protecting Janir from Saoven himself.

"How many courtesans does the Lord Argetallam have at one time?" Karile's rambling thoughts had gotten the better of him.

"Three," Janir replied, then realized she probably should have shut up and stayed silent.

"Why three?" Karile wondered.

"Two is not enough, four is an unlucky number, so three is perfect," Janir explained.

"As much as I would love to go on discussing Argetallams and their warped society for hours, I believe that you two must get some sleep." Saoven rose to his feet and winced as he removed the poultice from the side of his head. Like a molted duck's, his face was styling a large bruise over his right eye. His eye was bloodshot and red. He had numerous other bruises and scratches on his face and arms. Janir realized with a slight pang of guilt that she had given him at least half of them.

Karile obeyed immediately, seeming to have completely forgotten that he thought Saoven was a goblin. As if he was suddenly exhausted, the boy turned, curled up next to the log he had been sitting on and began snoring within moments.

"You as well, Janir," Saoven commanded.

"What about you?" Janir was seated on the ground, hugging her knees to her chest.

"I will keep watch," he informed her.

"Elves don't sleep?" Janir incredulously challenged.

"Of course we sleep," Saoven corrected her. "But

we do not need nearly as much sleep as your kind."

He didn't even have a clue as to who her kind were. But she knew it was a good thing that he was ignorant of that.

Janir curled up like a kitten near the base of the tree, listened to the forest sounds, and tried to hear the lullaby that had lulled her to sleep these past few days. The soft flowing of the river. The hooting of the night owl. The wind dancing in the trees' leaves. She felt herself drifting off into the dream-world, sliding away slowly.

"Father, no!"

She bolted upright out of slumber. It was horrible, dreaming about her father and what he did to the people who were his captives. The fire had been put out and the world was silent, far too silent. Saoven was several paces off, standing alert. He heard her and glanced in her direction just long enough to convey she was to be quiet, then continued staring into the trees. Then she heard it, the soft snapping and bending of greenery as someone moved through the trees. With care, Janir silently rose to her feet, ready to run or fight, whichever became necessary. Her heart was pounding in her ears like a drum, her breathing was getting faster. She felt the old feeling of fear brimming over in her heart. It was a long time before the sound of bodies moving through the forest died down.

Saoven made a dismissive gesture after several

moments, indicating that the warriors had gone. Still cautious, Janir lowered herself to the ground again, but knew that she would not be sleeping.

At dawn, Saoven announced that they needed to leave the region as quickly as possible. Janir obediently saddled her tall bay stallion, but Karile whined and complained. "What about breakfast?"

Like a parent and a small child, Saoven and Karile argued about breakfast and the necessity of it while Janir saddled her horse. Several minutes later, Janir had mounted her steed. Karile stubbornly refused to ride.

"I tell you, I won't get on that thing," he resolved.

"You'll get on it, or you're staying here," Janir snapped.

"Horses are smelly and sweaty," Karile complained with passion.

"And you aren't?" Janir longed so badly to hit the enchanter.

Karile opened his mouth to retort, when Saoven suddenly picked him up and set him arguing and kicking on the saddle behind Janir. Kalbo balked for a moment, then settled down.

"Under normal circumstances I would leave you, enchanter," Saoven growled. "But I have a strange suspicion that you would point them in our direction if you saw those soldiers."

A question occurred to Janir. "Saoven, where are we going?"

"Higher into the mountains," he replied, swinging up into his white mare's saddle.

His brief elaboration would have to suffice. Now that the enchanter was up with her, Karile gripped Janir's waist like a lifeline. Undoubtedly, she would be bruised by the end of the day. Knowing that this was no time for complaining, Janir resigned herself to the situation and tried to pretend that Karile didn't even exist.

The gray marble had been polished to a shine. Incense burned along the gold-rimmed pillars. Like silent watchers, a row of palace sentinels stood guarding either side of the long hall, their swords glinting in the sun. Luxury and wealth were displayed everywhere, from the red carpet to the High King's golden throne.

Up the steps to the throne hall trudged Armandius. Like a common criminal he was being led in chains to face his judgment. But unlike a common criminal, only the prominent members of the Seven ruling houses stood by to watch his trial. They still stood whispering among themselves the way the leaves of a tree do in a wind.

One man stood apart from the others, an elderly courtier in his mid-sixties, a thin white scar over one eye and a gold-plated cane in one hand. In spite of his age, he was very lively in appearance. It had been nearly seventeen years since he and Armandius had last spoken. Now it seemed that he was here to see the downfall of a once loved son-in-law, now a bitterly loathed rival.

Beside the aged knight stood a man about thirteen years Armandius' junior. He had a conflicted expression on his face, one of both resentment and empathy.

Regarding this whole affair with a disinterested eye was Velaskas. As the chief emissary between the elves and the mortals, Velaskas was likely only watching because it involved the hated race of Argetallams. He would have to report on this whole business to the Elven King. Easily overlooked from his post near one of the guards, the elf stood intently inspecting his fingernails. The bent over old scribe in the corner jotted down every action and word he heard, especially the words of the king and Armandius.

The scribe's hands had become so shaky that years later, Janir would puzzle over the words for hours, trying to decipher their meaning.

Armandius bowed before the aged High King.

"Tell me, Armandius. My most faithful of subjects and brilliant of generals, why?" The king spoke in an authoritive and almost mocking tone.

"I must ask you to further explain your question, King Remian," Armandius respectfully stated, after pausing for several seconds.

"Why…" Remian paused for a space, as if unable to find words strong enough for his thoughts. "Why in the name of Amatahns, did you offer aid to an *Argetallam*? Why?"

It was Armandius' turn to carefully search for

words. "She was a child, milord."

"So was the first Argetallam, once. Have you forgotten what those people are? What they can do to us? That you once told me yourself there was nothing you so hated as Argetallam flesh?" Remian seemed both genuinely bewildered and angry at once.

"I have not forgotten, my liege…."

"Then why?" Remian cut him off. "Why did you help her?"

"Because I swore I would," Armandius firmly announced.

"Why did you swear to aid a child of the ones who took everything from you? Did they not kill your wife?" Remian probed.

Although she never asked him, Janir could guess that about then Armandius felt his blood beginning to boil at the mention of Aryana. It would have been easy for Janir's master to keep a calm, cool outlook had not that memory been refreshed like a lanced wound.

"No," Armandius snapped, undoubtedly struggling to keep his temper under control. "I only thought they did."

The High King gave him a confused and inquisitive look that mildly but firmly demanded more information. Janir could just imagine the man with the scar and golden cane leaning closer, with a new interest in this revelation.

"Nearly seventeen years ago, Saaradan fell while I was away in *your* army. I assumed that the Stlavish and their Argetallam allies killed her with the rest of those here when they took the city. But no, as many of you remember she was very beautiful..."

Several of the older courtiers standing by gave a hearty assent, but Armandius seemed to have ignored them.

"...and the Lord Argetallam noticed." Armandius paused, his anger wearing down as he remembered that which he tried so often to forget. "He took her as one of his courtesans and Janir was the result." Armandius told the story in a quick, matter-of-fact manner, trying to conceal the immense pain he felt. *I failed her.* Armandius must have been screaming inside, the way Janir suspected he did every time that he thought about it. *I left her to the Lord Argetallam and all that I know he must have done to her.*

"My daughter was a plaything for that monster?!" screamed the withered voice of the man with the cane. "You left her to be a source of his amusement?" demanded the aged knight.

"Father," began the man beside him, vainly attempting to calm the lord.

"Silence, Drianar," the old man snapped to the knight next to him.

Forcing himself to keep an outwardly emotion-less appearance, Armandius turned sideways to face Aryana's father. "Lord Loholt Meliard." He coldly uttered the name. "I did not abandon your daughter. Ever."

"When you married her, I was certain that you were worthy." The ancient voice of Lord Loholt was frail and raspy, but the words could still pierce Armandius' soul as if they had been made of steel. Like a hound, driven by the smell of blood after the first bite, the old man continued. "But now I learn that you not only failed to protect her, as you swore you would on your wedding day, but you spared and nurtured the child of the one who shamed both her and the houses of Caersynn and Meliard!"

"That child is your kin," Armandius coldly countered.

"A scion born of her father's lust and brutality, and her mother's fear and shame, will not be called kin of mine!" cried Lord Loholt.

"Father, please. Not here…" Drianar trailed off.

"Aryana loved her," Armandius quietly murmured to himself. Janir doubted that anyone beside the keen-eared scribe and possibly the nearby elf heard those words. "Loved her enough to die in order to keep her from her father."

Lord Loholt apparently did not hear, nor would he have cared if he had. "Look at you, standing here before the High King to face judgment for what? Showing your indifference to the pain and fear my daughter endured as a prisoner of that accursed man, that's what."

"That's enough, Father…"

"I loved her!" Armandius cried, drowning out the rest of Drianar's sentence. "It nearly killed me when I believed that she was dead and it would have driven me mad when I learned of her true fate, had I not had Janir."

Lord Loholt was quick to reply, judging by the rapid scratching the scribe made on the paper to keep up with the words. "Yes, I suppose that trading one for another was nothing difficult for you."

She knew him well enough to know that Armandius would have felt something snapping inside his chest. He told Janir that he had felt a certain connection to Lord Loholt once, the feeling that they had both lost something that was very dear to them both and that could never be replaced. But now the aged knight had crossed a line. Lord Loholt had made himself an enemy of his son-in-law. His words were unforgivable.

Completely losing his temper, Armandius jerked against the chains and would have most likely strangled Aryana's father or bashed in his brains then and there, had not the guards restrained him.

"I will kill you!" Armandius shouted. "I am now convinced that you begetting my wife was a flaw in nature. I *will* kill you!" He meant it, by the passionate description the scribe jotted down. Perhaps not that day, perhaps not the next. But without a doubt, he was going to kill that son of a…

"What? By now the Argetallam would be only two years younger than her mother was when you…" Lord Loholt was cut off by the king's interjection.

"Enough!" Remian shouted, hastily motioning for Drianar to take his father away before Armandius broke through the guards and throttled him right here. Lord Loholt left with a taunting glance back at Armandius. Drianar almost had to carry his father out of the throne room.

The High King was silent for several seconds, apparently stunned that the normally aloof Armandius Caersynn would react with such passionate vehemence. For a time, there was no sound but the scratching of the scribe's pen on the parchment.

Struggling against the sheer rage that was threatening to overpower him, Armandius lowered his eyes to the floor and concentrated on restraining the desire to snap Lord Loholt's neck in two.

"That still does not explain why you raised this child," Remian continued, compassion softening his voice slightly. "Does it not make sense to destroy the offspring of your wife's captor?"

Taking a deep breath to keep his emotions in check, Armandius continued. "Seven years ago I was in command of a legion near the edge of the Staspin Waste. A group of armed men coming out of the Norwin Pass was spotted and the captain in charge of a small force…"

Here Remian interrupted again. "Who was the captain?"

"Captain Hastell of Dove Rise," Armandius briefly noted. "In any event, the captain did not wait to receive orders. Although he had been commanded not to engage any travelers in the pass unless instructed otherwise, he did." Again Armandius paused, not wanting to relive that day.

"Go on," Remian insisted, out of curiosity.

"They attacked, assuming that all there were Argetallams and they killed everyone, though not immediately. My wife died several hours after from her wounds." Armandius would have tried to regain his indifferent air, but failed miserably. His vision was fogging and he knew that if he didn't stop it he would soon be crying like an infant before the entire court.

The king was silent, letting Armandius compose himself until something occurred to him. "Then how did you come to rear the Argetallam?"

"She was with my wife as they were being sent away from the Citadel of the Argetallams to the winter residence of Sanreal."

"You said that they killed everyone," the king pointed out.

"Almost," Armandius corrected. "Janir healed. It is common knowledge that Argetallams can sometimes heal after mortal wounds."

"How do you then know that this...child...was your wife's?" Remian interrogated.

"I told you that Aryana died several hours later from her wounds. I spoke to her...before she died." Armandius voiced the last word menacingly, as if not saying it had been a way of preventing its truth. "She pleaded for me to promise that I would watch over Janir. With her dying breath, she begged me. I had not the heart nor the will to deny her." Armandius' voice had grown loud and bitter, but at the last sentence, his tone had softened.

Another long silence ensued. "What happened to the captain?" Remian wondered, recalling an unelaborated detail.

Armandius didn't answer. Instead he gave the king a sideways glance that asked *do you really want to know?* Remian seemed to have decided that he didn't.

"Very well." The king had long since slipped out of an enraged king's dialogue into a more cordial tone. "So you spared her and raised her for your wife's sake."

Armandius had obtained control of the clouds in his eyes and regained his stoic pose. If he did not have to tell anymore of Aryana, he would be fine.

With the efficiency that is gained through kingship, Remian made up his mind about Armandius' punishment and turned his considerations to the Argetallam. "What are your thoughts regarding this Janir, this Argetallam?" Remian announced.

"That she is like no Argetallam I have ever known. She is more her mother's child than anything else, and a daughter of Brevia."

"All the other Argetallams you have known were standing at the other end of a karkaton, I assume?" the High King pointlessly mused. Another very long silence. An uncomfortable silence. The withered old man beside the king scratched at the paper, meticulously taking down every word and action.

"Tell me about the night that this Janir killed Duke Ronan. What have you to say in that matter?" Remian proceeded.

"Duke Ronan tried to kill me. Janir went into the Riangar and killed him first," Armandius replied simply.

"Riangar?" Remian sought to confirm.

"Yes."

"Would you mind explaining what that is?" The king had no inkling.

Armandius restrained a sigh of frustration. "It's a state of selective bloodlust and complete invulnerability, brought on by an act of violence toward the Argetallam," Armandius summarized. Had he read that definition somewhere?

"Then why did she go into it to save you?"

"Because he struck her first, as she came between the duke and myself," Armandius elaborated.

"*Why* would the duke try to kill you?" Remian inquired.

"I do not know." Yet another silence. A painful silence. The scribe caught up with their words and there was no sound but the occasional uneasy swish of the courtiers' clothes.

"Why do you judge Janir through me?" Armandius mildly demanded, shattering the silence like an earthen vessel, causing the scribe to hastily take it down. "Is it not more fitting for her to stand here herself?"

"Oh, that is so. The Argetallam escaped, did she not?" Remian briefly considered and then returned to his deeply contemplative state.

The silence stretched on, as the king became immersed in his own thoughts. No one dared speak or move. Time itself seemed to have halted in favor of the monarch's inner contemplations. Perhaps he was considering whether or not Armandius would be able to control this girl. Undoubtedly, he was contemplating the possible military advantage he would have with an Argetallam at his disposal. But his next words came as a mild shock to all those standing by.

"If you can find her and bring her before me," Remian pondered "I will grant her amnesty for this crime. However, if she fails to appear before midsummer's eve, she will be judged guilty in her absence and banished from Brevia under pain of death."

There was an unrelenting finality in the High King's voice that made even the unerring scribe shiver from his small wooden desk.

CHAPTER 3

Separated

She should have left when Karile was still hanging from the tree. That was all Janir could think about as the day wore on and on. As if the world owed him something, he complained at every opportunity. He claimed the sun was too bright, riding the horse was too bumpy, the birds were too loud, the hills too steep, Saoven was too ugly to be with them. That was where Janir took the most offense. She secretly thought Saoven quite handsome. The midday sun was beating down on them and the wooded hills were growing into mountains with each step of the horses. The trees were scrunched close together on either side of the little group, as if trying to form a wall to enclose them. The path they followed was narrow, probably made by deer and other game. Grass grew so close to the path that the horses' legs brushed it with each step.

"Are we there yet?" Karile whined.

"No," Janir retorted.

"Are we there yet?"

"Shut up!"

For several strides of the horse Karile was silent.

"Are we…"

Janir lost control of her temper and elbowed him as hard as she could.

"Ouch!" Karile screamed.

"Karile," Saoven called back from his place in front of them, "if you refuse to cease antagonizing the lady, you will be forced to walk."

"Lady?" Karile mockingly asked. "What lady? I don't see any lady, just this…"

Janir sighed. "I apologize for hitting you, Karile," she amended.

"Well at last she apologizes! You know that's the first apology…"

"Silence!" Saoven hissed abruptly.

"Oh, no. Not you, too!" Karile moaned.

Saoven turned a menacing glare in the direction of Karile and the young enchanter decided to obey.

They halted in a small clearing, no more than three sword-lengths wide. Like a hawk, the elf sat perched on his mare, listening intently. Silently as an owl lands in a tree, Saoven swung off his horse and briefly motioned that they were to stay where they were. Like a deer he slipped through two saplings and vanished into the greenery like a phantom. Janir could feel Kalbo tensing. Whatever it was, the stallion sensed it, too.

Once Saoven was presumably out of earshot, Karile could barely contain his excitement. "What do you think it is?" Karile's voice had a childlike eagerness to it.

"Saoven will tell us when he returns." Janir was quite content to let Saoven do the scouting.

But Karile wasn't. Karile plopped off the side

of Kalbo like a sack of potatoes being dropped from a balcony. The horse nickered in confusion and awkwardly side-stepped to avoid the boy. After landing in a jumbled heap of robe, the young enchanter clambered awkwardly to his feet.

"Come now, Janir," Karile suggested eagerly, "let's find out what it is that our friend heard."

"So he's *our* friend now," Janir scoffed.

"Come on," Karile beckoned, then disappeared into the trees where Saoven was last seen.

Saoven had told her to stay put, so Janir did. That nutty little enchanter could be eaten by werewargs for all she cared. She was not going after him. There was no chance she would save his valueless hide. Then she considered how inept he must be when it came to self-preservation. So what if he started trouble and she wasn't there to rescue him? Why did she care? Hadn't she just been thinking that she should have left him the last time? But then again…..

With a meaningless shout of frustration, Janir swung off Kalbo's back and followed the mad wizard. "Karile!" she called.

Twigs snapped under her feet as she ran after him. Although Karile was almost half the size of Saoven, the elf had slipped through the trees like an eel into water, while Karile was plowing through the forest like a blind wild boar. The path the enchanter had taken was obvious. Janir merely had to follow the bent branches and fragments of torn robe.

"Karile!" Janir angrily shouted. "Karile!" The forest wasn't as dense here, so she had lost the enchanter's trail, but she could look about her surroundings.

The tall pines stretched heavenward. Ferns on the forest floor served as homes to the small forest life. A wood pecker was drumming in rhythm to some unknown beat. The sun poured through the pine needles, casting sunny patterns on the forest floor. All seemed silent and peaceful. She followed a game trail covered in deer and badger tracks. It seemed the easiest path to follow, all the while searching the greenery for more signs of Karile.

An alien set of noises caught her attention. The breaking tree limbs, the shouts of men, the scream of a wizard. Karile shot out of the thick brush like a rabbit chased by a hound, shrieking for help.

Not paying attention to his path, Karile hit Janir and tackled her to the ground.

"What have you done now?!" Janir demanded.

"No time to explain," Karile panted, and tried to escape. No sooner had he scrambled up, than he collided with a very angry and feral-looking man, who shoved him back down on the ground. With panic, Janir realized that they were surrounded on all sides.

They were encircled by wild-looking men as lanky as foxes. Covered with ragged skins, with matted hair on their heads and beards, they had a very scruffy, unkempt appearance. Their weapons were primitive. They held spears with stone heads and arrows with bone tips, but Janir knew that a rock can be deadly and that these weapons were, too. One of them stood towering over the wizard, shaking his fist violently and was doubtlessly elaborating all the things that he and his comrades were going to do to Karile when they took him back to their camp. The enchanter had a way of getting under people's skin.

Janir couldn't understand a word they were saying. It must have been some obscure dialect. But she did understand their apparent glee when they spotted her, greedily, the way they eyed her. She didn't like their looks. It gave her pinpricks of ice-cold fear along her spine and a sinking feeling of dread in the pit of her belly. Suddenly feeling like a child again, Janir wished that she could fling her arms around Armandius' neck as she used to when afraid.

One of them said something in the guttural tongue, to the effect of 'let's take them back to camp,' and another one, apparently their leader, seemed to heartily agree. Then another one skirted up, with several scratches on his face and a few pine needles in his unkempt hair, and excitedly informed the others of something new.

It seemed that there was a deer nearby, or something else to eat, because several of the by-standing warriors licked their lips excitedly, showing rows of yellowed teeth. Janir wondered how these people could catch anything, even a blind and deaf animal. If the creature didn't see or hear them, it would definitely smell their unwashed bodies and know immediately that it was being pursued. But, Janir reminded herself, she had been caught.

The leader made huge motions with his hands to emphasize the words and Janir was able to guess that some of them were going to chase the animal and others were going to take Janir and Karile back to the camp. Janir wondered if all the people in the camp smelled the same as these men, because if they did, she had no idea how anyone could endure such smell. Several of them went off into the trees and the others closed in on Janir and Karile.

What was she supposed to do? Where was Saoven when she needed him most? Janir frantically tried to conjure a way out of this predicament, but nothing came to mind. Why was it that when she tried to think, tried to come up with some clever scheme, she never could? She could hardly call Saoven. If she did, the feral-men would know that he was here and that would spoil his main advantage. But what was she supposed to do? In the end, it was Karile who had the idea, not her.

"Janir," he quietly murmured in a squeaky tone.

"Yes?" Janir quivered, crawling backward, away from the advancing warriors.

"I suggest a grossly over-rated, but highly successful battle tactic," Karile whispered, edging closer to her, as if for protection. Janir was ready to listen to anyone's suggestions.

"What is it?" she frantically whispered.

"Run! Run! Run!" he screamed, popping up off the ground and running under one of the primitive warrior's legs. The one he had run under bent down to stare after the enchanter, shouting protest. Janir seized the opportunity and raced after Karile. Why hadn't she thought of this? It was so simple.

More shouts of anger came from the others, and the chase was on.

Running faster than she ever had in her life, Janir fled after Karile in the direction of the horses. The thump of their pursuers' animal skin boots seemed to shake the earth with each step, spurring Janir faster and faster. They were gaining ground, of that she was certain. The noise was growing louder and louder as she ran with Karile screaming behind her like a fearful girl. Soon she wasn't sure if the sound was their pursuers' footfalls or her heart pounding in her ears. Her face was hot and the pine boughs whipped her arms as she shoved her way through the dense brush.

Just as she burst into the clearing with Karile right behind her, she tripped on a fallen branch. The wizard practically trampled her to get away. Having returned sometime earlier, Saoven stood by his snow-white mare waiting for them. The elf seemed about to demand as to where they had been when their pursuers came into view.

In hindsight, Janir thought Saoven had killed one or two of the feral men, but she couldn't be sure. Whatever the case, even though she had landed flat on the ground and scraped her face on the rocky terrain, the primitive warriors never caught her.

Her eyes locked on Kalbo. To her surprise, Karile flipped up into the saddle faster than a blink. Janir jumped up behind him and before she knew what was happening, Karile was holding the reins of the horse and she was clinging to his skinny waist for dear life. Galloping through the trees behind them, Janir heard Saoven's steed following. Several of the feral men, the ones who had apparently gone off to catch an animal, came out of the trees on their other side and began shouting furiously as the riders charged past.

"They were going to eat the horses!" Janir shouted against the wind. "What kind of barbarians are these people?"

Karile was an amazing rider. With practiced skill, he steered Kalbo through the maze of towering trees away from the tribal men. Left, right, right again. The skill of this young wizard was most remarkable. Never once did Karile mislead Kalbo as they raced through the trees, trying to outrun their pursuers, whose cries were growing ever fainter. The stallion seemed to sense the danger, and showed no qualms about their speed or direction. Trees zipped past them like insects and the horses and riders pressed on. The five of them were traveling uphill when they came out of the trees onto a narrow ledge that led around the edge of the cliff to the far side of the mountain. Down, down, down below them was a camp that looked the size of an ant hill. A band of about twenty men with fires and deer-skin tents lay below. Janir stared down on the troop for several minutes, then realized that she was leaning towards them. Shivers shot through her when she internalized how far *down* it was. Or how high *up* they had gone so quickly. Rocks slid underneath Kalbo's hooves, clattering down the mountainside, as if to show her just how far one could fall from here. Finally the horses left the gravel and zipped around to the other side of the mountain, where it was grassier. The horses pounded deeper into the mountains, running at an angle along the steep slope of the giant earthen mounds. Kalbo's breath was coming in ragged gasps, and Janir was beginning to worry about him. Behind them, Saoven's mare was thumping her hooves hard against the earth with no signs of tiring.

Deciding after a harsh gallop that they had outrun their hunters, Karile checked Kalbo to a halt on a green meadow with lush grass. Janir swiveled around in the saddle to see Saoven rein in his steed behind them. Now both the horses were heaving from the effort and the riders were heaving from the rush.

"We shouldn't stop," Saoven breathed, "the horses should keep walking for awhile."

Karile nodded and kicked Kalbo into a walk.

"Where did you learn to ride with such skill, Karile Kerwyn?" Janir inquired, very much impressed, but for some reason a little angry.

"Oh, Daddy made me learn," he dismissively replied.

"One doesn't teach a wizard to ride like that," Janir countered.

"No, but you do teach a knight to ride like that," Karile carelessly explained.

Saoven was glancing about, searching the countryside for any signs of intruders. "Your father is a knight?" Saoven asked in a disinterested tone, he might have been speaking to a two-year-old.

"Yes, he is. Always wanted me to take up the family trade, but I never liked the armor. Too hot." Karile seemed to think it unimportant.

"If your father is a knight, how did you end up as a tramp in Green Haven?" Janir skeptically demanded.

"I ran away," Karile explained.

"Right," Janir scoffed.

"No, really. Daddy wouldn't let me study magic like I wanted to. He burned my book of incantations and told me that if I didn't start playing more with swords, he would make me sorry." Karile shrugged, as if it was nothing serious. "I thought to run away to the Wizard Temple, but then decided on a bigger quest." Karile seemed about to laugh. "If only Daddy could see me now."

"Is your father the steward of a fief?" Janir pried.

"As a matter of fact, he is," Karile announced, as if it had just occurred to him.

"Which one?" Janir pressed after the enchanter remained silent for several seconds.

"Ivy Down," Karile replied. "But I ran off for the Wizard Temple about two months ago."

Janir didn't ask anymore questions. Where Karile was from explained why he held such abnormally strong opinions concerning Argetallams. The boy's father was doubtless in command of the garrison in Ivy Down, and that would be enough reason for his disdain of her race.

The two horses walked side-by-side for a few hours after the incident. They left the meadow and ventured into the trees, continuing higher up into the mountains. The steep hills with their tall grasses and treeless landscapes blended into a single image in her mind. Janir noticed that the air was cooler. At least twenty miles from where they had lost the feral men with their crude but potentially fatal weapons, Saoven announced that they should stop for the night. The horses were tired and so were their riders. They made their camp near an outcropping of trees on the top of a slope that overlooked the valley below. Although they could see for miles, there was no sign of the feral men chasing them. The tall, green grasses bent in the wind, the cold wind. Janir secured her cloak about her shoulders. The elf made camp on this spot because of the view they had on three out of four sides. Janir protested that it merely meant other people could see their fire from three sides, but Saoven told her there was no need to worry because no one would be looking for them. When Janir reminded him of the feral men who had chased them there, he told her that these people had never chased him more than ten miles before, and he didn't expect them to change their ways now. She started to ask him what he meant by "before," but decided to hold her tongue.

Saoven seemed distracted, as if he were thinking very deep inside himself. Still, Janir didn't question him as they unsaddled the horses. They cleaned a brace of leverets Saoven had caught and built a fire.

At length, the three of them sat around the fire. Karile stared intently at the young rabbits on the spit, watching them the way an eagle watches its prey. Saoven stared meditatively into the flames and Janir stared with concern at Saoven.

"I am going to have to leave you, Janir," Saoven reluctantly announced.

Taken aback, Janir hesitated several seconds before responding. "Why?" was all she could manage to reply.

"You are in the mountains now, and I must inform

the Brevians of the Ralissian band that is here."

"Ralissian? Those people were from Ralissia?" Janir repeated. "I thought that people from Ralissia were dwarves and mountain trolls."

"The famous ones, but a great number of its inhabitants are mortal. Like you." He added the last two words sadly, as if that was a terrible problem.

"Also, I must tell my people about the Argetallams' search for the Key of Amatahns."

Janir bit her lip. Saoven and Karile hated her people so much. It could become dangerous or fatal for her if he found out.

Misinterpreting her expression, he offered consolation. "I am certain Armandius has worked things out and that you will be able to return to Green Haven soon."

Smiling faintly, Janir wanted to change the subject, but couldn't think of anything.

"While you're there, ask the Oracle why it is he let the Argetallams live," Karile interjected.

Janir tensed. Hadn't they discussed this topic enough already? Thankfully, the issue was dropped right after that as Saoven didn't reply.

"I thought the Ralissians were famous for their metalwork, not their thugs," Karile continued, as if he wasn't paying attention to his own words.

"Silver is the main export of the dwarves. Yet in some parts of the mountains there are tribal mortals who make war on whoever is weaker than themselves." Saoven was considering something again. "The dwarves have kept them in check for decades, but it appears that for some reason they are spreading. It seems my father will be paying the dwarf king, Vladimir, a visit about this soon." Saoven seemed to contemplate something deeper than his words. Everyone knew that dwarves and elves were as incompatible as oil and water; however within the last few years they had reached a sort of agreement. The elves stayed away from Ralissia and the dwarves stayed away from Silverwood. Brevia was the only place the dwarves and elves could both be found, but even then they had their own trade routes and port cities, at opposite ends of the country. As for any elf or dwarf found wandering in a territory belonging to the other race…..Janir didn't want to think about being hated because of one's blood. She wanted to ask Saoven why a human emissary couldn't be sent, but Karile spoke before she did.

"Odd how people seem to take a disliking to me easily."

No one paid attention to the enchanter's comment.

And now a new thought occurred to Janir. "The Ralissian Mountains are many days from here, why would such a band with no apparent motivation be in Brevia?"

Saoven shrugged, clueless. They were all quiet for a very long time.

"What am I to do?" Janir inquired. "Where am I suppose to go?"

"Stay in the mountains," Saoven replied. "As high up as you can go without endangering the horse on the slopes. Keep a low profile and avoid all other travelers when possible. Hunt at night. That is when most hunters have returned home. Watch for were-wargs. If you move every other night or so they should not find you. If they do, remember that they fear water. And stay away from cliffs. Griffins may be nesting there." Saoven seemed to have completed his advice. Not that he needed to tell her half of it.

"Will you know where to find me?" she ventured.

He gave her a sideways glance. "I am an elf," was his simple reply. "I can usually find anything and anyone in creation, as long as I know what or who I am searching for."

Janir nodded. Of course, she had forgotten that.

"Though," Saoven remarked, "I did have a slight bit of trouble finding you this time. I could not feel you at all. I must be getting lax." The elf seemed to genuinely believe it was his own mistake that had kept him from sensing her. "Hardly matters. If I happen to err again, I can do what I did this time, search for Kalbo," he declared.

Saoven left them the next morning. "May the sun, moon, and stars guide you until we meet again," Saoven blessed her as he turned his pristine white mount toward the hills.

Unmoving, Janir just stood and watched him disappear into the trees while Karile chattered about something she wasn't listening to. Even though Karile's voice was running in the background, she felt suddenly so alone, naked on the hillside. Everything she had come to depend on for safety and protection was gone. She wondered if this was how fledgling birds felt when left on their own for the first time. Bracing herself to face the enchanter, Janir turned toward the direction of Karile and Kalbo again. Karile was standing beside Kalbo, standing on his tiptoes, trying to lift the horse's saddle onto the stallion's back.

"What are you doing?" Janir demanded. "Let the poor boy rest, he ran a long way yesterday."

"Oh, that's okay. I had no intention for either of us to ride him," Karile pacified.

"Then why are you saddling him?" Janir probed.

Karile grunted as the saddle finally reached its desired altitude. "Because if we're going to find the Key of Amatahns before those blasted Argetallams, we had better start moving. And I don't want to carry the saddle, do you?"

"Who said we were going?" Janir demanded "Why don't we just stay here and let people much more qualified than us find it, whatever it is?"

"You don't understand, do you Janir?" Karile sighed and sounded remotely sane for a change. "By the time Saoven reaches his people, tells them the story, they assemble a group to go after it, the group is ready to move and those people find where it's hidden…the Argetallams could have found it and delivered it to their client a dozen times over. They have a head-start on us." Karile looked suddenly more serious than she had seen him in the few days she had known him. It was very unnerving.

"Why should I care?" demanded Janir. "You and Saoven kept talking about 'nearly unlimited power,' but you never even explained yourselves. Why should I care about this Key?"

Karile sighed, "Do you remember the story of Amatahns, the great savior of the world?"

"That antediluvian tale about the wizard who saved the three races from the mazag? You are referring to that Amatahns?"

"Yes, do you remember it?"

"It was something about there being a great warrior race that led a war against the three and Amatahns took their magic and knowledge," Janir recalled. "But there is nothing in the story about any Key."

"Not many people know the rest of the story," explained Karile. "Their knowledge the enchanter contained in an orb and kept for himself. It was lost to our realms when he sailed across the sea."

"And the point of the story is?" Janir pressed.

"I haven't told you what he did with the other thing he took from this race," Karile qualified, impatient at her impatience. "Their magic."

The enchanter paused, as if for dramatic effect. Janir raised one eyebrow. "What about their magic?" she prompted.

"He sealed it in a crystal chamber, and if anyone can stand inside the chamber they can absorb the power of an entire race!" Karile exclaimed.

Janir was still not impressed. "And what does this Key have to do with anything?"

Karile sighed and made a frustrated grunt. "You need the key to open the chamber!" he shouted.

"What exactly will you do with this Key once you

have it?" Janir pressed.

"Hide it from the Argetallams. I would never use it," he assured her.

"How will you keep it from the fiercest band of warriors ever to walk the earth?" Janir demanded.

The enchanter was quiet for sometime before admitting "I don't know."

"Figures."

"But that's not important right now. We just need to keep it from the Argetallams until we can hide it again."

"No," was her firm response.

"Come on, Janir," Karile pleaded.

"No."

"Please. It's just in the province of Ivy Down, not three day's ride away."

"Conveniently, the province in which the Key is located, happens to border with the Staspin Waste," Janir muttered to herself.

"Listen." Karile sounded almost desperate. "I can't do this alone. I need you, Janir. Terrible things will happen if the Argetallams get this key first."

"I want nothing to do with Argetallams," Janir resolutely decreed.

"We'll be there and gone before they ever arrive," Karile assured her.

"You said they had a head start," Janir contradicted.

"True, but they don't know where the Key is. I do. Remember I told you about how I was putting the pieces together? Well I know where it is for certain and they don't."

"Karile, something has been bothering me since you said it. How do you know that the Argetallams are after this Key?"

"My father runs the Ivy Down garrison." Karile was only confirming what she had already suspected. "A few weeks ago, they spoke to someone, a convert spy named Camak or something like that. But this person told them that the Argetallams had been hired to find the Key of Amatahns and that the prince was being sent to find it."

"*The* prince?" Janir skeptically repeated. "Do you really think that with three courtesans, the Lord Argetallam has only one son?"

Deciding that his clueless shrug was the best response she would receive, Janir went on. "Another thing, why did Saoven believe you? You're obviously mad."

"An elf knows that no enchanter, whether of the Tenth or First Degree, would lie about a matter concerning the Key," Karile gravely explained.

"Even a mad one?" Janir demanded.

"Alright! So they have ways of telling whether or not I'm lying," Karile admitted. "Call it a sixth sense or whatever."

"So you expect me to risk my life for a 'sixth sense' and the supposition that you 'wouldn't lie' about this?" Janir queried.

Karile considered her words for several more seconds. "Yes. That's right."

With a sigh, Janir resignedly capitulated. "Very well, I'll go with you to find Amatahns' Key."

"The Key *of* Amatahns," Karile corrected.

Janir had been about to indignantly shout that she could call it whatever she wanted when Karile continued.

"I'm so glad you decided to come. I'll need help when we face the monsters that guard it."

"Monsters?"

Chapter 4
The Key of Armatahns

It was just an ordinary cave, nestled on a small ridge that overlooked the rest of Ivy Down. Janir had not originally wanted to come to this precarious spot, but Karile had convinced her after several hours of arguing, that it was safe to go down, even though they could see the lights of Laress, Ivy Down's castle, from their lofty perch above the valley. Strangely, Karile had never once questioned why she wanted to remain out of sight, nor why she was a fugitive. Rain poured on their heads as if the sky itself was trying to hold them down to prevent their entry. Like stern commands to leave, thunder and lightning split the night sky every few moments. The mouth of the cave was in the side of a treacherously steep mountain, with only one way to enter. This whole place seemed to have been engineered to strike terror in the heart of all who drew near.

Mud and steep terrain not being very tractable, the maiden and enchanter had nearly fallen off the narrow goat paths which led to the cave several times. Dirt and grime had spattered their clothes and hair. Janir had the rope coiled around her shoulders with a pack she had put together before they left. It contained a flint, steel, a canteen which hardly seemed necessary at the moment, leather straps for quick repair of practically anything, and several other odds and ends. The mahogany box was inside the pack as well.

Karile swallowed, and took a step in the direction of the cave. When Janir didn't follow, the enchanter paused. "Well, come on," he prompted.

"I am so glad we left Kalbo at the top of the mountain," Janir sighed.

"That's not important," Karile dismissed.

Looking one last time up at the pouring rain, Janir dove into the blackness of the cave with Karile. The first thing she realized was that they should have brought a torch and wondered why she hadn't thought of something so basic. She decided she should ask him, but then a shadow flitted off to her right and she swirled to stare fearfully toward it.

Karile muttered something that sounded like gibberish to Janir and clapped his hands six times. Lights glowed along both sides of the cave immediately. Torches left behind by someone or something, flared into being. With a cursory glance at Karile, Janir stepped to one side and gingerly lifted one of the torches out of its iron ring. Picking her way through the stones which were strewn about as if from a giant's tantrum, Janir again thought she spotted a shadow whoosh past. The flames on the torches stirred, but then all was quiet. Karile didn't seem to have noticed; he was staring down at an antediluvian-looking piece of paper, trying to keep it from rolling back into a scroll. While he pored over it, Janir was nervously glancing at the many tunnels and passageways that led off to their left and right. Any one of them could be hiding some horrible and carnivorous monster.

"Where did you have that?" Janir wondered.

"In my robe," Karile quickly replied. "And thanks to you not wanting to come earlier, it was soaked in that downpour and now it doesn't want to unfurl."

She thought it would have been soaked anyway. Janir ignored his accusation and surveyed their surroundings. The cave seemed to grow wider the further it went on. The torches stopped just ahead and the ground seemed to sink. Red soil was sticking to the hem of her dress and her boots. The smoky smell of burning torches wafted about them along with another smell, a musty, scaly and strange smell. Janir didn't like that smell.

With a little shout of triumph, Karile finally unrolled the scroll and began to decipher it. He muttered incomprehensible words of a dozen syllables or more, as if they had some special meaning to him.

"Straight ahead," Karile announced. "Janir, could you do me a favor?" he requested. Without waiting for a response, he continued. "Please make sure that nothing jumps out at us from those tunnels to the side?"

His request was unnecessary, Janir was already watching each tunnel for any signs of malign movement.

WHOOSH!

The two of them stopped instantly. Frozen by

fear, the pair stared with wide eyes into the shadows.

"What was that?" Karile whispered at length.

The young wizard had hidden behind Janir as a strange red shadow, shapeless and almost soundless, had swooped in front of them. It had come as quickly as it had gone, there and away in half the time it takes for a heart to beat. Terrified, Karile gripped Janir's skirt as a child might. Janir's skin felt like a blanket of ice had been laid over it and she was acutely aware of everything about her: the soft drip of cave water, the chatter of Karile's teeth, each individual shadow cast by the torch. They had reached the edge of the dirt cave, and now beheld stone as flat and smooth as a frozen lake walled in all four sides as far as the torch cast its glow. Janir waved the torch in her hand from side to side. Nothing was there. They stood completely motionless for several minutes, afraid of what would happen if they stayed put, but more afraid of what would happen if they moved. Janir's knees were shaking, knocking together like branches in a wind, but she tried to conceal it from Karile. The wizard was already frightened enough. Tentatively, like a fox entering a meadow, Janir stepped forward. As soon as her foot pressed down on the stone they heard a rumbling sound, as if the whole mountain was groaning. They whipped around terrified in time to glimpse two huge stone slabs close the mouth of the cave. They were trapped with no way of escape.

As if on cue, the torches closest to the cave mouth winked out in rows simultaneously, until the only one still lit was in Janir's trembling fist. Karile was too scared even to blame her for causing the doors to close. Deciding that they had no where else to go, Janir took another step forward. She waited. Nothing happened. She began slowly advancing into the perfectly square stone tunnel with the enchanter clinging to her for dear life. Her footsteps and Karile's shuffling echoed softly in the tunnel. They deliberately inched forward, barely taking half-steps at a time. This seemed to go on for hours. Step, look. Step, look.

As the pair crawled along at a turtle's pace the tunnel's ceiling abruptly became much higher. Janir realized that they were walking toward a ledge that led just two sword-lengths lower into the mountain, made of solid granite that glistened in the torch's glow. Recalling what had happened the last time she stepped on a strange surface, Janir hesitated a very long time before deciding to step down onto the granite. Taking a deep breath, Janir dropped onto the ledge and hopped down into the next chamber. Karile, not to be left behind, jumped after her.

The young enchanter had barely clambered to his feet when they heard the rumbling sound again. When Janir glanced up, three heavy slabs of stone had already sealed the path behind them.

Deciding that there was nothing she could do, Janir held the torch up as high as she could. They were inside a huge domed room with mosaics on the walls, colorful mosaics which told of mortals, elves, dwarves, beasts, and birds.

Karile muttered meaningless words again and the room was instantly illuminated by a glow which seemed to come from all directions. The torch winked out immediately, as if it couldn't compete with the glow. Having no more use for it, Janir tossed it aside. Karile was standing before one of the walls, almost leaving nose prints on the mosaic he was so close.

"They tell a story," Karile decided.

"What does?" Janir absently inquired, searching the walls for a way out. She paced the circular room, about twenty sword lengths in diameter, searching for an exit. Any exit. Every crease in the stone seemed solid, every crack sealed. Janir noticed what appeared to be the remains of a human skeleton lying at one end, but it was so old it had mostly turned to dust and she couldn't tell for sure what it had been. Perhaps thousands of years old? This discovery motivated her search for an escape. Karile's ramblings interrupted her frantic quest.

"The mosaics, they tell the story of Amatahns," Karile announced. "See?" He pointed to a piece on the wall. Janir knew that the pictures were very vivid, but she wasn't paying attention to them. Still continuing her search for a way out, she examined a set of four pillars erected in the very center of the room. These pillars had no mosaics and were simply blue granite towers to support the ceiling. Karile's voice was running in the background like a river's murmur, but Janir wasn't listening.

"Oh, look Janir!" Karile exclaimed in delight. "Look at this mosaic of a dragon, isn't it amazing?"

Janir stopped her seeking long enough to behold the mosaic Karile was so enthusiastic about.

It was of a monster; that much was certain. The

creature had a thick, rectangular body, like a cow's with stocky, muscular legs, and webbed toes, long black claws on the ends that were digging into a rock in the artwork. Its body was red, like the flames of the torch that had just been extinguished, with blood red spikes running along the beast's spine from the back of its head to the end of its whip-like tail. The creature's eyes were yellow with tiny slits for irises, a wild, hungry look in them. Whatever this creature was, it had two half-jaws on top and two on the bottom. The jaws were spread apart, to reveal a thin, forked tongue that was coiled as if ready to strike. Its short, muscular neck was twisting around to stare at some unknown foe.

Janir was amazing by the detail of the piece. She could almost see the individual scales on the beast's body, hear its heavy breathing. Again, she smelled that musty, scaly scent. Such great attention had been given to the beast's eye, she thought she could see it moving. It flickered from side to side......See it moving? That meant.....

"Karile, get down! It's real!" Janir screamed. She tackled the wizard to the floor just as the beast pounced. It missed and overshot, skidding to the other side of the dome.

The dragon spread its four mandibles to reveal two rows of needle-point teeth along each jaw. An ear shattering roar of anger shook the dome as the beast turned to renew its attack. Janir shoved Karile to one side, and she jumped to the other. Not certain which one of them to take, the beast hesitated a split second before batting at Janir with an iron claw. She felt the beast's powerful muscles ripple as it tossed her like a toy. For several agonizing seconds, she couldn't breathe, her chest wouldn't expand enough to inhale. The pack she had been wearing had protected her somewhat from the claws, but now its contents were strewn about her. In front of her, lying just out of reach, was the mahogany box. It seemed to be calling her, beckoning her to open the polished lid. Strangely, it hadn't been damaged when it had flown out of the pack.

Open me, open me, the box called. She heard the words like whispers in the wind. They could have just as easily been her imagination gone rampant. Open, open. This time, she had to open it. Janir coughed, and tried to push herself off the granite floor. Almost of their own volition, her hands snatched up the box, turned it around so that she would face the opposite side of the hinges, and ripped it open. Even though the box had stayed closed for years, the lid opened easily. She forgot everything, the screaming wizard, the roaring beast, her own bruises and cuts.

Inside the box, placed side-by-side, were the two most beautiful objects Janir had ever seen. She couldn't understand why she thought them so beautiful. They were a pair of black rods, perfectly round and perfectly straight, lying lengthwise on a purple velvet cushion inside the box.

Touch us...touch us...

Janir had to. She couldn't stop herself. Gingerly, she wrapped her fingers around one of the rods. She immediately felt a huge wave of excitement wash over her. Janir had to pick up the other one. Slipping her other hand around the rod felt…right. Like this was how things belonged, were supposed to be.

In a flash, the beast had turned its attention to Karile. The wizard was in the four pillars, trying to keep the snapping jaws from reaching him.

She had to help Karile. Janir rose to her feet, clenching a rod in each hand. Before she realized it, she had reached one of the beast's powerful hind legs. Driving the rods down with a force that showed uncharacteristic strength, she struck the beast in two places at once.

She became aware of a droning, wailing sound coming from the rods, and a high-pitched scream of distress coming from the monster. The beast flopped on its side, shaking on the ground, yelping like a beaten pup. Flipping on its side, out of reach, it wobbled to its feet, turned and clacked its mandibles together in warning. Janir advanced toward it, her rods held in a firm grasp. The beast tried to intimidate her, striking out with its powerful forelimbs again, but she kept coming toward it. Realizing its bluff was futile, the creature turned and staggered away from the girl. As it turned, Janir spotted two black welts where she had jabbed it on the thigh.

The monster wobbled toward the wall, whimpering pitifully. As if to offer refuge for the beast, the walls parted into another tunnel, allowing the monster to escape. The doors closed behind him immediately, again sealing them in the chamber.

Janir no longer felt the need to grasp the rods, but she held onto them anyway. Lying on his back, Karile was still shouting with terror.

"That thing's alive!" he shrieked.

"Yes, it is Karile," Janir replied. She felt strangely calm, quite the opposite of what she had expected.

"What do we do now? Who knows what other horrible things could jump out of the walls at us?" Karile seemed on the verge of tears.

Before Janir answered, they heard a rumbling in the earth again, the sound of a mountain groaning. A third tunnel opened. A crease in the stone that Janir had thought solid was now parting. Feeling relief, she barely had time to seize the wizard before the doors began to shut. Frantically, she shoved Karile forward and clambered after him herself.

This time she dropped down three sword lengths. Karile was moaning at the bottom and she missed landing on him by inches. The ground was soft, and her landing was cushioned by the loose earth. Still, she didn't move for several seconds because of the jarring the fall. They were in total darkness. She blinked several times trying to see. A small point of pale bluish light shone ahead, but it was so small or so far away it didn't light their way. She groped for Karile in the darkness, trying to find him. To her surprise, she was clenching a rod in each hand. Was it possible that she had snatched them up again as they were fleeing? She hadn't had time to grab any of the other objects that had been in her pack. Janir cautiously probed the darkness with one of the rods, in case they had landed next to another monster. The rod softly scraped along the loose soil. The cave floor gave way to what seemed to be a channel of some sort. A channel meant to conduct water, perhaps?

They would need water, so Janir pushed the rod along, and into the channel.

A terrific shrieking, ear-shattering sound split the air, so high pitched Janir could feel the vibrations. A huge spark lit the cave and embers rained toward Janir, stinging her cheeks. Then came a loud whooshing sound as fire spread from the rod into the channel. Janir recoiled as fast as she could, scrambling away from the fire. A moan of protest came from Karile when she slammed backward into him.

The rod in her hand had somehow set off a spark, lighting whatever it was, most likely oil, that flowed in the channels. Flames advanced around them in an arc, illuminating a huge room, bigger than any they had seen before. This room was rectangular and more of a corridor than a room, with two rows of thick pillars running its length. The fire spread in a straight line through the pillars, lighting the darkness. This part of the caves felt as if it had been made when people were just learning about art. Instead of mosaics, clay had been used to color the vivid shapes and faces. Strange characters, meaningless scratches, as if drawn by claws, in a seemingly random pattern, decorated the ceiling.

"Hmm," Karile mused. "It seems you found the lights."

Ignoring him, Janir clambered to her feet and gripped the rods tighter in her hands. Karile popped upright beside her.

"Look Janir! This room has drawings too!" he whispered with delight.

"You told me that the monsters were dead!" Janir

indignantly retorted. "That they had died out thousands of years ago, remember?"

"Yes, well it seems I was wrong, doesn't it? They are still here to guard the power that was taken from them," Karile admitted. "But at least we know where they will be because the last one came from the mosaic."

"Well, do you see any more mosaics of monsters?" Janir inquired, her back to the wizard as she surveyed the shadows for movement.

"No, but look here!" Karile giddily exclaimed, pointing to a place on the ceiling with wild scratches. *"Only the child of Compassion and Strength may vanquish the Gifted One and deliver Mankind.'* An odd prophecy, wouldn't you agree?" Karile inquired,

Janir was too distracted to pay attention. She thought she saw something moving. In the orange glow from the flames, it was hard to tell if she had seen a red-scaled body, or just a shadow.

"Get behind me, Karile," Janir commanded, taking up a defensive stance.

"Why? So you can see all the interesting things first? Not a chance!" the little enchanter retorted.

"Get. Behind. Me." Janir repeated each word emphatically. Now she was certain, she had seen a pair of yellow eyes glowering at them from the shadows. As the fire at the far end of the caves died down, darkness was slowly reclaiming the chamber. The eyes blinked and reappeared, closer this time. Again she smelled a musty, scaly scent that reminded her of slime and dust mixed together.

Karile followed her gaze. It was easy for Janir to

know the exact moment he spotted the eyes, because he suddenly tensed like a bowstring and gripped her madly again. He whimpered, and Janir disgustedly rolled her own eyes in the spreading darkness.

The yellow eyes drew closer. Karile gripped Janir tighter. Holding the rods out in front of her, she stepped to one side and Karile quickly followed.

They heard a clacking sound.

Tck, tck, tck… the beast smacked its four jaws together. Now the only usable light burned behind them, casting eerie shadows of the pair far along the corridor.

Then they saw it. This one was far bigger than the first, which was the size of a small horse. This creature towered above them at twice the height of a man.

The clicks didn't seem random to Janir. They seemed calculated, as if they had some meaning she could barely decipher. If she tried very hard to understand, she could see rather than hear meanings and ideas that her mind translated into words. It was like untempered thought being transmitted through sound.

"It has been many freezes since I last laid eyes upon your kind," the clicks seemed to say. The monster craned its neck to survey them closer and seemed to be waiting for something to happen.

"We don't want any trouble," Janir commented, because she felt like she should say something.

"Then don't start any, Invulnerable."

Shivers shot up and down Janir's back as the beast unerringly identified her as an Argetallam.

"Please, we need the Key," Janir explained.

"Why are you talking to it?" Karile whispered. He couldn't understand the beast. Not having time to argue with the wizard, Janir again turned her attention to the monster standing over them.

"The bane of my race was the creation of your forefather. Drell was the pinnacle of power for men, and the downfall of my kind. Tell me, fleshling, what is your name?"

Surprised that the beast would care, but feeling obligated to reply, she answered, "Janir."

"She-hawk. Not a very fitting name for one so timid. Perhaps it is because you are, as of yet, only a fledgling?"

The beast made a clicking sound that sounded like a snarl, and began flicking out its tongue experimentally, as if testing its limits. *"I long to taste the flesh of Drell's wretched spawn. You still hold his scent, even though it has been, what? Four hundred-and-twenty-odd generations?"* The clacking was growing hungry, hateful. The brief courtesy, however small, was gone.

"Karile," Janir quivered, "be ready to run."

The enchanter was too frightened to argue with her or question her motives. A squeak was all she received by way of acknowledgment.

They waited. Janir wanted the beast to make the first move so she stood still, waiting for it to come within reach of her rods. Time ticked away slower than ever. The beast seemed cautious of Janir, as if it knew about the rods. The monster might have heard the other one whimpering, but the girl doubted that any sound passed through these impenetrable stone walls. The creature again craned its short neck, Janir intently, auditing her capabilities as an adversary with a practiced eye.

"You trust your karkaton, I see," the beast sneered. *"My people have fought against karkaton for eons. Do you think I would not know their weaknesses?"*

The beast lunged at them with a pent-up fury that seemed come be from millennia of hate. Janir dove toward the beast and Karile followed closely behind. Desperate for an idea, Janir raised her rods above her head and dragged them along the underside of the creature, marking its soft white belly with black streaks.

Screeching an ear-splitting cry, the beast leapt out of the way and flopped to one side, yelping as Janir had hoped. Not easily defeated, the monster lashed its tail after them, falling short several inches and smashing a solid stone pillar instead. Recoiling its tail the way an ox driver recoils his whip, the beast roared and clacked with rage. It sent its tail after them again, this time tripping Janir lightly with the tip, bringing her to the ground. The rods flew out of her grip.

The beast snarled with fury and leaned closer with clacking jaws. Janir tried to scramble to her feet and run, but the monster was quicker. It dove in for the kill like a swooping bird of prey. Janir would have died right there had it not been for the one who entangled her in this whole affair to begin with. Thinking quickly, Karile had taken the largest remnant of the smashed pillar he could lift and with a heave sent it hurdling through the air toward the creature's snapping head. The beast made a weak groaning sound and staggered sideways.

Fearfully, Janir leapt nimbly to her feet, snatched up the rods and pointed frantically toward the blue light ahead. Karile understood the cue immediately and took off running at a full-gallop. Janir had to scramble to catch up with him. The pair raced blindly toward what they perceived to be that bluish-white glow at the end of the hall. With her knees beginning to ache and her breath coming in gasps, Janir began to think the light was an optical illusion. Perhaps this hall went on forever, Janir wondered in terror. No, of course it didn't go on forever. Those kinds of things were in stories. But so were monsters with forked tongues and whip-tails, she realized. Forcing herself not to think, she sped on faster as the thunderous lope of the monster boomed in her ears.

"Run faster, Karile!" Janir panted, screaming over the beast's angry clicking.

"Do I look like I want to be eaten?" the enchanter shouted back.

"Just run!" Janir snapped.

Closer. They had to be getting closer to the light, of that she was certain. Determined not to be eaten herself, Janir pounded frantically toward the glow faster than before, trying to escape from the monster, outpacing Karile, zooming past him.

As she drew nearer, she realized with despair that the point of light they had staked all their hopes on was nothing but a small crack in the ragged stone wall before them. Janir skidded to a stop at the wall, hurriedly trying to concoct a new plan. Racking her brains for an idea, she drew a blank. Karile went charging straight at her, screaming like some terror-stricken animal. His arms flailed wildly at his sides. The beast was directly behind him. The enchanter's eyes looked the size of charger plates.

Janir raised the rods, ready to ward off another attack, when Karile slammed into her like a load of bricks. The wizard had been running too fast to stop, too terrified to care that he was headed straight for a stone wall. Whatever the case, he collided with Janir, shoving her against the rock wall like a battering ram, driving her through it with a force she would never have suspected to be within Karile's power. The wall gave way easily, as if it had been waiting to break. Janir realized with astonishment that they were rolling down a slope of red sand, bumping into rocks every few turns. The frustrated clacking of the monster seemed distant now. There was only the unhappy shouts of Karile as he did somersaults down the slope. Red sand was everywhere, in her hair, in her eyes, up her nose, in her mouth. She tried to grab onto something, anything to stop this tumbling, but nothing checked their down-slope roll.

Finally, they rocked to a stop at the bottom of the hill. The world still felt as if it was tilting, spinning around her like a wheel. Janir coughed out sand, tried to brush it off her face. It was even sticking to her soaked dress. Not any more, she thought grimly; now the sand was wet and clinging to her in the process.

"I hate sand," Janir groaned, spitting out the abrasive grains.

"Scratchy, sticky and grainy," Karile weakly remarked, "what's not to hate?"

Her eyes began to focus. Janir surveyed the enchanter. He looked as if someone had powdered him with sand. Janir knew she did, too. The beast clacked furiously from the top of the hill, able to fit one clawed paw out the hole they had made, unable to force the rest of its hulk through. Then it occurred to her, she could *see* it. They were at the bottom of a small cavern with a narrow river flowing through it. Above them a huge orb hung, bathing the whole cavern in a gentle, bluish glow. Sheer-looking, jagged walls lined the other sides of the cavern. The ceiling was far overhead. At their feet, the river flowed through and under two of the walls. Janir staggered to her feet. Karile was still moaning on the ground behind her. The world had stopped spinning and she could see clearly again. Scanning the opposite bank for an exit, she spotted what appeared to be a wooden door, incongruously placed in the wall. She roughly dragged Karile to his feet.

"Help me find a way to cross this river," Janir commanded. She retrieved her rods from where they had slid and stored them in her boots.

"Oh, it's shallow," Karile assured her, wobbling like a newborn colt, "we can wade across."

Janir stared down at the lazily flowing water. It was so clear that she could make out the white pebbles on the bottom and see silvery fish that swam almost gleefully about their feet.

"Come on then," Janir urged. "We need to cross

before our hunter breaks through the wall."

She half-carried Karile to the water's edge. Not wanting the rods to get wet, she drew them out of her boots and tossed them to the other side of the river before turning to Karile.

"Can you walk now?" she inquired.

The wizard gave an exhausted nod and they stepped into the water. To their surprise, it was over their heads. They plummeted to the rock bottom, the water was much deeper than first anticipated. Janir thrashed frantically to the surface and Karile flopped up alongside her. Even though she was underwater, she could see clearly. Karile didn't notice the novelty. Bubbles rose from his mouth, as if he were screaming. She shoved him up out of the water on the opposite bank and came up gasping after him.

"As I was saying," Karile panted, "the riverbed must've changed."

"Certainly," Janir sarcastically retorted, "from the moment we surveyed it, to the moment we stepped in it, the riverbed changed from less than a half to several sword-lengths deep!"

Karile shrugged and clambered to his feet. "Where to now?" Karile inquired, exhausted and resigned. Now he was asking her for directions, even though this whole idiotic quest had been his idea.

"That way." Janir pointed toward the wooden door.

"But there's no mention of a door on my map!" Karile protested.

"Double-check it," Janir suggested. "See if you can figure out where we are."

"I seemed to have....er...lost it," Karile sheep-ishly admitted after searching frantically through his pockets.

Tired of arguing, Janir just repeated herself. "Go that way!" she firmly ordered.

With a shrug, the enchanter obeyed.

She stooped down, picking up the rods and again storing them in her boots, marched toward the wooden door, her in the lead. The door swung open easily when she pulled the handle. Karile obediently plod through, too tired to question their route. They stood in a gray stone hall, much like one inside her master's castle back home. If Janir had closed her eyes she could have imagined herself there.

Carefully, as a precautionary measure she bran-dished her rods from their place in her boots. Janir had no inkling what these rods might be, nor why her father had given them to her in the first place, but they could be used against the monsters and that was all she needed to know for now.

With renewed enthusiasm, Karile took the lead again, leading them down the hall and toward an orange, fiery glow that seemed to be coming from ahead. Janir followed, but much more cautiously.

The hall wasn't nearly as long as it appeared at first. Janir followed closely after Karile and entered a dome-shaped stone room.

Arches around the edges were etched with more meaningless scrawls carved into the stone supports. The orange glow seemed to come from between the arches that laced the inside of the dome and the wall itself.

Everything was stone: the ceiling, the arches, the floor and the walls, all made of gray rock that was beguilingly normal. Janir noted another hall leading away from the chamber. Already she began concocting an exit strategy. Karile was standing in the middle of the room, staring down at a small, slender pillar with a glass box resting precariously on its top.

"This is it!" Karile squeaked with delight. "*I* found it! *I, Karile Kerwyn! I* did!"

Janir felt uncertain what to say now and decided that when in doubt with Karile, argue. "*We*," she corrected. "*We* found it."

The enchanter ignored her. "Look at this, Janir!" he smiled. "The Key of Amatahns!"

Janir peered over his shoulder to behold a silver object the size and shape of a large goose egg resting on a tiny stand inside the glass. The egg was engraved with twisting runes and scrolls and was very pretty. But Janir couldn't see why it would be worth guarding, or how it could lead to almost limitless power. She was not sure what she had been expecting, but certainly not this little egg-shaped object.

Janir had been about to say as much to Karile when she heard a pounding on the wooden door. The beast had gotten through the wall and was trying to break down the door. Its furious clacking echoed through the passage.

"Hurry up and grab it, and let's get out of here!" she screamed.

Karile nodded nervously and began surveying the

glass box from different angles. "Now, there is a trick to opening this," he hurriedly explained, fumbling for the scroll in his robe that was thoroughly soaked.

"I thought you said you lost it?" she pointed out.

"That was my map-scroll, this is my glass-case-opening scroll," he explained.

Janir sighed and rolled her eyes before bringing down one of her rods onto the glass with a loud smashing sound. Karile jumped back a good three feet and gave a shout of surprise.

"I suppose…" he seemed to be searching for the proper words. "I suppose that would work, too."

Not waiting for him to pick it up, Janir raced toward the other hall, with Karile squawking for her to wait. But she had no intent of waiting for anything. That monster was coming through the door and she didn't want to be around when it did. The unceremonious smashing of the case and grabbing the key had not been quite what she had anticipated. Janir had hoped more for music and a choir, not that she had truly expected either, but there had been no time for anything of the sort. She tore through the darkness, hoping that there were no more beasts or rocks in the way. The tunnel twisted and turned like a serpent through the mountain, changing direction every few strides.

Janir heard Karile's frantic footsteps and the loud clicking sound of the beast as it tried to wriggle its way into a tunnel. All this running was so exhausting, Janir thought to herself. But she kept going, through the black depths of mountain, onto whatever awaited them at the end. Janir spotted light ahead for the first time. With renewed purpose, she charged toward the faint glow. Around every turn the lights grew brighter, stronger. She had to keep going, she just had to or she would die at the hands, or claws, of that beast behind them. As she reached the end of the hall and the source of the light, Janir halted suddenly. They had apparently run upward, because now she stood overlooking the same river they had forded earlier, but directly above it. Janir stared down. How deep had it been? Three sword-lengths? Perhaps more?

Karile panted up beside her, followed closely by a loud clacking echo. "What do we do?" Karile shrieked.

"Jump!" was the first word out of her mouth. She shoved Karile forward, tossing her rods across the river to the bank, and leapt herself. As the water rushed to meet her, she thought this idea incredibly stupid, what if the water wasn't as deep as she remembered?

With a splash the water was up her nose and in her mouth. Janir paddled evenly, reminding herself that she always rose to the surface of water after diving. She burst out of the current gasping, and Karile popped up next to her.

They clambered onto a red-sand shore, having safely escaped the monster, at least for now. Janir stumbled to gather up her rods that she had thrown across the river, and with a sloshing of water crammed them into her boots.

"Well, we lost..." Karile didn't finish his sentence because at that moment he noticed several scaled bodies floating in the water. The monsters raised their heads above the water and hissed with rage. Janir brandished her rods again and Karile took up his battle station behind her.

"Just stay calm," Janir murmured, even though her heart was beating like a wardrum.

The beasts slowly rose out of the water like ghouls, snorting and clacking their displeasure. Deliberately the monsters came closer and the two friends receded backward. Two beasts leapt off the cliff, surrounding them on all sides. The clacking grew louder, as if the creatures were preparing to strike. The large monster they had hoped to have lost burst out of the rock and stood behind the smaller monsters encircling the pair. It flicked out its tongue tantalizingly, as if already tasting their flesh.

"*I am impressed, Invulnerable,*" the biggest monster, the one who had spoken to them earlier, clicked. "*Sebile, I call you. The cunning one. But not cunning enough. Give us back the egg. It is ours. Return it and we will spare your life and the life of the enchanter.*"

This offer was tempting, but Janir knew that if she could capture the Key, then it would be easy for her father to do the same.

"I'm sorry," Janir apologized. "It's not safe here anymore."

"*I say it is,*" was the indignant reply. "*And although it is such a shame to destroy one of the finer creations, you have chosen death.*"

The pair was backed against a wall of the cave with the river to their right, surrounded by dragons.

"Janir?" Karile whimpered, "I have a plan."

Normally, she would have dismissed the idea of Karile having a plan, but she was out of ideas herself, so there was no better option. She whispered in a low voice so that just maybe the monsters couldn't hear their deliberations.

"What is it?"

"We could jump back in the river," he suggested.

"Why? Would you rather be eaten in the water? If so, I'll watch from here," Janir replied, regretting that she had even considered listening to an idea concocted by the mad enchanter.

"Because, the river must flow under the mountain and back out into the valley," Karile meekly explained.

Janir hadn't thought of that. "But you saw what good swimmers they are; we wouldn't stand a chance."

"Do we stand a chance now?" Karile quietly inquired.

No, they didn't, but a fool's plan was better than no plan, Janir reasoned, so she agreed. "On the count of three," she whispered. "One…"

Karile threw himself at the water. Janir shouted angrily, took a quick gulp of air, and dove after him. They were swept under immediately by the current, dragged down like river debris. Janir still clenched her rods tightly in both hands. The blue glow came from the stones that lined the bottom of the river, so she could see everything clearly, including the confusing figure of Karile, writhing and twitching madly, as if he were in pain. Her head scraped against the top of the rocks, as they were shoved along by the powerful current. The rocks had barely grazed her, however, she was certain she would be bleeding. Her head hurt, but she forced herself to keep from screaming and losing air. Her chest burned, she wanted to breathe so badly. A sharp ache spread through her whole body; she needed to breathe; she needed air now. The water surged on, flowing under the jagged rocks, whisking her further through the mountain. Faster, faster, they went, swirling in circles as they bumped into rocks that spun them off balance. Finally, after what seemed like days, the mountain ended and Janir was propelled like a missile into a rushing open river. Almost immediately she was dragged back down by the racing current. Several seconds later Janir was shot over a waterfall, and landed in a pool of water under a night sky. She came up gasping desperately for air. She didn't remember Karile until she had flopped onto the bank, breathing like a beached fish.

Realizing that the wizard could very well be drowning at that very minute, Janir struggled to rise to her feet. It seemed to take a superhuman effort, but she forced herself to release her grip on the rods and stagger back into the water to fish out the bobbing mass of robe that was Karile. Once on the bank, Janir shoved down roughly on the enchanter's chest.

"Karile!" she frantically shouted. "Can you hear me? Are you dead?"

The boy coughed, a hard, racking cough and murmured distantly. "It hurt, it hurt so much." The enchanter was still gripping the Key, much the same way Janir had gripped her rods. A loud clacking came from above the waterfall.

"Karile, we have to go, now!" she frantically shouted. Cramming her rods into her boots, Janir slung one of Karile's arms around her shoulders and struggled away into the forest with the wizard limping beside her.

"It hurt, it hurt so much," Karile whispered again.

Janir ignored him and continued their flight into the trees, tripping over stones and roots in the strange terrain. It was no longer mountain pines but lowland shrubs and mesquite trees that they were running among. This land was barren, almost dead. A mesquite thorn stabbed Janir's foot; she stepped on the branch with her other foot, tearing out the thorn, and pressed on. The monster could still be heard, crashing through the trees after them, clicking its anger.

Glancing down, Janir confirmed that Karile was still gripping the egg-shaped Key in his other hand. After all this trouble, she thought, they had better not lose it. She stumbled on, half-dragging Karile through the sparse greenery.

Now she could hear the beast coming closer, ever closer as they blundered through the harsh landscape. Janir lost her balance, tripped forward and sprawled on the ground between two trees. The beast was upon them. It flicked out its tongue, hissed at them spitefully, and lowered its tongue to sample them before eating.

But first the monster negotiated. "*You are the embodiment of all we loved and loathed the mortals for: their stubbornness and strong will. Return the Egg to my people and this will be the end of it."*

The creature held out its tongue as if to receive the egg. Janir defiantly whipped out one of her rods and struck the tongue before shoving the rod in her belt and charging off with Karile. There was a droning, shrieking sound and the yellow eyes went wide with pain. The monster screeched its ear-splitting scream and recoiled its tongue.

"Come on!" Janir cried. To her surprise and delight, Karile was still holding the egg.

The horrible stench of the beast's tongue seemed to waken Karile, who stumbled groggily after Janir back into the forest. The creature writhed in pain behind them, screaming its displeasure as loudly as possible. Spotting lights through the trees, Janir decided to run toward them. Following lights had worked thus far. Half-dragging Karile behind her, Janir plowed through the dense shrubbery toward the flickering glow. Her feet slid on rocks; her chest wasn't expanding as it should, but she pressed on, towing Karile like a wagon. The pair burst into another clearing just as the beast caught up with the pair and flicked out its tongue to trip them both.

They tumbled to the ground. Janir landed flat on her stomach, Karile flat on his back. Karile stared at the Key contemplatively. What did he find so appealing about the egg?

The monster reared its ugly head above them, roaring angrily.

"I tried to show you mercy. I tried to show you reason. But you spit upon my offers and now they have all expired!"

This time, the beast stepped forward, raising a clawed, webbed foot above them, about to crush these little pests and do away with them, once and for all.

Then Janir heard a sound that she remembered quite well, the sound of arrows zipping through the air. The arrows whizzed toward the beast and buried themselves in its seemingly impenetrable hide. The monster yelped in pain and staggered to one side. A shout rose from someone hidden in the mesquite trees and another volley ensued. Arrows rained down to pierce the animal's flesh. Janir couldn't help feeling sorry for the creature. The creature stumbled and fell to the ground motionless.

Janir glanced up to see men clad in black and carrying torches step out of the trees. Their chain-mail glinted in the moonlight and their hoods made them even more mysterious. When they moved at the right angle, Janir spotted bands of what appeared to be closely-fitted silver around their necks, like a collar for an animal. Instead of rings where a chain would be attached at the center of the throat, there was a circular indentation about the same circumference as her rods. Several of the men marched past the pair of intrepid survivors to check that the beast was dead.

One, who apparently was the leader since he had no ring around his neck and was not carrying a torch, stepped out of the shadows and threw back his hood. It had been seven years since she and the leader had last seen one another, but she still recognized him. There was something about his presence, an indescribable essence that undeniably declared his identity. Dark, tanned skin covered him and dark eyes stared after the men who were checking the creature.

"Is it dead?" he called.

In response to his question the monster struggled to raise its head again, groaning in pain. Quick as a flash, it wrapped its tongue around one of the soldiers and with a swift motion, squeezed the screaming man in two. Janir looked away, not wanting to watch. She heard shouts and more screams as several other men were torn to shreds by the desperately snapping jaws and squeezed in two by the powerful tongue. This final act of defiance ended quickly when the monster was stabbed in the eye with a javelin. Seeing that his orders to finish off the creature were carried out, the commander turned his steely gaze to Janir and Karile.

"Thank you, my friends," Karile smiled graciously, "although I didn't expect to meet people from the Ivy Down garrison here. But I guess you need to be on the lookout for those nasty Argetallams all the time," he surmised.

"Karile, I wouldn't say anything like that, if I were you," Janir cautioned, her voice quaking.

"Why?"

"Because," Janir was nearly trembling with fear now, "I don't know about the others, but this man at least," she indicated the commander, "*is* an Argetallam."

CHAPTER 5

The Staspin Waste

"Oh…dear," Karile stated woodenly, as if he wanted to say other words but didn't feel that they would be appropriate around a girl.

"Whatever happens, Karile," Janir hurriedly summarized, "no matter what is said next, or you hear, you must remember that I risked my life for you there in the caves. And I saved you."

The Argetallam surveyed them for several seconds, as if he were heating their fear, the same way you might warm a drink on a cold day.

"Welcome to the Staspin Waste, travelers," he mildly greeted them. Those few words were equivalent to a vivid description of torture methods to Janir. She knew she was trembling, staring up at him slack-jawed. She also knew from what she remembered of him that her reaction was giving him great pleasure. Apparently the caverns had led them through the mountains that separated Brevia and the Staspin Waste. They should have turned the other way.

"I am sure that the Lord Argetallam will be most pleased to have such a lovely young girl and sprightly young wizard in his realm," the leader continued.

Inside Janir was thinking so hard, hoping in vain that maybe if she thought the words hard enough Karile would hear them. *Please don't use my name. Please don't use my name.*

"My lord Lucan," shouted one of the soldiers, "what should we do with the dead?"

"Leave them, Camak," Lucan dismissively gestured with his hand.

"But milord," the one called Camak began, stepping toward Lucan to protest.

Lucan spun around like a snake and sliced cleanly through Camak's throat with a dagger from the soldier's own belt. Gasping, Camak fell to the ground, blood seeping out of his body and onto the ever-thirsty earth of the Staspin Waste.

Carelessly rolling the dying man over with the toe of his boot, Lucan leaned close enough so that the soldier could see his dark silhouette against the moonlit sky. Karile had rolled over onto his stomach beside Janir and buried his face in her shoulder to keep from seeing the rest of this cruel business.

"Did you think I hadn't spotted you? Only a defective convert could challenge my authority. Were you waiting to escape, hmm?" Lucan was so cheerful. He was even more ruthless than Janir recalled.

As Camak died, Lucan stepped back toward Janir and Karile, surveying them intently. "I know you were after the Key of Amatahns," Karile hesitantly began, his voice shaking like a leaf in a storm. "I have it, and I will help you find the crystal chamber if…" he hesitated for a very long time, while Lucan seemed terribly amused by the whole spectacle.

"Just let Janir go and I'll help you with whatever you want," Karile bravely offered.

Angry that he had used her name and confessed to having the Key, but very much impressed with his bravery, Janir stared at Karile. She wanted to say "thank you."

Contrary to her fervent hopes, Lucan did recognize the name. Like a whiplash, his gaze instantly switched from the enchanter to her.

"Janir?" he repeated. "I once had a sister named Janir."

"Did you?" Karile seemed to be slipping back into his usual self now, the clueless wizard. "Isn't that coincidental? But then you would want to let this one go, right?"

"I hated her," Lucan snapped, the old disdain and malice suddenly swelling in his tone. "However, my mother arranged for her to be killed in the Norwin Pass. It was easy, really. All she had to do was send a message to the Brevians that an armed band would be coming through the mountains and there they were." He elaborated effortlessly with a conceited and self-satisfied air. "Mother has a knack for arranging for people to be killed. Take for instance, this Lord Caersynn …something, down in Brevia. He would be a problem for us Argetallams. I forget why, but we needed him dead. She bought off a duke, *a duke,* to kill him," Lucan seemed very pleased with the fact his mother was so successful at the dirty side of politics. "I mean, consider the true brilliance. No one expects another noble to be an assassin. They expect assassins to be low-lifes and tramps," Janir's brother elaborated. "All the same, I never received the pleasure of punishing my older sister again. And that has been something that I have missed for seven years." Lucan's dark eyes stared suspiciously into Janir's hazel eyes.

"Why punish her?" Karile obstinately inquired.

"Three hours!" Lucan suddenly shouted with distilled fury. Karile and Janir jumped in surprise at his spontaneous outburst of passion. "Three hours nearly cheated me of my inheritance!" he screamed.

For years after, Janir wondered why she had been so stupid. Perhaps it was the sudden anger at learning her mother had been murdered indirectly by Bricen, Lucan's mother. Perhaps it was the result of leftover energy from being chased by the monster, but whatever the case, it was incredibly foolish what she said next.

"It's not my fault I was born three hours before you!" Janir screeched indignantly. "Is that why you always beat me? Is that why your hag of a mother had mine killed? You wanted this barren wasteland? Fine! Let's go talk to our father and arrange it!"

The very instant those haughty and enraged words passed her lips, Janir realized that she had just committed the most idiotic and dangerous mistake of her life.

Still, Janir had very few times in her life beheld Lucan truly speechless. And had she realized that this was one of them, she would have relished the moment far more. He stood stock still, his countenance one of confusion and uncertainty. Janir quavered at his feet, all her terror renewed.

"It's you," was all Lucan could manage. Even in his shock, her brother held the tone of a great wordsmith.

After a brief pause, Lucan's surprise wore off. "Well, I can use the wizard to help me find the crystal chamber for our master's client. As for you," he turned a malicious, cruel grin in Janir's direction, "it will be nice to again have a playmate."

"Liar!" Karile screamed with righteous fury. "Liar! Liar! Liar! L-l-liar!"

"I never told you I was anything besides an Argetallam!" Janir helplessly protested.

"Liar! Liar! Liar! Liar!" Karile angrily refrained, leaning toward Janir from his spot tied to a sapling.

"If you don't stop repeating that word, I will cut your tongue out myself," Lucan threatened, glowering from a log by the fire.

After making certain that the beast was indeed dead this time, the Argetallam had commanded his dozen or so soldiers to make a camp here. Lucan and the others now sat by the fire, eating something that appeared to be a snake while watching their prisoners bicker. The crescent moon hung high above them, a solemn face among the twinkling stars so bright that they silhouetted the towering mountains against their sparkling display.

Karile glanced at Lucan, wondering whether or not he would make good on the threat. After staring for a spell, the enchanter decided that the Argetallam most certainly would and reasoned that it was wise not to upset him.

"Here I was going to offer myself in exchange for your safety from the Argetallams, but lo and behold, you are one!" Karile furiously screeched.

Janir would have leaned toward Karile, but it would have chafed her wrists that were tied around the slender tree trunk, so she remained straight. "I saved your life, thrice now!" Janir countered.

"Only because you wanted to help your people get the Key of Amatahns. And congratulations girl, you did it," Karile hissed.

"Does it appear to you that I am on good terms with my blood family?" Janir demanded, indicating her bound hands.

"Well," Karile muttered, "I'm not on much better terms with mine."

"They tried to have me killed, you dunce!" Janir shouted. "How close to my brother can I be if he tries to have me killed?"

"Strictly speaking, he didn't try to have you killed. His mother did," Karile pointed out. "This does explain how you knew one of the Lord Argetallam's courtesans, though. She must have been the only one here who was nice to you, right?" Karile's voice was now full of sympathy.

"She was my mother," Janir rigidly responded.

Karile sensed her reluctance in answering. "It's okay Janir," he soothed. "It's not as if the Lord Argetallam is your father or anything, right?" he reassured her.

Lucan made a sound that seemed to be the closest

to laughter he could get. Janir suddenly felt very sickly and nauseous, not wanting to say what she had to say next. Was there any way she could evade this question without lying?

Seeing her green expression, the enchanter second-guessed his own conclusion. "Is he?" Karile's eyes went wide in terrified anticipation.

Janir hesitated and then sheepishly admitted "Actually..."

"Oh, my gosh!" Karile hurriedly gasped, trying to whip his head away, but instead slammed into a stray branch. "That hurt," he moaned.

"Didn't you hear what I said to Lucan? Didn't you realize it then?" Janir pressed.

"I wasn't exactly listening," Karile confessed.

With a deep sigh, Janir leaned against the sapling again and stared helplessly at Lucan, who was holding the silver egg, tilting it this way and that to reflect the firelight, examining the intricately carved runes with a mild curiosity. In the distance a cougar roared after its prey; a distressed bleating from a desert goat followed the triumphant snarl. The fire crackled contentedly, feasting on deadwood from a tree that had only died days ago. But the desert had already reclaimed its precious moisture. A hawk called to its chicks in the darkness, and an owl hooted from somewhere nearby.

"Beautiful, isn't it Janir?" Lucan murmured, not even glancing in her direction.

She wasn't certain if he was referring to the animals or the egg, so she said nothing.

"Unlimited power," Lucan absently mused.

"Imagine what it would be like if we could use this?" He held up the Key.

Janir was very grateful that her people couldn't use its power.

"Our master is brilliant, is he not?" Lucan proudly stated, turning to a different subject. "He knew that if even a whisper of our search for the Key was heard, every wizard in Brevia and elf in Silverwood would soon be trying to keep it from us. 'Let someone else find it,' Master said to me, 'then take it from them when they flee the caverns.' After all, there is only one true way out once reaching the Key." He gestured to the surrounding barren countryside. "The Zebulun, that river is, of course, the water supply for this land," he explained with an arrogant air.

As there was nothing she could do at the moment, Janir resigned herself to listening to Lucan's haughty words until dawn.

"However, what I find most interesting in all of this, is that Master trusted you with a pair of karkaton at eight, whereas I still have not received mine," Lucan held up one of the black rods disdainfully. His lip curled slightly. "Interesting, don't you think?" Lucan bitterly added. "He used your blood to make them."

"Used my blood?" Janir repeated.

"Yes. You don't recall him cutting you and soaking something with your blood?" Lucan added, his ridicule and mockery as clear as words.

Now that he mentioned it…

"Werewarg's scales, griffin's tears and the blood of their Argetallam are all that is needed to make the ultimate torture device and weapon."

Lucan suddenly dropped the karkaton and it fell into the sand. Then he added in a quieter tone, "As your brother, they resent me, but I can still use them if I am willing to endure the pain." He disdainfully stared at her and the wizard. "Sleep well you two. We have a long trip tomorrow."

"Faster," Lucan hissed.

Karile flopped his head toward Janir, "I am beginning to think 'faster' is his favorite word."

The oppressive sun beat down cruelly on the surrounding wasteland. Off in the distance heat waves shimmered like mirages in the desert. Where they were headed in such a hurry, Janir didn't know. Nor did Karile have the audacity to ask. They were heading east, back toward the mountains and the fateful Norwin Pass. Janir was dressed for the mountains, certainly not for the desert, and sweat was trickling down her temples and into her eyes. The slaves, Lucan's soldiers, pressed on silently, never stopping, never once hesitating at his commands.

"They seem good-natured," Karile remarked to Janir in an undertone as one of them dragged him up a rocky ledge.

"They have no choice," Janir replied.

One of the slaves nearly threw her up the ledge after Karile, shoving them together for a moment.

"They're slaves, most likely common Stlavish men broken to my father or Lucan," she explained.

"I seem to recall something to the effect they always have to obey their Argetallam. But it's been so long. I can't be sure."

"So, they have to obey Argetallams?" Karile asked to confirm.

"Yes, that's right."

Lucan was choosing a path much more precarious than the one Janir had traveled seven years ago. The ground they tread was like a raised road that wrapped around the cliff, rising and falling with the valley below. Now they were walking in the shade of the cliffs; however, it was still hot.

"Faster!" Lucan shouted again. The slaves pressed on obediently to catch up with Lucan on the next rise ahead of them.

"So, maybe you could command them?" Karile suggested.

Janir considered this. "Perhaps. It's a possibility."

They were both quiet. Two of the soldiers hefted them over a shoulder to cross a ditch and then continued marching after Lucan.

"So?" Karile prompted.

"Let us go!" Janir commanded, in the sternest tone she could manage.

The minions halted abruptly and dropped the two companions on the ground. The grass and rocks were not comfortable, but it had worked! Janir stared gleefully at Karile for a moment in pleasant surprise. The converts did have to obey Lucan, but they also had to obey her!

Just then, Lucan glanced back. "What are you doing?" he demanded.

"Restrain him!" Janir severely ordered.

The warrior-slaves glanced down at her and stepped toward Lucan, ready to obey their new leader.

"Ignore her," Lucan overruled.

To Janir and Karile's dismay, the warrior-slaves halted abruptly and snatched up the pair again before they could flee.

"You stupid little girl," Lucan laughed. "I am more powerful than you. They have to obey me." As if to make his point, he added "Slap her for me, Trevae."

The convert who was lugging Janir, obeyed immediately. Striking Janir with so much force she was surprised he didn't break her neck. Tears welled in her eyes as the sting reached its height, then abated.

"I'm sorry," Karile sadly tried to console.

Janir admitted to herself that there would be no escape for now.

Merciless as the terrain they traveled, Lucan kept them going well past dusk. How did he keep going when the rest of them were on the verge of collapsing? Perhaps if she had not been living in the mild climate of Brevia for seven years, and if she hadn't been wearing clothes so unsuitable to the weather, she might be tireless as well. But she wasn't. Blisters were forming on Janir's feet, rubbing them raw, and her lips were parched with thirst. She wondered if Kalbo was still at the top of the mountain where they had left him, or if he had been eaten by werewargs or possibly stolen by horse thieves. Or maybe he had come untethered and was on his way back to Green Haven. Whatever his situation, except for being eaten, it was most likely better than theirs. The sun sank steadily behind them as they pressed on toward the Gideon Mountains and the Norwin Pass. Wherever it was they were going, Lucan seemed extremely eager to push on. Rocks slid under Janir's boots and sand somehow managed to get into everything, even her hair. Desert lizards and rodents skittered away at the sight of the company while desert predators watched from a distance. Vultures circled over head as if anticipating a meal, causing Karile to gawk up at them nervously. In the fading light, Janir spotted a tan cougar with black-tipped ears peering around a boulder, observing them with a cautious contempt. Falcons and hawks watched the group's progress across the landscape from their perches in thorny mesquites. A group of travelers in this land was such a novelty that even the beasts stopped to stare.

Lucan apparently did feel exhaustion because he finally had the slaves throw down Janir and Karile and make camp. The enchanter and she-Argetallam flopped side by side onto the spiky crab-grass, not wanting to move. They just stared at each other with bleary eyes. Karile's eyes, red and puffy, were circles of darker skin where there was no sand, giving him the appearance of an owl. His lips were cracked and dry; his hands were tied in front of him like Janir's. She wondered if she looked as awful as Karile. She certainly felt it.

Both of them were in no mood to speak. Lucan commanded the warrior-slaves and made whatever arrangements that he seemed to be so preoccupied making. He posted sentries and assigned hunters. One of the warrior-slaves designated as hunter caught some game within several minutes. It appeared to be a rodent of some sort, but Janir was so hungry that she would have eaten almost anything. The warrior-slave sat on a large stone and began skinning and cleaning the carcass with a curved, evil-looking blade.

Spontaneously, Lucan snapped a quick command to the warrior-slaves, and the slave who had been cleaning the rodent responded immediately, placing the knife on the rock, grabbing Karile by the collar and dragging the wizard toward Lucan.

"Show me," Lucan commanded, pointing to a map spread out over a large rock of Brevia, the Staspin Waste, Ralissia, Silverwood, Stlaven and Arisillia beyond. "Show me where the crystal chamber is."

Karile stood wobbly and sun-baked before Lucan. "You know I really don't feel like it," Karile replied with a child-like air.

Lucan raised his chin, made a comprehending sound and nodded. "I am not one for playing games, wizard," Lucan replied in a hostile tone.

"Pity, you should play more games. It would do wonders for your people-skills," Karile suggested.

Janir had been left to her own devices, lying out of the way some two or three paces off. Now she fumbled frantically with the knots on her wrists, trying to loosen them. Her eyes locked onto the blade lying on the stone, left behind by the hunter who now stood behind Karile, just three sword-lengths out of her reach.

Lucan's short fuse reached its limit and he seized Karile by the back of his neck. "Show me now, wizard." Lucan shoved Karile's face near a section of the map marked *Gideon Mountains*.

The warrior-slaves stood still as statues. The ones who hadn't been posted as sentries stared at Lucan with blank, emotionless eyes.

"I told you that I don't feel like it," Karile protested. Janir noticed the muscles rippling in Lucan's arms as he gripped Karile in fury. It escaped her understanding how someone who was actually younger than her could seem so much older. Lucan had always spoken as and appeared to be years her senior.

Carefully, Janir began edging toward the stone with the knife lying on it. None of the soldier-slaves noticed and Lucan was busy shouting in Karile's ear.

"Do you have any idea at all what I can do to you?" Lucan hissed.

"I don't know. Why don't you enlighten me?" Karile suggested in an innocent tone.

Lucan began spewing out all the horrible things his father had taught him, and Janir was very glad that she had been raised by Armandius these past seven years.

"Then I drive a one and one quarter-inch blade into your side, right here and..." Lucan was shouting louder than ever, but Janir ignored him to concentrate on reaching the blade lying before her. Inch by inch she slowly made her way to the rock.

She happened to glance at Karile and saw that the enchanter's eyes were the size of pies as Lucan extended his knowledge of Argetallam skill.

"After that, I twist the blade at a precise thirty-degree angle here..." Lucan jabbed Karile and continued his elaboration.

Janir was almost to the rock. Carefully, she eased the knife off the stone and turned it around in her hands. It was sharper than she had expected, sliced neatly through the ropes and nicked her wrist. Stifling a shout of pain, the girl glanced about for her next move. She was free. Now what?

If she acted quickly she could kill Lucan and then the warrior-slaves would be under her control. A vague memory that she wasn't supposed to harm Lucan for some reason came from her subconsciousness. Her mother had said something about this. She was to spare Lucan. Why? Staring at Lucan, holding Karile down on the large stone by his neck, she had no inkling.

"Once it has pierced the second layer of flesh here, I insert another blade..."

The image of Duke Ronan's motionless face flashed across her mind's eye. She vividly recalled how it had felt to kill. Recollections of the horror she had felt at slaying a man and having no choice in it flooded back. Now that she did have the choice, even though she knew it might very well be the best one, Janir couldn't bring herself to kill again. The very idea was sickening. Janir laid the knife down. She could always kill Lucan another day, if it became necessary. If she were to kill him now, it would be irreversible. Instead she snatched up the stone that the knife that had been resting on and brought it down on the back of Lucan's head.

Like a dead bird, Lucan crumpled to the ground in a heap.

Karile turned around in surprise and was about to ask what had happened. The warrior-slaves had already begun to advance toward them, with weapons drawn. But without Lucan to command them, they seemed lost, like children who have just witnessed a murder and don't know what to do next.

"Run! Run! Run!" Janir shouted urgently. Best to flee while the warrior-slaves were standing about clueless. Karile was quicker to obey this time than ever before. Like an arrow from a bow, he shoved past the line of warrior-slaves, shot into the spiny mesquite trees and sparse shrubs. With his robe spreading out like a sail, it must have been difficult to run in that thing. Janir raced after him, musing on how her life had become mostly running and shouting.

Into the darkness they went, fleeing blindly from her brother who would soon be awakening. He would doubtless be clearing his head, while the warrior-slaves knelt around him asking how he was and what they should be doing. Lucan would shout and tell them they were imbeciles, then command them to chase after the two fugitives. Staggering like a newborn fawn, he would follow after them at a slower pace, cursing and angrily shouting unkind words. However, there was no time to think about Lucan, she needed to think about escaping from him. With dismay, she realized that she and Karile were running south, away from the Norwin Pass and the Gideon Mountains. Too bad. They would have to circle back later.

Lucan still had the Key! That was another "too bad" and it also would have to wait.

Keep running. There was nothing else she could do. Karile made so much noise as he ran that he could easily have been a horde of fleeing wizards. Janir felt her heart pounding in rhythm with her foot falls, thudding to the same beat. On through the desert they fled under the sparkling sky. Shadows flitted under the mesquites as small desert life moved for the bolting pairs of feet. Faster. They mustn't be caught again, because this time Lucan would be raging mad. Janir heard the boots of the warrior-slaves behind them. They were gaining ground. Propelling herself faster, she caught Karile by his robe and jerked him behind a line of juniper bushes.

They were breathing so hard Janir wondered that their pursuers couldn't hear them right away. They backed several feet away from the line of shrubs. Here there was nothing between the row of junipers and the jagged cliff rising behind them, not a shrub or tree of any kind. Janir wondered why, but there was no time to think about it.

The pair edged carefully away from the trees as the lights of torches flashed through the branches. Karile was gripping Janir just like he had in the caves, trembling like a leaf in the wind. His teeth started chattering again and Janir jabbed his jaw to make him stop. Although he gave her a glare that could have incinerated stone, even Karile knew that this was not the time for protesting another's actions.

Indistinct shouts from the warrior-slaves and inaudible commands from Lucan met their ears. Her brother was very angry, that much they could tell.

"We must be very quiet," Janir whispered. Karile gave her a look that showed he had been thinking of telling her the same thing.

The shouts began to fade away and the pair breathed a little easier. Janir tried to take a cautious step forward. But her feet wouldn't move. Frustrated, Janir glanced down to see that sand covered her ankles. Panicking, she tried to jerk her boots free of the sand, but her struggling only made her sink deeper. Glancing at Karile she saw that the sand was almost to his knees. The enchanter had deer-eyes as he stared down incredulously at the sand that was swallowing him.

"Quicksand! We're caught in quicksand!" Karile squeaked.

"Actually it's dry, so I think it's called sucking sand," Janir corrected on impulse.

"Well so much the better!" Karile hissed. "We'll be suffocated instead of drowned!"

Janir glanced about for anything that she could grab. A branch from a tree dangled nearby. She stretched out to reach it. Straining, she wrapped her fingers around it and pulled. There was a loud snapping sound, and the next thing Janir knew she was holding the branch, detached from its tree, and was several inches deeper in sand.

"Why does everyone always get caught in quicksand?" Karile moaned, and Janir didn't bother to correct him again. "All the heroes in stories, always get caught in quicksand. They're also supposed to be rescued!"

Staring helplessly at the severed branch in her hand, Janir sighed. She heard a pop, and sand showered into the air as if a small bubble under the sand had exploded. As soon as it popped, they began sinking at an alarmingly faster rate.

"This is the worst day of my life!" Karile screamed, waving his arms wildly. "I am being eaten alive by dirt!"

"Don't move," Janir snapped, "moving seems to make you sink faster."

"What do we do?" Karile wailed.

Janir had no clue. No options were within reach. Everything useful, such as branches and vines, were either out of reach or unattached. All their gear had been taken away or lost, or else Janir could have swung the rope around that branch there and pulled them out…but it was useless thinking about it. Sensing her helplessness, Karile seemed to grow suddenly very angry.

"This is all your fault!" he shrieked.

"My fault?" Janir repeated, nearly up to her waist in sand.

"It's your fault we escaped from Lucan!" the enchanter accused her.

"Karile, he was going to do all those things he was telling you about, if you didn't tell him where the chamber was!"

"So? I would have told him if he wanted to know that badly," Karile snapped back.

"You would tell him? Then why were you so set

on not telling him earlier?"

"Because he wasn't sticking me with tiny knives then!" Karile announced, as if it were perfectly obvious.

"Weakling!" Janir angrily hissed.

"Weren't you paying attention to what Lucan was telling me? Your daddy is extremely creative. And I would rather not experience his genius, if you don't mind!"

There were no real words that would describe what Janir wanted to say, so she shouted meaninglessly up at the sky. All was silent for several seconds, as the pair sank deeper into the earth. Karile tilted his head sideways, expecting her to say something.

"Our only hope is for Lucan and his minions to find us," Janir reluctantly stated. The sand was now over her waist.

"So the same people we just escaped from are our only hope?" Karile clarified.

"Yes," Janir closed her eyes.

Karile didn't seem to hold as much disdain for the thought as she did, because he immediately began calling for them. "Scary knife boy, we're this way!"

Janir couldn't bring herself to call out to Lucan.

"Do you think they can hear us, this far away? Karile wondered.

"It hardly matters if they can. We're dead either way," Janir hopelessly sighed.

"Why? Why are we dead?"

"Once they find the chamber, they'll kill us because we'll no longer be valuable," Janir moaned sadly.

"You don't know that," Karile cheerfully replied.

"You don't know *them*," Janir glumly replied.

Karile seemed to consider this for a moment, then resumed his cry for help. "Scary knife boy! Scary knife boy!"

The sand was beginning to come over her shoulders, her arms were reaching upwards in case anything useful might land in them. "Karile," Janir morosely tried to spot him above the sand. "It's been an honor knowing you, even though we're most likely the imbecilic fools who just enslaved the world by giving my brother the Key of Amatahns. And we'll most likely die here for our sins."

"Oh, don't say that," Karile nervously attempted to brush off her statement. "I think that my toes are touching the bottom," he added. "No, wait, it's rolling. Bugger, it has a rough side. I think it's a skull."

"As I was saying," Janir impatiently continued. The sand was up to her chin now. "It has been an honor and…" just then sand began pouring into her mouth. Karile said something that sounded like "Umph oomph," but she couldn't be sure. He was sinking beneath the desert floor.

Soon all that was above the sand was her hands. She couldn't breathe at all. This was much worse than riding the river out of the caverns, because she knew for certain that she would never reach the other side of the sand. She struggled to breathe, but the sand filled her nostrils. She tried to gasp for air, but only sand came in her mouth. Perhaps she fainted, because suddenly everything went black.

She awoke lying on sand with crab grass poking her stomach, something soft and warm blowing on her hair, and something like leather straps on her neck. A voice was enraged and indistinct in the background. A hard fist slammed down on her back, making her rack and cough. Janir spat out bitter sand and gasped for air.

It was Lucan's voice in the background. "If she was here, then the wizard can't be far off, find him! I need him!"

Raising her hand above her head, her fingers brushed a soft nose and long head. "Kalbo," she softly whispered. "You stupid and faithful horse, I love you."

The stallion nuzzled her hair with concern. It had been his nose and leather reins Janir had felt. The must have been the reason Lucan had found her and…..with a jolt she recalled Karile.

Janir tried to twist around to see Lucan, but she was too weak to do much of anything. Still, she managed to swivel her head around to spot the other Argetallam standing by the edge of the slip sand, with the warrior-slaves leaning out over it holding branches, trying to find Karile. The warrior-slaves brushed their sticks along the surface, searching for any trace of the enchanter.

Not Karile. Please, not him. Janir silently pleaded.

"Here," shouted one of the warrior-slaves excit-edly, as excited as any of them ever became.

There was a flurry of action as they hauled Karile out against the pull of the sucking sand. And then the enchanter was unceremoniously deposited beside

Janir on the solid sand. He coughed as she had, rolled onto his back to behold Lucan staring down at him with crossed arms and a vicious expression.

"I have no clue where the chamber is, but according to my sources, the seeress, Zeerla, does," Karile blurted out.

"Thank you," Lucan mildly seethed back. "Let's see. Where would I be if I were a disgraced seeress….." Lucan seemed to be gathering his thoughts outloud. "Since I can hardly go to a Wizard Temple for protection, I would seek shelter somewhere that being an anomaly would be nothing uncommon. Not in the mountains. I would want to be somewhere crowded. The Vermilion Market!" Lucan exclaimed joyously. "Even if she is not there, someone there will know where to find her. I am as brilliant as our master, am I not?"

Casually he stepped between Janir and the stallion. Then her brother maliciously drove the toe of his boot into her back, as he used to do when they were little. The impact was even stronger than it had been then and drove her breath out of her lungs. She couldn't breathe for a time that seemed to last forever. Just as before, she stifled a scream.

"There, you see my sister?" Lucan stooped down, slipped his fingers under her chin and pulled her closer to him so he could easily whisper in her ear. "I always win." He slid his hand around to the side of her face and shoved her back down into the sand.

"Yes, I would call you brilliant," Janir snapped, spitting sand, "if the Vermilion Market even existed. My master has friends who have searched for it.

Enchanters have never found its location. Even the elves my master knows couldn't tell where it was."

"That may be true, Sister, but…" He glared down at her. "I am not an elf."

Sparing him had been a huge mistake. She should have driven the knife into his spine. Why had she not?

The two were dragged back to camp and tied to trees more securely than ever. Lucan and the warrior-slaves fed on the rodents and didn't share any of the meat. Karile's stomach growled so loudly, that Janir began to wonder if there was something alive in there. Lucan did let them have water, for which Janir was grateful. It had become clear that he wanted them to be as uncomfortable as possible, but not dead.

Kalbo was tethered to a tree, a little scratched, but none the worse for wear, with his saddle still intact. Lucan had been kind enough to have one of the warrior-slaves unsaddle the stallion and now Janir was staring with consternation at the sores on the horse's back from wearing the saddle too long. Still, Kalbo didn't seem to mind. Janir wondered why he had come looking for her instead of going back to Green Haven, as would have been normal, but she really didn't need to know. From his place across the fire, she could tell that Lucan was planning their route to the Vermilion Market.

CHAPTER 6

The Vermilion Market

For many days and nights they pressed onward into the Gideon Mountains, toward the Vermilion Market. Janir's brother never once passed up an opportunity to make their lives miserable. Simple things, such as tying them next to gorse bushes at night, seemed cruel torment. Poor Kalbo was laden with most of the gear, while Lucan shrieked for them to move faster. They wound their way between the steep mountains, crawling between the bases of the colossal titans. Often, they could not see the sun at all. Snow still blanketed parts of these obscure corners of the world, even though spring had come long ago to Brevia. Lucan and the converts seemed to be suffering more than she and Karile. Brevia received snow every winter, but the temperate Staspin Waste seldom saw rain, let alone a freeze. Irritation at the weather seemed to irk her brother.

Slush lubricated the path they trudged. Janir worried about Kalbo more and more. The poor stallion slipped on the soggy terrain often but always staggered to his hooves again and plodded on behind the convert who led him. Like a tired plough horse, Kalbo seemed worn down to shreds. Although treated better by Lucan than she and Karile were, Kalbo was by no means a guest of honor. At night, they all tried to gather as close as possible to the fire, but naturally Lucan made it difficult for them.

After several days of short rations and cold nights, they came to a place that peaked over a leveled out pocket between two mountains. No more than a hundred yards in diameter, the pocket of flatness was strewn with large boulders and scraggly, leafless trees. Here the path became clearer. Down from the small peak they marched. Trails the right size for mice led off from their own path. It was so narrow that it might be mistaken for a game trail, but Janir noted all the curiously angled trees and strangely formed rocks. Several rocks stood in a hodge-podge fashion, but when a double of the non-descript pile of rocks came into view on the other side of the narrow path, Janir realized with a shiver of frightened excitement that it was not a natural occurrence. There was a whisper, a chitter, to their right. A flicker of pale blue motion to the side, and then nothing. The chilled group of travelers came out of the stark trees and were blocked by a stream that ran across the shadowed pathway. A medium-sized waterfall poured down to their left, spitting cold foam into the frigid water.

After a moment's hesitation, Lucan whirled to the left and strode toward the waterfall. Not even waiting for a command, the warrior-slaves followed after their master with Janir and Karile in tow.

Rounded rocks lay on both sides of the waterfall, resting close together and leading underneath the flowing curtain itself. With an impatient glance back at his companions, Lucan stepped gingerly onto one of the stones. Like a child playing with bricks, he skirted from one to the other, holding his arms out for balance. He swayed precariously at times, but kept upright and out of the water, wobbled straight to the waterfall, braced himself for the cold, and dove into the pounding veil. The warrior-slaves shoved Janir and Karile across the round stones without a single misstep and thrust them into the icy waterfall. With a backward glance, Janir saw with satisfaction that one of the warrior-slaves was staying behind with Kalbo.

At the other side, Janir shivered and brushed water off her face. The enchanter said something about "bloody cold water." Concealing the entrance to a hollowed out, craggy passageway, the waterfall playfully splashed at their backs. Before them, Lucan stood sputtering and cursing the engineer who had designed the entrance so effectively. With an impatient snap, Lucan spun on his heel and marched deeper into the earth.

The tunnel continued at approximately the same level, arching to the left in a sinuous curve. Stones that seemed like cobblestones lined the floor of the passage, but were more natural in shape and texture. On either side of them, the craggy walls guided their path. At first, Janir wondered why her brother had not ordered torches to be lit. But no sooner had the light from the waterfall side begun to die down, that the light from the other side shone through. They continued on toward it until they came out of the tunnel and into the light of cloudy day.

Janir poked her head out, then ducked back in. Ahead lay a winding ledge that seemed to have been fashioned into some sort of a road. Below was the fief of Ivy Down, far, far below. Lucan's converts caught her and dragged her onto the ledge. Trying to attain control of her fear, Janir stiffly followed after her brother, constantly reminding herself not to look down. Thankfully, it was not long before they came to a door, if it could be called a door. At first glance, Janir mistook it for a fault in the cliff. It was a very subtle, sketchy round outline in the rock.

Lucan stepped up to the center of the huge round trace and dusted earth off of a section. Once it was cleaned, Janir saw a series of five cylinders in a vertical line. Small, narrow, round pieces of metal faced sideways and spun around with a clicking sound. As her brother absently spun the top one with his forefinger, Janir noted that each one had five odd symbols marking its sides. Lucan spun the cogs contemplatively, as if trying to refresh a forgotten memory.

"What was the order of the symbols?" Lucan mumbled to himself. "Elf," he softly resolved, spinning the top cylinder so that a particular rune was facing out. "Followed by….. Mortal, Dwarf, Mazag, and Troll," he answered himself, spinning each cylinder into place as he recalled its proper symbol.

Janir heard a clicking sound as something behind the wall of earth moved and adjusted itself. Then the earth seemed to shimmer like a curtain, and slowly the veil of soil parted and opened to show the strangest place Janir had ever laid eyes on.

Now she understood why it was called the Vermilion Market. The ground, the ceiling and the sides of the narrow walkways were all made of bright red dirt. A reddish tinge seemed to have settled over the market, like a fog of light. The expected sounds of a market were there: gruff voices protesting prices, vendors calling out their wares' superiority to the other vendors who screamed the same message with as much conviction. Children ran about playing. Beggars at the street corners and scavenging animals prowled about, the only things remotely normal about this place.

Two heavily built, wrinkled trolls with triangular, pointed ears and mostly naked bodies argued over the price of a strange little animal in a cage. The animal had a young eagle's wings covering its head, with a lion's muscular tail nervously twitching from side to side, a griffin.

Vendors were selling things such as "invisibility amulets," "sleeping potions," "scent eraser," and other things that Janir didn't recognize. Several dryad children, normal in appearance aside from being no taller than chickens and purple, loped underfoot, laughing while chasing an animal that greatly resembled a rat, with yellow scales all over its body. A willowy, long-limbed creature in rags sat on the corner of a narrow street, holding out a wooden mug and asking for alms.

White rabbits, or animals that appeared to be rabbits, foraged the leftovers and scraps of the marketplace, like rodents. Janir realized that they were not rabbits when one of them spotted a piece of pastry that had fallen off a baker's cart. Like a wolf, the small rabbit-creature hunched its shoulders as if readying for the kill. Then, to Janir's amazement, it shot out a long red tongue, just like a frog's, revealing two rows of needle-point teeth, and gulped down the crumb. Lucan dragged them into the crowd with unhidden impatience. No one even looked up from their business as the abnormal band of travelers melted into the crowd of unusual market-goers.

Jostled by the strange pedestrians, Janir tried to stay close to her brother and his converts. Somehow being of the same race felt unifying. Every so often, Janir would catch a glimpse of an elf appraising something very refined and expensive-looking. One or two dwarves bartered for a piece of especially rare metal, and thrice she spotted mortal enchanters and an enchantress mingling with the throng. But for the most part the scene was populated by the strange beings of secrecy. Even though she and her mortal counterparts were misfits amidst the others, no one even gave them a second glance. Lucan stopped to ask a troll selling mushrooms where a seeress might be. Not having any real interest for his conversation, Janir's eyes aimlessly wandered about the market. Her gaze fell on an angry father troll scolding his son. They were too far away for her to hear their words, but she could see the boy apologizing. The father sighed and stared wordlessly for several moments, shook his head, smiled and wrapped the boy in a forgiving embrace. Janir glanced back to Lucan and the converts.

Where was Lucan?

A frantic search of everyone in sight only revealed that he was not in sight. He must have neglected to check that she was with him when he and his converts moved on. Karile was important, he had information, whereas she did not. Janir stepped too close to the mob of market-goers. Suddenly, she was being shoved along between two foul-smelling and fat trolls. Fighting against the current of the crowd, Janir forced her way out from between the trolls. When shoved, the huge mountain-dwellers protested loudly and called her Trollish words that she had never heard before, and doubtless did not want a translation. For a second, the crowd thinned between waves, and she was able to whip a frantic gaze around the intersection of narrow streets. Her brother was nowhere to be seen. Panic mounting in her breast, Janir pushed through the mass of unhurried bodies, battling to reach a spot where she could get up high enough to watch the ever-mingling crowds and spot Lucan or Karile.

As she cast a searching glance behind her, she spotted a cloaked figure who seemed to be moving against the flow of the crowds. At first she thought him no more than another one of the strange clientele of this odd market. But with each step she became more and more nervous. Deciding to test her paranoid conclusion, Janir broke into a frantic gallop, tearing her way through the placid crowd. She dodged a swinging basket of pears that hung from a large troll-woman's arm and swerved around a cart full of pigeon feathers, ducked under the arms of some creatures and leapt over the heads of others. Taking a sharp turn to her right, Janir rounded a corner in the narrow street. Pausing for breath by a rat-on-a-stick stand, Janir glanced back at the crowd. With consternation she spotted the cloaked one forcing his way through the crowd with as much haste as she had. A stocky dwarf stood in his path, and didn't move fast enough to get out of the way. Her pursuer bumped into the little person, his cowl slipping backward off his head and his cloak becoming disarranged at his sides.

With terror she saw the slender swords gleaming on the left and the right about his waist, and the subtly pointed ears of an elf.

Their eyes met for a moment as the dwarf sputtered and cursed the elf in Dwarvish. The elf stepped around the furious little man and stood there staring at her calmly. There was an agelessness about him that seemed to be about all elves, but he lacked the knowing, wise essence of one who has lived for eons. In several ways he was like the other two elves she had met. His face had the same angular shape, his midnight-black hair had that same slight sheen to it. But in others ways… nothing like Saoven, or even Velaskas, this elf's bright blue eyes held a cold darkness. Shadows and ice immediately came to mind the moment she met his brutal gaze of anger and fury at an unspoken injustice.

Janir thought him the ultimate epitome of "deadly beauty."

He held out his hand in a commanding gesture, and Janir faintly heard him say something in a strange tongue that definitely was not Elvish. Something translucent shot toward her from his outstretched hand, something that made her think of a spider's web made of water. It hurtled toward her so quickly that she barely had time to react at all. Instinctively, Janir ducked to try and avoid it. It struck her anyway.

'Twas a strange feeling, a feeling of something colliding with her body, but something that wasn't solid, just wispy force, almost like a mist. The next thing Janir knew, it had knocked her off her feet and she was sprawled on her back, lying in the red soil. She sensed, rather than saw, the pieces of magic lying about her, shattered like an earthen vase. Enchanter. Undoubtedly, this elf was an enchanter, and she was guessing that because his magic had affected her, even though not at all in the way he had meant, that he was of a much higher Degree than First. Leaping to her feet, Janir heard the elf cursing in his native tongue.

A surge of the crowd came between them and Janir wasted no time. She sprang to her feet, whirled around and bolted through the wiggling mass of bodies, trying to put as much space as she could between herself and her hunter. Nothing came to mind when she tried to find a reason why he would be chasing her. The idea occurred to her that he could have been sent to protect her now that Saoven was no longer doing so. Then why would he be shooting magic at her? There could be a reason. Just as she began to believe that thought, she remembered his eyes. The distilled fury behind them. If he was here to protect her, she would rather suffer Lucan than the company of this man.

Ducking under a line of hanging rugs made from some slimy fabric, Janir emerged on the other side with what seemed to be pond scum clinging to her hair. Glancing left and right, she made for an intersection of paths up ahead.

By the time she reached a stout fountain in the middle of the crowded intersection, she had been cursed in approximately nine different languages ranging from Trollish to Dwarvish. Apparently people here did not appreciate pushy little girls. Bubbling as if it was doing the world an immense favor by flowing, the fountain consisted of three gray, unadorned stone basins with the two smaller basins rising above one large one the size for a horse to wade in. Bright red, glowing fish that resembled coy swam placidly under the lapping water. Janir tried to spot a better place to hide, but saw none. With resolve, she clambered onto the side and stepped to her right. She slipped into the basin with a loud splash, and prayed that the elf wouldn't hear. In an instant, the water was over her head and she couldn't touch the bottom. To reach the surface, she had to claw and scratch at the inside of the basin to find handholds and pull herself upwards. Poking her head barely out of the water, Janir glanced left and right, searching for the frightening elf who was trying to catch her. Nobody even glanced at her when she dove into the water; they just continued about their business. Not seeing her pursuer, Janir carefully lowered herself deeper into the water and under the inward curving rim of the fountain.

It seemed an eternity that she remained in the cool basin with fish nibbling at her exposed skin and fishy water seeping into her mouth. For several minutes she didn't move. Waiting. Waiting. Eventually she lost her patience, eased out from beneath the curved lip and raised herself barely an inch high to check if the coast was clear.

Cautiously she peered to her left. Not spotting her pursuer, Janir glanced to the right. The crowds were moving at their usual pace, everyone mostly ignoring everyone else except to curse at someone they considered particularly rude.

So quickly that she didn't even realize until it was too late, a hand swooped down and snatched her up by the back of her dress collar. With consternation, Janir found herself staring up into the icy blue eyes of the elf. Ungraciously, he jerked her out of the water with an astonishing strength and proceeded to drag her toward a narrow back alleyway. No one heeded Janir's screams of distress, nor even turned their heads at the sight. Struggling gained her nothing. The elf ignored her rebellious kicking and frantic punching.

"What are you doing to that girl?" demanded a hefty troll, passing by. He had warts over most of his body and black hairs growing out of his ears. Rotting teeth were falling out of his jaw line, but at that moment he was the most gorgeous creature Janir could have seen.

The elf snapped his head to attention. "Nothing inappropriate, I assure you." The elf spoke with a refined, cold voice. If frozen silver cold speak, it would have sounded like him.

"What then?" the troll inquired.

"He's…" Janir began, but the elf imperceptibly clamped a hand over her mouth and the troll seemed not to notice.

"The girl owes me money," the elf explained.

The troll grunted in understanding, made some remark about lazy borrowers, and shuffled off about his business.

Having handled the inquiry, the elf whirled around and strode with confident, masterful steps toward their destination. They reached the alley, and after the elf dragged her several paces into the narrow space between buildings, he raised her off the red soil and slammed her back into the hard terracotta wall. Groaning faintly from the impact, Janir tried to remain calm. There had to be a misunderstanding, there had to be.

The elf stared at her with a penetrating gaze, glaring deeply into her eyes, as if he was trying to see her thoughts even though she was an Argetallam and should have been unreadable by anyone except an especially skilled Argetallam. He held her firmly by her throat with a claw-like grip.

"How interesting," he mused, "you must be at least fifteen, but you still have not learned how to create a shimmer."

"There must be some mistake here…" Janir hesitantly began, but he glared at her so hard that she decided to hold her comments. Suddenly, she felt something inside her head, something that wasn't supposed to be there. A hazy idea or image. With horror, she recognized the presence of the elf, he was in her mind! Panicking, she tried to get him out of her thoughts. Imagining a battering ram, Janir flung her consciousness at his mental presence with all the force she could muster.

The elf let out a stifled hiss of pain, tightening his grasp on her neck. Janir sensed his mind withdraw from hers with the rapidity of one who has been bitten by something inside a box. Ramming her head into the wall again, he muttered in his native tongue, regularly repeating one word that she did know in Elvish.

"*Stultus, stultus. Stultus de me.* "

Stupid, stupid. Stupid of me.

Janir glanced from side to side, trying to find a way out.

"Where is it?" he harshly demanded.

"Where is what?" Janir moaned, petting the spot where her head had struck the earthen wall.

"Do not jest with me, mortal!" the elf snapped, "Where is it?" he repeated. "I know you had it. I learned that much from you, in spite of you recently handling karkaton."

With a driven air, the elf groped through her pockets and felt her all over with his free hand. Janir kicked his shins.

"Get your hands off me!" Janir hissed, struggling in vain.

"Where is it?" the elf repeated after thoroughly frisking her body.

"Let me go!" Janir shouted, kicking wildly.

The elf leaned so close that she smelled night-time, even though she had never thought of a time of day having a scent before. Now she knew exactly what it smelled like. The aroma of midnight was accompanied by the sweet odor of evening stars, which she would have found appealing under any other circumstance.

"Where is the Key?" he demanded.

"I don't know!" Janir defiantly shrieked, fighting to pry his fingers off her throat.

"You will tell me," the elf growled, tightening his grip even more on her throat.

Just then someone smacked the elf on the back of the head with a shovel.

He cried out in pain, drew one sword and whirled around, holding his head with his left hand. It was the dwarf he had bumped into earlier, along with half a dozen others, all of them carrying shovels, jeering at the elf.

"Ye think that just because ye've got pointy ears and longer legs, ye can shove us around?"

The elf said something haughty in Elvish, something Janir didn't catch. It was likely something that enraged the dwarves, because all at once the one who appeared to be their leader angrily cried out.

"Get him, lads!"

Dwarves are masters in shovel-combat, as Janir learned that day. With a fierce battle cry, they expertly wrenched his swords away from him and set to taking out his knees. The elf was quickly brought to the kneeling position by several well-placed shovel strikes to the back of his legs, and then the dwarves set upon him mercilessly, hitting and kicking him with their heavily built fists and stocky legs. Two of them started head-butting him like miniature, two-legged bulls. One of the dwarves grabbed the elf's flailing hand and crunched his fingers between two rows of stout teeth.

Janir stood there watching the dwarves' retaliation toward her assailant for several moments, not having anywhere to go. Seemingly from nowhere, a dark, lithe woman, appeared from the crowd and laid a hand on Janir's arm.

"Come with me, Janir," the woman beckoned in a voice like wind in a tree, in a foreign accent that seemed somehow familiar. She was clad in a loose beige gown that flowed about her like a living garment, which seemed to be a being unto itself when it shimmered in the crimson glow of the market.

Surprised at the woman's recognition of her, Janir obediently followed her back through the crowd. Just as a wave of the crowd swept between them and the elf, she spotted the elf snap to his feet and all the dwarves fly backward, away from him. One hand went angrily to a cut on his temple, and the other snatched up his swords. Then his menacing eyes began scanning the crowd for her.

"How do you know me?" Janir wondered, stooping low to avoid a dead hanging animal by a vending stand that the other mortal easily slipped under.

"What Argetallam maiden besides the daughter of the Compassionate One would have been without karkaton and lost in the Vermilion Market?" the woman rhetorically remarked.

"The daughter of who?" Janir asked.

"In good time," the woman replied.

The woman led Janir to a quieter street, far away from that part of the market. This part of market had flowers growing from the upper stories of the buildings, and potted plants in front of the house doorways. The woman guided the maiden up the steps of a terracotta abode, ducked under a low doorway with wooden beads and a ragged cloth flap hanging down for a door, and into a cozy room. Herbs and flowers hung from the ceiling and lay in disorganized piles on the floor. A loom was set up near the small fireplace with fresh flax lying beside it. The furniture was fitting for the surroundings, roughly made and very natural in appearance. Another low doorway led to the rest of the house, the kitchen, and a bedroom. What caught Janir's attention was the golden orb set upon a small round table in one corner of the room.

"You are a seeress?" Janir inquired.

"Who else keeps such an orb?" the woman curtly replied. "My name is Zeerla. I am the one your brother is searching for."

"But how could you know that?"

"I cannot see through Argetallams, nor their slaves, but I can see through enchanters. Karile was warning me with his thoughts, though he knew it not." Zeerla stepped like a wraith over to her small wooden table and laid her wispy fingers over the orb protectively, like a mother stroking her baby's head.

"Then why are you still here?" Janir demanded.

"My brother will not be good to you when he finds you."

"No," Zeerla agreed "he will not."

Janir waited several moments for a response. "Well?"

Zeerla sighed. "I have had a vision of my death, Janir."

"What does that have to do with anything?" the maiden demanded, irritated at this seeress' behavior.

"I have my powers when I die; your brother or any other Argetallam, will not take them from me now, or ever."

"He could still kill you without claiming you!" Janir shouted impatiently.

"No, I do not die by the hand of an Argetallam, nor do I die here," Zeerla sighed, casting a loving gaze about her small home. "These visions are such a curse," Zeerla morosely moaned. "All of us learn that, including your mother."

"My mother?" Janir balked, feeling the acute sense of bitter loss that still accompanied any reminder of her.

"How else would I know your name, unless she told me? Before she even saw your father she had a vision. In that vision she met a girl, who was an Argetallam and addressed her as 'mother,'" Zeerla sighed again. "Poor Aryana, it nearly drove her mad after that, realizing she would bear the child of an Argetallam."

Janir fell silent. She had been born as much a curse to her mother as Amatahns was to the mazag. Tears came to her eyes when she thought about it. Her mother had been in love with a man, had been that man's wife. But Aryana's only child was the offspring of her abductor. How could her mother have even pretended to love the child of a murderer? Janir didn't want to think about what else he must be. Armandius was loving and kind.

"Why couldn't I have been born Armandius' daughter!" Janir suddenly shrieked, breaking a long space of silence.

"You would not be yourself, if that had been," Zeerla coldly replied.

"But I *hate* being an Argetallam," Janir screamed, slamming her hand into the terracotta wall.

"You think I enjoy being a seeress?" Zeerla retorted. "Seeing people's deaths, people I love. Knowing all the painful and horrible things that are going to happen to me before I finally die…you think I relish that?"

For awhile Janir couldn't find words. She had not considered that. "It can't all be bad," Janir hesitantly responded.

"No, it is not. I do see joyful things occasionally, happy visions. Like everything, it is two-sided, as is being an Invulnerable." Zeerla calmly removed her hands from the orb and folded them in her lap.

"I just…" Janir sighed and eased herself into the small chair opposite Zeerla across the small round table. It creaked slightly as she sank into its seat. "I don't like being such a monster," Janir moaned. "My people are the cruelest and most brutal to live," she complained.

"Take care when using superlatives to describe someone who you do not know well," Zeerla chided.

"Don't know them? I am one of them!" Janir

snapped.

"Very well," Zeerla dismissively allowed, "I suppose being one makes you an expert on them. But it still does not make you an authority on all the other people in the world. And you must know everyone, ever in existence, to know who truly are the worst and best."

Janir had never thought of it that way. She had simply accepted the general opinion that there was no more wretched form of life than that of an Argetallam. Intently, she studied the red dirt on her hands, wondering what made it that color.

"Do not flee," Zeerla stated, a soothing tone creeping into her voice for the first time.

"Flee from what?" Janir wondered, looking up from her fingers.

"Yourself. Do not flee from yourself." Zeerla leaned around the table and laid a thin, long-fingered hand on Janir's arm.

"What is that supposed to mean?"

"Do not flee from who you are. You will never get away," Zeerla sympathetically placated, staring at Janir with luminous, cat-like eyes. "Take it from someone who knows. It is impossible to escape, believe me."

Janir had almost forgotten the elf, but now she remembered. She asked Zeerla about him.

"That was Malkalar," Zeerla emotionlessly stated.

"And I take it you know him?" Janir pressed.

"Oh, yes," confirmed Zeerla.

Realizing that Zeerla preferred only to answer questions and did not enjoy giving information freely, Janir reconstructed her query. "Who is the elf? Why is he chasing me, and why did he search me?"

"He is a very important person. As to who he is, I am not to tell you. Ask your friend, Saoven." Zeerla laid her hands on the orb again. "Malkalar is chasing you, and he searched you for the same reason. You had something that he wants."

Janir stared blankly at Zeerla. The seeress had replied to all her questions honestly, without giving any explanation.

"Is it so secret?" Janir moaned.

"Why be secretive, unless it is a secret?" Zeerla retorted.

Perturbed by the seeress' deft avoidance of straight answers, Janir sat back in the wicker chair and stared at the other woman. The seeress went back to stroking the glowing orb, seemingly absorbed by its presence. Behind Janir the jangling of wooden beads being shoved aside caused her to twist in her low seat. Janir spotted a young mortal girl of about twelve, gracefully stooping down into the house. She had the look of a foreigner, as did Zeerla. Dark eyes like onyx and smooth, honey-colored skin. Earth-tone clothes raggedly hung loosely from her slender shoulders and draped down to the ground. At first she wore a joyful smile, until her gaze fell on Janir. With a start, the foreign girl glanced sharply at Zeerla, who had looked up from her orb to meet the girl's nervous stare.

"Argetallam!" she exclaimed in a heavily accented voice, reaching behind her with a swift motion. In less time than Janir could react, the other girl had a short stone dagger in her hand and looked ready to charge Janir like any one of the fiercest warriors on earth.

This market had to be one of the most inhospitable places in the world, Janir thought. Children had knives for use especially on unwanted guests.

Seeing the imminent danger, and not sure how to react, Janir tried to leap backwards but forgot that she was still seated. The result was that she flipped the chair on its back and hit her already sore head on the terracotta wall.

"Peace, my child," Zeerla placated, smoothly and swiftly rising like an apparition to calm the girl. "Florete, I have warned you about only reading half of a person's thoughts," the seeress chided. Janir remained uncomfortably prone on the ground and with baffled and nervous eyes watched the other girl's very sharp stone blade.

"But she is an Argetallam," Florete protested. The girl spoke clearly, carefully, with perfect grammar, never letting two words slur together.

"And a friend," Zeerla added.

"The Argetallam…is a friend?" Florete incredulously repeated and cautiously lowered the stone knife.

"Yes, and the daughter of Aryana Caersynn," Zeerla explained.

"I am honored," Florete smiled brightly, curtsying with the knife still in one hand.

Janir racked her brains. She had heard that accent before, perhaps in a dream, long, long ago. Both

Florete and Zeerla spoke with the same accent, and so did someone else from Janir's distant memory. Catching herself in time to return the courtesy, Janir popped upright and since she had never been taught to curtsy, bowed to Florete in turn.

"Mother has told me much of your mother. You should be proud," Florete beamed, slipping the stone knife back into its place.

"'Mother'?" Janir repeated, seeking clarification.

"I was a slave girl in Stlaven when I bore her," Zeerla explained. "I was allowed to bring her with me once I discovered that she had the Gift."

"I am an enchantress," Florete proudly announced, neatly setting herself down in another chair near the small table.

That explained the accent. Janir had heard Bricen, Lucan's mother, speak with the same inflection.

"Mother's friends taught me to use my Gift," Florete explained in a sweet voice that told of an innocent and guileless nature.

"Enchantress? But then, how could you read a person's thoughts?" Janir inquired.

"It is a slightly hereditary trait occasionally passed onto the children of seers and seeresses," Zeerla explained.

"But I don't have it," Janir protested.

"Being an Argetallam cancels out any hereditary magical gifts you might have received from the other parent," Zeerla explained.

Florete smiled again at Janir and the Argetallam felt her heart filling with dread. Even if Zeerla was meant to get through this with her powers intact, did that mean that Florete would, too?

"Florete, my child, would you see to the fire, please?" Zeerla asked in a very maternal tone. Janir immediately felt a pang in her heart, tugging on that sore place where her mother had once been. Almost gleefully, Florete popped to her feet and stood before the fireplace. With exaggerated motions and clear words, she raised several logs into the air from beside the hearth and arranged them in a perfect pyramid for a fire. As Florete practiced her skill with great concentration, the young Argetallam's mind had already moved to other things.

"My brother is coming," Janir whispered frantically to Zeerla. "As is our friend from the market, they will be here any minute. We should go."

The seeress took on a very sad expression and stared mournfully toward young Florete. Exhausted by the work of using magic, the young girl sat cross-legged in front of the fire watching the leaping flames with a blissful ignorance that Janir found heart-wrenching. For some reason, she had felt an instant bond with the young enchantress and Zeerla. They were like living reflections of her mother, seen through textured glass. Inexplicably, Janir felt that they were like her mother in some way. It was as if they had been crafted of the same material as Aryana. The idea of them meeting their fate at the hands of Lucan was unbearable.

"Oh, child," Zeerla sighed, shaking her head despondently. "They are already here," she whispered. Janir immediately bolted upright just in time to see Lucan force his way through the low doorway of Zeerla's house. Behind him followed his warrior-slaves dragging Karile.

"Janir! I was worried about you!" Karile cried. Lucan cast a poisonous glare in the enchanter's direction that demanded silence. Her brother surveyed everything with a painfully familiar, quick and decisive glance. Irritation was apparent when he spotted Janir standing between Zeerla and the stunned Florete.

"Rushing ahead of me, were you, Sister?" Lucan snapped.

"Please, Lucan," Janir supplicated. "Don't claim them."

At her plea, Lucan's eyebrows raised. "So they both have powers, do they? But only one is the seeress, so then the girl is an enchantress?"

Her brother noticed Florete sitting by the fireplace. The light in his cold eyes when he stared at the young enchantress made Janir uneasy.

"What do you want with us, son of the Staspin Waste?" Zeerla stoically inquired with the authority of a queen.

"I want to know the location of the Temple of Amatahns from you, but I may want something else from your young companion." Lucan had not taken his eyes off of Florete.

Janir knew full well what happened to enchanters or enchantresses who were claimed by Argetallams, and she had no desire to see that happen to this smiling young girl. Florete stood bravely, even though Janir knew that her knees must be knocking together. The young Argetallam admired her courage and wished that she could do more.

"That I cannot tell you," Zeerla announced, a note of sadness in her voice, as if she knew that he would not be satisfied with that reply.

"I think you can," Lucan icily replied.

"Do you know what will happen if you succeed and deliver the power of Amatahns to the purchaser?" Zeerla questioned. Janir could see that the seeress was afraid, and she spoke to Lucan in a pleading tone.

"How is that relevant? Tell me where the temple is!"

"I have seen him taking control of all the races…"

"No one can control our race," Lucan snapped. "As for the others, we could not care less."

"He will destroy the Argetallams!" Zeerla cried. "Once the other races are under his control, they will march against you. Even the Children of the Karkaton cannot stand for long against such an alliance!"

"I'll leave that for the Lord Argetallam to decide," Lucan retorted.

"After you are destroyed, he will command what he believes to be the inferior races to destroy themselves. This world will become a wasteland and soon even his race will perish for lack of sustenance," Zeerla concluded. She gazed at Lucan beseechingly, trying in vain to appeal his cruel resolve.

Lucan was not one to be reasoned with. Letting off an irritated sound, he drew one of Janir's karkaton from his belt, made a determined grimace as the karkaton rebelliously stung him, and strode firmly toward his sister and Florete. Janir tried to block her brother's path, but he shoved her into a pile of rosemary next to the wall and grabbed Florete by the hair.

Struggling, Florete tried to reach for the concealed dagger, but to no avail. Lucan dragged her to the middle of the room and forced her to her knees.

"This girl is very dear to you, is she not?" Lucan inquired of Zeerla.

Clambering to her feet, Janir tried again to intervene, but with a sharp command from her brother, the warrior slaves snatched her up and took her to stand beside Karile. The enchanter looked sadly at Janir and then pityingly at the young enchantress. With tears streaming down her face, Florete tried to keep her composure.

Lucan did not wait for the seeress to reply. He simply drove one of the karkaton into the back of Florete's neck, right at the base of her skull. Florete screamed with the indescribable pain that coursed through her veins. Like a mocking refrain, the karkaton wailed with her, a droning, shrieking sound.

Having made his point, Lucan released Florete from the karkaton's touch. The enchantress gasped, coughed and slumped forward weakly. Where the karkaton had been, a blistering welt appeared.

"Will you tell me now?" Lucan demanded, stiffly bracing himself against the sharp bite that the karkaton inflicted on him in umbrage. Zeerla had risen to her feet and was staring horrified at her young daughter.

"I...I cannot..." Zeerla repeated, less resolutely

this time.

With a slight sigh and shake of his head, Lucan drove the karkaton into Florete's back this time. Janir hated being so helpless, being so powerless to stop him.

"Tell me," he snapped

Zeerla was quiet and looked down into Florete's pleading eyes. Already all the light and laughter were gone. Beside her, Janir could see Karile out of the corner of her eye, shifting his weight.

"I am sorry, it is multitudes or you..."

Zeerla never finished her sentence, because Lucan savagely ground the karkaton against Florete's flesh again. The brave young enchantress screamed helplessly as the pain consumed her.

"Tell me!" Lucan shouted.

"No." Zeerla had tears streaming down her face. Janir thought she heard something below the demands of Lucan and the screams of Florete, but she could not be certain. It sounded like something very soft, more an idea than a sound.

Rolling his eyes in frustration, Lucan jerked Florete around to face him and caught his hand under her throat. "If she means so little to you, then perhaps you will not mind if I claim her as my own," Lucan jeered, turning his dark, flashing eyes to the whimpering Florete.

"No!" Zeerla wailed.

Florete weakly tried to struggle with Janir's brother. But her futile resistance only served to annoy him.

"Then, and this is the last time I will offer you this

chance, tell me!" Lucan shouted, brutally clenching Florete's throat harder.

Zeerla hesitated for several seconds before she gave in. Lucan seemed to know that she would, and waited.

"According to my visions, the Temple of Amatahns is on the tip of the Rivellis Peninsula. In the forest," Zeerla sighed.

"Thank you." Lucan said it in a way that seemed more of mockery than anything else.

Janir's brother stared down at Florete with a hard, cold gaze. He stared directly into her terror stricken eyes. Janir found it difficult to explain, but it was as though Lucan was seeping into Florete's mind. Or perhaps drawing her out of hers. Vaguely, Zeerla screamed in the back ground.

Janir felt a deafening silence, a noiseless void, pound over her ears. It was like the feeling of thunder, but only one pulse. The world itself seemed to hold its breath, then breathe again once it was done. The seeress screamed again, and Florete slumped limply to the ground. Rushing to the side of her young daughter, Zeerla's tears flowed freely.

"I led them here," Karile whispered to Janir. "This is my fault." He was beginning to weep.

Although she had just been blaming him for this in her mind, Janir touched his arm in a sympathetic gesture. Lucan stood straight and stared down at his hands with a hard interest. He closed his eyes in concentration until orbs of flowing light appeared in both his upraised palms. As he used her powers, Florete gasped as the strength was taken from her to serve Lucan.

"And that is the best part," Lucan sneered, extinguishing the orbs. "Not only can I take your powers, but you pay the price."

This time Janir was certain that she heard something. Faint whooshing. Glancing to her right, there was nothing. Checking her left...with a start, Janir beheld the elf Malkalar, standing before the low doorway that led to the rest of the house. He seemed to have simply appeared, materialized out of thin air. His dual-wield swords were drawn in both hands. A look of confidence and cruelty was on his face.

"Holy fewmets!" Karile exclaimed in alarm. Janir felt much the same way at the elf's sudden emergence, but chose not to show her astonishment.

"I will be taking the seeress with me," Malkalar mildly stated, sounding remarkably casual for the circumstances. Zeerla looked up, frightened.

"Who are you?" Lucan demanded in a deliberate tone, separating each word clearly to express that he was by no means impressed with the elf.

"Someone who demands your compliance, mortal." The elf spat out the name of the race as if it were poisonous. At a command from Malkalar's lips, a loose piece of clay in the wall sprang up like a living thing and charged at Lucan like an arrow.

Raising his hand, Lucan stopped the potentially deadly missile mid-air. It stopped, hovered for a moment, and retraced its course back toward the enchanter.

Malkalar ducked his head to one side so that it missed, and uttered something that sounded like:

"Damn Argetallams."

"An enchanter, are you?" Lucan asked, despite the answer's obvious nature.

"An Argetallam, are you?" Malkalar sarcastically retorted.

It occurred to Janir how alike Lucan and Malkalar were. Both were so cold, so calculative. They might have been two different versions of the same man. Seemingly bored with the conversation, Lucan bent his fingers in a practiced pose and like magic, it was magic, Janir realized, a tongue of flame appeared on his finger tips, grew stronger, then roared toward Malkalar.

In a motion almost too quick to be seen, Malkalar held his palms out before him and traced the top of something large that surrounded his entire form like an invisible screen. As the fire collided with it, the outline shimmered like a luminescent curtain of protection. The flames died as if they had struck water, having no effect on the Elven enchanter.

Florete moaned weakly as Lucan used so much of her power at once. When Zeerla cried out in anguish, Janir knew that her brother had killed the smiling and innocent young enchantress. A grimace creased Lucan's face as he glanced down furtively at the girl's lifeless form.

Realizing that the victor could not be decided by magic, and that they were indeed foes, elf and Argetallam prince were both still unwilling to fight the other. Lucan must have noticed the assured and confident air about Malkalar that spoke of lifetimes' worth of training and experience. As for the elf, he was doubtless uneager to risk his powers, which appeared to be substantial, in a tussle with this sturdy Argetallam youth.

"Where is the Key of Amatahns?" Malkalar demanded, with the air of one who is accustomed to swift and truthful replies.

"Go to hell!" Lucan defiantly snapped back.

Janir didn't pay attention to the rest of what Lucan and the elf said, though it was certainly a string of inquiries and insults flying both directions. She stared sadly at Zeerla, wishing she could do something to help.

Leaping sideways, the elf sheathed his swords, snatched Zeerla's arm and in less than the time it takes for a heart to be beat thrice, dragged her to the low doorway that led to the rest of the house. With a few hasty words from Malkalar, Zeerla's glowing golden orb flew up from the table and rested in his other hand.

Janir couldn't help but notice Zeerla's devastated eyes and sorrowful face staring at the lifeless body of Florete. Hardly able to help herself, Janir glanced to the girl's still form herself. When she glanced up again, the elf and seeress were gone.

"Oh, well," Lucan shrugged. "We got what we wanted anyway. He can have the seeress for all I care. Come along, we have a temple to find."

Janir didn't know what she would do, but pulling against the convert's hold, she reached toward Florete. The girl lay still and motionless, just an empty shell of the very alive and joyful child that had been breathing moments before. Having seen people die and killed before, Janir did not expect Florete's death to be so devastating. But it was. The converts grappled with Janir for several seconds, and then dragged her after Lucan, away from the lifeless enchantress and the seeress' cottage.

CHAPTER 7

Avenport

The city was placed squarely at the water's
edge, like a boxy giant just dipping his toes
in the quiet bay. It was built against the side
of a seacliff that overlooked the narrow straits of the
harbor and beyond, the vast nothingness of water
that is the sea. The city made a formidable defense.
Soaring watchtowers and stern soldiers faced out
from all four sides, as if daring an enemy to try
and take the massive city. Officially, the city was a
principality of the King in Brevia. Realistically, they
did business with whoever paid for a place in their
harbor.

Lucan had decided that the fastest way to the
Rivellis Peninsula would be to charter a vessel
here in Avenport, and sail. Not looking forward to
sailing, but not having any choice in the matter, Janir
followed after her brother with reluctance.

Lucan was before her, riding Kalbo and pretending
that was where he belonged. From behind, it was
obvious to Janir that Lucan had not ridden a horse
in awhile. He was sliding slightly to the left and had
a stiff posture, as if he was using muscles he hadn't
even remembered he had. She and Karile were in

wrist irons that had been obtained in Ivy Down. It was amazing how questions of blacksmiths could be quelled by a few well-worded threats. They were being led by one of the warrior-slaves and were surrounded on all sides by the others. That had its advantages: no one jostled Janir and Karile as they trudged behind Lucan.

They had been traveling with Lucan for two or three weeks now. Janir had stopped counting the days after day eleven. All that time her brother had been a cruel task master, forcing them to keep pace with him even though he never seemed to tire. He did let them eat eventually and soon learned that it is unwise to let a hungry wizard have free access to a cooked animal meant to be shared between fifteen people.

They neared the gates at what seemed to be a continent's pace, but at last they were standing beneath the brooding stone archway that spanned the gate. A guard stopped them and pulled them to the side.

"Name?" he inquired in a disinterested, matter-of-fact tone.

"Lucan Caersynn," Lucan coolly replied.

"What?" Janir indignantly demanded. One of the warrior-slaves clamped a rough hand over her mouth before she could say anything else.

"Business?" the guard wearily continued.

"Seeking passage to the Rivellis Peninsula, where we will meet elves who wish to purchase these Arge-tallams." Lucan was motioning to her and Karile!

"Destination?"

Lucan balked. "The Rivellis Peninsula."

"Vocation?"

Lucan apparently hadn't expected this question. "Mercenary," he honestly replied. His answers seemed to satisfy the guard and the man moved aside, motioning for them to continue on.

Once out of an earshot of the guards, Janir snarled at Lucan. "Vanmar. Vanmar is your mother's surname, not Caersynn."

"I know, you little minx," he hissed, "but I can hardly confess to being of Stlavish nobility and a mercenary, can I?"

After commanding one of the converts to strike her, Lucan continued on. The Staspin Waste must have been very out of touch with the rest of the world if Lucan thought using Armandius' name was safer. As Janir considered it, he would have been better off confessing to be a Vanmar, as there was only one full-blooded Caersynn left alive.

They entered the city. The inside was just as crowded as the outside. They forced their way through the inner courtyard and ultimately through the second gate, into the actual city.

Lined with street vendors and barking dogs, the place was noisy and chaotic. Shouting fish mongers promised the lowest prices and people on the side of the streets with their wares laid out on display tried to attract customers any way they could. Janir and Karile weren't given much time for sight-seeing as Lucan made an almost straight line through the chaos toward the shipyards. Not that they needed to see, Janir could guess just by the smell. She was certain that all the fishmongers were lying about the fish being caught that morning.

Lucan hastily arranged a full charter on a small ship called the *Sea Queen*.

"*Sea Queen?*" Karile scoffed, "Looks more like a *Sea Skiff.*"

Indeed it was little more than a skiff, but Lucan gauged that it was all they would need for the three-day voyage to the tip of the Rivellis Peninsula. He paid the grungy, burly and excessively hairy sea captain half of what he was to receive in all, then told him they would depart in the morning, and to be ready. Janir was beginning to wonder how the warrior-slaves carried all this money.

When it came to his personal relaxation, Lucan didn't concern himself overmuch, but he did concern himself all the same. He chose a comfortable, but aged inn for them to spend the night. Contrary to Janir's expectations, the sight of fifteen nearly disparate people and a horse did not raise an alarm. Instead, Lucan showed a side Janir had never seen with the landlady. He complimented the middle-aged woman on her hair, and smiled a charming, warm smile that Janir would never have suspected him of. His charm worked so well, that the air-headed woman didn't even ask why two of his companions were in shackles.

Lucan realized that they would need to have the horse taken care of, so once they were locked in their rooms, he grudgingly commanded Janir to go down and see to the beast, as his men and himself knew hardly anything about tending horses.

"But if you are gone more than one hour," he threatened. "I will kill the wizard, do you hear me?"

Janir understandingly nodded. Lucan unlocked her shackles with the keys he was wearing around his neck and told her to be gone. She glanced Karile's terrified expression as she slipped out of the room, but Kalbo needed to be tended, so she went anyway.

The inn was one of many buildings lining the street, seemingly built into the wall. They were all flat in front and their owners tried to make up for this with colorful banners and hanging shade cloths. The inn was at the end of the street, within sight of the well-guarded shipyards, with a stable around back.

Janir took the stallion from one of the warrior-slaves, who unquestioningly relinquished the reins, and led the horse around to a side way to the stables. The stables were where an alley would normally be. But apparently it had made more sense to make a stable for the inn instead.

The thatched roof over their heads seemed a direct defiance of the brick and mortar of the rest of the city. Nondescript timbers lined all sides and rough juniper logs formed stalls for the animals in the straw. A doorless opening in the stone led from the stables back into the inn. The sounds of people milling about on the outside faintly spilled into the relative peace of the barn.

A few donkeys and oxen chewed their cud peacefully while a barn cat cleaned itself from atop a stall post and a litter of puppies barked playfully below. This place was quiet and peaceful, as stables often are. It smelled the unparalleled scent of hay and manure mixed with animal sweat and worn leather. The afternoon sunlight filtered through the timbers, flashing frequently as people moved on the other side, blocking the sun every so often.

Kalbo was used to such places, having traveled a bit with Armandius before, so he followed Janir without argument. She chose a stall near the middle of the stable, so no one prying about would be likely to spot the tired bay stallion amidst the content beasts of burden.

Janir unsaddled him and tended to his cuts with care. Trustingly, the stallion stood without protest as she dug stones out from under his loosening shoes and eased a mesquite thorn out of the soft part of his hoof. All in all, he was not in irreparable condition, but still, she cringed every time she found a new scratch. She twisted a handful of straw into a short cord and rubbed him down, avoiding the bruises and abrasions where she could.

"I'm sorry," Janir whispered. "I know I am the one who got you into this."

The stallion either didn't understand, or didn't hold a grudge in the first place, because he shook his mane and continued munching on the hay in front of him. The crunching of straw beneath footsteps caused Janir to freeze in fright.

She doubted it was anyone hostile, but still. There were three of them, heavily built and clumsy from the sound of it. The footsteps halted directly behind her. Icy claws of fear wrapped around her heart, and her breathing quickened with dread.

"What have we here?" a gruff, uncultured voice

growled behind her. Most likely a sailor, she was guessing.

Janir had been bent over one of Kalbo's fore hooves, but now finished, she straightened her back deliberately and turned slowly around to face her antagonists. Sailors, just as she had guessed. They were on the chunky side, with a week's worth of greasy stubble on their chins and several month's worth of grime under their fingernails. One still held an overflowing tankard in a clenched fist. She wondered how she hadn't smelled the pungent scent of beer before, but now it was overwhelming. They stared at her with beady, dangerous eyes. Cautiously, Janir slipped under the bars of the stall and tried to walk around the trio of drunken shipmen. They staggered into her way, blocking her off.

What was she supposed to do now? It hadn't been a full hour yet, but she needed to get away from the stables immediately. The one with the brimming tankard took a faltering step toward her.

"Excuse me, but you're blocking my way," Janir stated, making what she knew was a vain attempt at cordiality.

"That's right," he mumbled.

That tact had not been successful, not that she really expected it to be. There didn't seem to be many choices as to her course of action.

With a swift motion, Janir upset the tankard and splashed its contents on the face of the sailor standing before her. He spat and cursed while Janir tried to dash past him, which she did, only to meet the angry fists of his compatriots. The one to the left grabbed a fistful of her hair, while the other tried to catch hold of her thrashing feet. The latter received a kick in the jaw, with a hard-soled boot for that, but the one who had her hair was dragging her toward the pile of straw near the back of the stable.

"Let me go!" Janir shrieked frantically.

The one she had splashed the tankard on had stumbled toward her, and struck her in the face with a brutal fist. Janir struggled, kicked one in the knees who had tried to grab her earlier, sending him toppling over. The one who still had a grip on her hair, jerked her up and locked her neck in a choke-hold. Gasping, Janir remembered something Armandius had once mentioned to her. Fighting to ignore the natural instinct to grapple with the arm that was over her neck, she flexed backwards and reached for his face. She located one of his eyes and clawed viciously with both hands. The sailor screamed in agony and threw her down like a poisonous snake.

The next one, the one she had kicked, was coming toward her; he grabbed a hold of her arm and twisted malignantly.

Janir cried out with the sharp pain and tried to reach his eyes, but to no avail. He flipped her on her stomach and stomped a rough boot in the middle of her back. It seemed to crush the very beat of her heart and for several moments she couldn't think or hear.

"Release the maiden and depart," came a voice toward the entrance of the stables. Janir couldn't see anything besides cobblestones and straw, but the voice was familiar.

"Why?" the sailor, with his boot still on her back, gruffly demanded. "So you can have her for yourself?"

"Believe me, she be too much for one man alone," another remarked.

The replying voice was calm, calculated. "I said, release the maiden and depart. Shall you do that willingly, or must I force you?"

"We found her first, get your own wench," the sailor she had spilled the tankard on snapped in a surly tone.

"Let the maiden be, sailors. You have no idea who you are dealing with," came the third warning. This was followed by the ringing of steel as a pair of swords were flicked out of their scabbards. That was the ultimatum.

The sailors seemed to consider this for a moment. The one with his boot on her back twisted her arm a little harder. But then, they suddenly began scrambling to get away from Janir and her rescuer faster than they had moved at all since Janir had met them.

The fumbling boot steps of the sailors receded into the street, and the man who had protected her sheathed his swords. He knelt beside Janir, gently lifted her chin so he could see her face and tenderly stroked her cheek with his fingers. Seeking something warm and solid at the moment, she wrapped her arms around his neck. He smelled of pine needles and rushing rivers, even in the city. Comfortingly, he laced his hands behind her back. Somehow she felt safe now, as if nothing in the world could hurt her.

"Are you well?" he inquired with concern.

"Now," Janir coughed. Carefully, he gently peeled her arms off his neck and lifted her to her feet. But he kept a hand on her back, gently reminding her that he was still there. Janir leaned against him for a space and rested her head on his chest.

"You should have killed them," Janir murmured.

"Perhaps, but I did not wish to cause any trouble for myself, and especially no additional trouble for you."

"But now they will simply go and torment another girl," Janir countered.

"I would not be so certain," he remarked.

The maiden glanced up at him, searched for a further explanation, but received only a strange expression in response to her unspoken query. "Thank you, Saoven," she gratefully sighed.

"Why are you here? Did I not tell you to stay in the mountains?" he chastened.

"Yes, but first, why are you here?" Janir wondered.

"I was on my way from Saaradan to find you. The guards at the gate had someone using the name of Caersynn enter earlier today and I thought perhaps it was you. Considering that Armandius is still at Saaradan, according to last report."

"Is he alright?" Janir queried with unhidden concern.

"Yes," Saoven assured her, "his trial was held. But the High King is very forgiving apparently."

Master was safe.

Turning to other matters, Saoven rebuked her. "Really girl, you should not be so rash to use your name when you are a wanted fugitive, nor should you be traveling in such a city alone," he chided.

"But I *didn't* use my name, *or* come here alone!" Janir shouted.

"The wizard hardly constitutes a protector," Saoven briskly replied. "Speaking of which, where is he?"

"I'll tell you the whole story, but first, how did you know the guards had someone using the name of Caersynn enter this morning?" Janir reasoned.

"I have my ways," Saoven replied.

"Fine. Well it was my half-brother who used the name Caersynn to get into the city," Janir paused, realizing with dismay that now she would have to tell Saoven about who her blood family was.

"Your Argetallam brother?" Saoven inquired, as if that were nothing but a simple and harmless fact.

Janir balked. "Yes, how did you know?"

"I know that you are an Argetallam, Janir," Saoven blandly confirmed. "I learned after the verdict of Armandius' trial, remember? What I do not understand, is why you seem to think that would merit how tense you have suddenly become. I didn't know it was possible, but you seem to be tensing your eyelids."

"You hate Argetallams!" Janir realized that she had drawn away from him, shoved his hand off her back and taken up a defensive stance.

"I do not hate you," Saoven gently placated. "I could never hate you, even if I wanted to."

Janir cautiously let down her guard and relaxed her stance. "I was afraid of telling you, once I realized you didn't know. And frankly, I'm surprised that your father never told you."

The elf shrugged, an unbefitting gesture for him. "Velaskas? We are close only in that we both concern ourselves with the realm of mortals. Back home, among all the other elves, most of whom consider you unworthy of our attention, that can be rather uniting." Saoven added hastily; "Not all of them think that way, some merely have their own problems. Mortals are full of potential, and some of us, such as my father and myself, are committed to exposing such good as there is in your race."

"As I was saying," Janir grew suddenly uncomfortable, "Lucan, my brother, has the Key of Amatahns and is taking us in a skiff to the Rivellis Peninsula, where the crystal chamber supposedly is. Wait, did you say you came to find me?"

"I did," Saoven mildly replied. He was about to explain why to her, when a loud and now familiar voice rang out.

"Fifty seconds, Janir! forty-nine, forty-eight…" Remembering Lucan's threat, she scrambled back toward the inn. When she reached the door way, Janir realized she had best explain to Saoven why she was dashing off. She spun around to see that he had followed her, noiselessly.

"Lucan's going to kill Karile if I'm not back in…"

"Forty, thirty-nine…"

Saoven nodded, understanding. With her brother growing impatient, Janir whirled around again to race up to where Lucan would doubtless already be pressing a blade against Karile's throat.

"Janir," Saoven called, seizing her wrist and

pulling her back to face him.

She lightly twisted her wrist free and stared at him in hurried bewilderment.

"I shall return for the Key and you," he quietly assured, reaching down and grasping her hand in a comforting gesture. "We are friends, and that is what friends do."

Janir wanted to say something that befitted his promise, like maybe "I wouldn't blame you if you abandoned the child of an Argetallam warlord." But that hardly seemed appropriate, and although she trusted him utterly, her suspicious side didn't want to give him any ideas. As if she had been running, her heart was racing, and Janir wondered if it had anything at all to do with concern for the enchanter.

"Twenty-eight! Twenty-seven…" Lucan warningly announced.

"I should…"

"Go," Saoven supplied, giving it as more of a command than a completion of her sentence. Janir felt an understandable reluctance to leave, but spun around and rushed into the inn to find Lucan. The doorway led up a staircase, and ended in a bustling and noisy kitchen. The smell of onions and garlic hanging from the ceiling stung Janir's eyes, while the clang of pots and the yells of the cook assaulted her ears. The cook must have spotted her, because as she ran past there was a sudden flurry of intense hollering. Still blinking from the onions, Janir's eyes darted from side to side across the large room that served as a tavern. A roaring fire at one end was scorching the rest of the room with its heat, and all the clients nestled at one end like birds escaping a wildfire. In spite of the oppressive temperature, laughter and beer flowed as freely as any river. Mostly unwashed sailors with tankards in their fists, sat around the rough tables and crude benches. Now she realized with mild interest that her assailants must have come from here. Janir glanced around, but spotted no Lucan or warrior-slaves.

"Fifteen, fourteen…"

Directing her course toward the creaky wooden stairs at the far end of the tavern room, Janir bolted. Racing up the steep steps that were nearly vertical, she listened as Lucan continued his countdown.

"Ten, nine, eight…"

She reached the top of the stairs and beheld two rows of wooden doors staring out from the gray stone walls. They were all identical, and now she couldn't remember which one Lucan was in. Like a reminder of the life that was at stake, she could still hear Lucan counting down.

"Six, five…"

Janir held her breath, trying to pinpoint the exact location. There was a shuffling sound behind one of the doors, but Karile would be thrashing. She listened intently, attempting to hear even the slightest sound that might proclaim the proper location.

"Oh, for Amatahns' sake, where is the silly girl?" wailed a familiar, whining voice.

Her destination determined, Janir raced toward the third door on the right. She laid a hand on the knob and shoved it open, just as Lucan counted to one.

"There you are," her brother emotionlessly acknowledged.

Karile was kneeling below the casement, with Lucan standing over him, blade in hand. The warrior-slaves stood about, still as statues, staring blankly into space with absent eyes. Lucan stepped away from the cowering enchanter, took a set of shackles from one of his inert minions, and motioned for her to hold her hands out. Over the past days, this had become standard procedure. Lucan would release Janir for whatever reason, then when she came back he would slap the shackles back on her. Just like every occasion before, Janir searched her mind for an idea or a reason Lucan wouldn't be shackling her this time. But like every occasion before, she still held out her hands resignedly, and he roughly clamped the irons around her wrists. There would be no escape. Not this time. Janir didn't resist as Lucan roughly shoved her down beside Karile and maliciously struck her on the shoulder. Although tears brimmed in her eyes, she hid them from Lucan. Her body was already bruising on her back, now on her shoulder too; of that she was certain.

"Are you alright, Janir?" Karile whispered, almost inaudible, so that Lucan couldn't overhear. "What the heck happened to your face?" he motioned to where the sailor had punched her.

"Lovely, I'm fine," she murmured back. "It just hurts."

"Are you sure you're okay?" Karile whispered, then must have decided that he would receive no real response, because he silenced himself.

"Sleep well, you two," Lucan taunted. "We have a big day tomorrow."

With a start, Janir realized that she hadn't asked Saoven about who Malkalar was. That would have to wait for another time.

Early morning mist had settled over the harbor and the shipyards. The city was just waking up in the pre-dawn light, like a giant yawning before reluctantly rising. A few ships, from massive brigantines to fishermen's sloops, were slowly leaving and entering the bay, their crews probably only half-awake. Janir had not slept well, but better than she had on previous nights as Lucan's prisoner. Well before dawn, Lucan had awakened them, paid the innkeeper to house Kalbo until his return, and then dragged his captives out into the sleepy city. The warrior-slaves followed Lucan without a word as he marched with resolve toward the shipyards. Karile and Janir followed submissively, trudging along the slippery docks. She was sore from Lucan's strikes and those of the sailors the day previously, but she marched on obediently. Fisherman were on the distant beach, spreading their nets in preparation for the day's work, while the rhythmic clanging of a blacksmith's hammer rang like a bell through the salty sea air. Squawking gulls soared overhead, eager to steal what they could when the fishermen brought their wriggling catches back.

"What is it?" Karile quietly inquired.

"Hmm?" Janir turned her head and glanced at him before resuming her visual scan of the docks.

"You have been peering about expectantly ever since we left the inn, what's with you?"

"Nothing," Janir replied. Then added in a hushed tone: "Is it that obvious?"

"Yes, it is," Karile confirmed.

Janir didn't spot any sign of Saoven, but made it a point now not to keep surveying every corner for him.

The skiff was waiting for them at the docks. The "captain" of the skiff (who still hadn't bathed) welcomed them onto the deck, and showed Lucan a place by the prow of the vessel where he could deposit his prisoners. No questions asked. As one of Lucan's minions dragged her and Karile beneath the pathetically small sail to the front, Janir happened to glance back toward the docks. She thought she spotted something moving to the starboard side, something that moved faster than her eyes could see. The Argetallam and enchanter were dumped just behind the prow on the hard oaken planks. Like men in a trance, the warrior-slaves secured Janir and Karile's chains to rings, conveniently located in the front of the ship. Burly and filthy sailors heaved the oars up and down, throttling the small skiff onward.

Uncomfortably, Janir noticed as they rowed out of the harbor, the captain of the skiff was ogling her with beady eyes. Were all sailors the same? He even smelled the same as those others had, like reeking refuse. Lucan was shouting orders to his loyalists, telling the practically helpless warrior-slaves what they were to do.

The sea captain stepped toward her across the swaying deck, stooped down and reached out with one of his greasy hands to touch her hair.

"What have we here?" he mumbled.

Couldn't he think of anything more original? Janir jerked away defensively. Saoven had promised he would come, where was he?

Seemingly irked by her avoidance, the sea captain snatched her jaw in a cruel grip with that dirty hand and forced her to look up at him. "Perhaps you should be more cooperative, seeing as how I could make this much worse," he hissed. His breath stank, as if he ate nothing but onions.

Defiantly, Janir glared up at him, daring him to try something. Even though she was quaking inside.

"Get. Away. From. Her. Now," a firm, seething voice authoritively commanded from behind the sea captain.

Like a viper ready to inject venom into a sea rat, Lucan stood behind the sailor, with that deadly serious glare. A little surprised, the sea captain twisted around to look at Lucan, but didn't release Janir from his grasp.

"I'm sorry, is she yours? Do you mind?"

"Don't. Even. Think. About. It," her brother was speaking deliberately, spitting out each word as if wrestling with himself for control.

Lucan was in a plain fury now, his nostrils flared, his teeth grinding. An amber flicker went over his dark eyes, they rolled backward into his head for a moment and a racking shiver went over him, before setting back to normal.

Unnerved by Lucan's display of Argetallam power, the sea captain released Janir.

"Thank. You," Lucan stiffly acknowledged, then struck the sailor with a force Janir hadn't expected.

The sailor, who seemingly had prided himself at his toughness, sprawled on the deck of the ship like a sun-struck bat. He was mortified at being knocked down on his own ship, in front of his sailors, by a fifteen-year-old boy.

"You touch her again, I'll kill you," Lucan hissed, seizing the sailor's collar and pulling the confused sea captain up toward his face so that he would have no choice but to look Lucan in the eye.

"Do you hear me?" The amber flicker went over Lucan's normally dark eyes, and he shuddered convulsively again. "I'll kill you."

The sea captain's eyes had gone wide, and he nodded comprehendingly before scrambling to the back of the ship, away from Janir. Lucan suddenly seemed tired; he staggered to one side of the ship and slumped against the wooden planks, waving his concerned converts away.

Karile cautiously leaned toward her, still staring at Lucan, to whisper in her ear. "What was that?"

"I'm not sure," she hesitantly whispered. "If it was what I think it was…" Janir stopped. It couldn't have been. That couldn't be it.

"What?" Karile prompted.

"I think…" she hesitated again. "That's what happened to me before I went into the Riangar to protect my master. But that can't be it."

"Why not?" Karile pressed.

"Because my eyes turned green," Janir pointed out.

"Your eyes are green," Karile countered. "Well, hazel-green."

"But I was struck, thats what seemed to cause it," she pointed out.

"Okay; but what else could it be?" Karile asked.

Janir gave him a shrug in response.

They stopped at the mouth of the harbor to load supplies for the brief, but non-stop voyage. The skiff pulled close to the docks, and a series of barrels were dragged out of the warehouses to below deck by the hefty sailors. The harbor warehouses were an almost ramshackle collection of large wooden buildings, weathered by years of facing the harsh sea air and salt water. They were built up on stilts to hold them out of the water, resting against the jagged cliffs of the harbor mouth, with ramps that went down to the ships. Merchants and sailors alike moved about the warehouses like ants, each one to his duty without any concern for his surroundings.

Karile and Janir sat behind the prow, watching the proceedings without definable emotion. At this early morning hour, there were hardly any other vessels coming for supplies, so things appeared to be running smoothly.

On one hand, Janir was impatient for their departure because it was taking so blasted long, while on the other, she wanted Saoven to come so she wouldn't have to depart at all. Even though she feared and loathed him, Janir found a strange feeling of attachment to Lucan. There was a feeling of an invisible cord binding them together, like he was keeping her bound to him somehow, reaching out with…what was that feeling? It was an emotion she couldn't find words to describe. She needed to get away from him more than anything else, but at the same time, she felt that she didn't want to abandon him. She wouldn't be *abandoning* him. She would be *escaping* from him! Why did she need to remind herself of that?

Lucan and his warrior-slaves had not gone onto the docks, but stayed behind on the skiff, not helping load, just standing there like statues.

Janir tried to close her eyes and imagine herself back in Green Haven, the green fields that gave the province its name spreading in all directions, mourning doves fluttering in the oak trees, children laughing in a distant meadow, the gurgle of a stream.

"Bloody…" Lucan exclaimed, not finishing his sentence. Saoven had appeared, seemingly from nowhere to stand behind her brother and his converts.

"Release the girl and the wizard," Saoven declared simply.

"Kill him," Lucan barked to his converts.

Obediently, the converts stepped forward with brandished weapons to engage Saoven. Flicking out his pair of swords like a cat unsheathing his claws, Saoven blocked and parried effortlessly. Within seconds, one of the converts dropped to the deck, dead. Realizing that his converts were no match for the Elven warrior, Lucan wasted no time. Her brother swiftly drew the karkaton from his belt and held them an arm's length apart, before driving them together with all his might.

A high-pitched screaming, screeching wail shook the air and sent tremors through the boards of the wooden skiff. Janir clamped her hands over her ears as the noise stabbed at her head cruelly. Karile did the same and several by-standing people on the docks covered the sides of their heads and searched about in bewilderment for the source.

The sharp noise was hurtful to Janir, but she couldn't imagine what it must have felt like to the elf. His sharp and fine-tuned senses were used to Lucan's advantage as the karkaton's wail grew even louder. Dropping his swords reflexively, Saoven fell to his knees, gasping in pain. Without a second's hesitation, Lucan strode across the short deck and jabbed Saoven in the neck with a karkaton. The elf slumped limply to the ground. Where the karkaton had struck, a blistering black welt appeared.

"Put him in chains with the others," Lucan commanded his converts. "I may have use for him later."

"Saoven…" Janir whispered.

"Oh, shut up, he's alive," Lucan snapped. "Friend of yours?"

"You know he is," Janir bitterly replied.

"Indeed I do. One of my converts spotted you with him last evening and when you began glancing about like a sheepdog waiting for his master, my suspicions were confirmed. Of course, the docks or the city would be the obvious place to try and rescue you, so I assumed he would be here. And I was right!"

The converts slapped Saoven in chains and secured him beside her and Karile. She hesitated, then carefully she touched the welt on Saoven's neck. It felt hot and inflamed. An oily black substance clung to her hand as she drew it away. She stared at the black oil in bafflement as she rubbed it between her fingers.

"Karkaton ash," Lucan remarked. He seemed to be telling her out of sheer arrogance, displaying his superior knowledge of all things Argetallam with haughtiness.

"Why do you want the power of Amatahns, Lucan?" Janir gently probed. "Do you think you can use it?"

"Use it?" Lucan scoffed. "Shows how much you know. The power contained in that chamber is powerful enough, that it will undoubtedly kill any Argetallam foolish enough to become trapped inside. No, I am going to use either the elf or the wizard or both to contain the magic, and then deliver the living vessel to our master's client." Lucan put away the karkaton, flexed his fingers experimentally and winced as he struck a sensitive spot.

"Kill an Argetallam? But…"

"No, that makes no difference," Lucan haughtily corrected. "This magic was taken from our original foes, the mazag; even you remember them from the caverns? So it can effect us, as long as it is raw. Once contained in someone else, however, it will integrate into them and we will live fully to our name and be truly invulnerable."

"So that's what this is about?" Janir demanded. "Our father wants to give this power to someone else, so that no one will ever be able to use magic on us?"

The sailors finished loading the few barrels into the bottom of the ship, had separated the skiff from the ramp and were pushing off into the open sea. Waves rocked the sides gently and the sail was idly lolling in the breeze as the oars dipped up and down in the water. There was the creaking of wood as the oars twisted in their sockets and the sound of distant gulls.

"You may not be quite as stupid as I first thought," Lucan mildly stated.

"But if it's in the chamber, how could someone use it in the first place?" Janir pressed.

"There are ways to use magic that do not involve taking it into one's body," Lucan replied, seemingly amazed at her ignorance.

It occurred to Janir that even though the sailors had doubtlessly overheard their conversation, no one raised so much as an eyebrow. They probably knew what she suspected, and that was--if Lucan thought anyone would reveal his presence to anyone in authority, both the informant and the authority would be dead before the words passed their lips.

"Who's the buyer?" Janir continued.

Lucan glanced at her sideways with a suspicious light in his eyes. "Commercial confidentiality," he brusquely snapped back.

Janir heaved an inward sigh; that was something she would never learn from Lucan.

"If only I had my own karkaton and father hadn't had them imprinted on you," Lucan seethed, more to himself than to his sister. "Then I could use them so much more effectively."

"What can the karkaton do?"

Lucan stared at her for a moment, narrowed his eyes and smiled a crafty smile. "You're very good," he grinned. "Getting me to tell you what you want; well, no more. I shall not tell you anything else. I find your ignorance amusing," Lucan added.

They sailed, if it could be called that, well into the day and into the evening. Janir was beginning to wonder why the term "sailing" was associated with a smooth and uninterrupted ride. That image was wrong! Sailing involved swells and waves and ornery winds. Karile had turned eleven different shades of green, and had fed the fish his meager breakfast by midday, while Janir was no better. The only comfort she received was that Lucan's tan skin was a most unusual color, a color she couldn't quite describe. Her own face was sunburned, along with all the other skin that was showing. Her skin would be flaking off in scabs soon. Karile resembled a pouting green and red lobster.

Toward midnight, when a crescent moon hung like a sickle in the night sky, when the Brevian coast was just a dark sliver on the horizon and all other ships were out of sight, Lucan stared from the back of the skiff. The water had grown calmer now, and the eerie dip of the oars in the water was one of the few sounds in the crisp sea air.

"What does he see?" Karile whispered.

"I don't know; if I knew, I would have told you!" Janir hissed.

"Quiet!" Saoven scolded. The elf gained consciousness around noon and had since reacquired all his unnaturally keen senses.

Lucan appeared to purse his lips, then spun around and made for the front of the ship. He went immediately to his prisoners and produced the keys from their place around his neck. Without a word, Lucan undid the chains binding them to the prow of the skiff.

"Come with me," he commanded, and led the three of them past the heaving oarsmen to the back of the ship. The sea appeared calm in their wake, past the ripple caused by the craft shoving through the water. Karile bumped into Janir.

"What is it?"

Lucan gave the wizard a harsh glare and hissed for him to be silent. He pointed to the distant horizon. "What do you see there, Elf?" he demanded.

Saoven gazed out across the water, peering into the shadows. Janir strained to see what it was that her brother had spotted, but she could only see several dark shapes in the moonlight. Briefly, she thought she saw one of them raise slightly out of the water, but then she decided it must have been her imagination.

"I see trouble, for you," Saoven announced. "A group of four mazag, swimming toward us."

CHAPTER 8

The Magag Want Their Key

"Throw the Key back, Lucan!" Janir shouted.
"Not a chance," Lucan calmly hissed
back. Karile was staring with wide eyes
at the dark shadows that were slowly but steadily
gaining on them.

"Don't you see they're relentless? They're going
to kill us all if we don't give them what's rightfully
theirs!"

"Ah, yes. And I suppose you'll ask me to give
them you and me next, seeing as how we are argu-
ably theirs as well!" Lucan jeered.

"It was stolen from them; we weren't!" Janir
protested.

"Correct me if I have the facts wrong, but I seem
to recall that *you* were the one to steal it. True?"
Lucan countered.

"Don't you see? You killed one of them! They will
show us no mercy!"

The small crew was comprised of about ten
oarsmen in all. Everyone of them and the captain

was staring at the brother and sister, with bewildered expressions.

"I didn't agree to flee mazag. When fireside fables start coming to life, the deal's done," the captain piped up, stepping past Lucan. "Turn around men!" he hollered.

Before the sailors could obey, Lucan gave an angry cry, slashed the captain's throat with a concealed dagger and a swift motion.

"No one leaves this ship!" Lucan screamed. "Row! Ahead!" Glancing down at the still gasping body of the captain, and nudging him dismissively, her brother added, as if an afterthought, "Toss this in the sea."

She felt no real sympathy for the sea captain, but still she cringed inside at the emotionless and seemingly effortless way that Lucan could kill.

"You fool!" Janir screamed. "They fought our forefather, do you think that they will not know how to defeat us?"

"How far away do they look to you?" Lucan demanded. "Twenty, twenty-five miles?" he sneered.

"Nineteen," Saoven blandly interjected.

"It hardly matters, onward!" Lucan snapped back, seizing Janir's chains with fury and shouting for his converts to bring the elf and enchanter. Jerking her chains mercilessly at every opportunity, Lucan dragged her harshly back to the front. He snapped that she and the other two should be chained together, to keep them from escaping. After roughly securing all three of them near the prow again, Lucan strode back to tend to the ordering of the sailors.

The mazag were relentless in their pursuit, but Lucan was just as relentless in his flight. By dawn, there was no sign of the irregular shapes and sulking scales. Still, Janir had no doubt that they would be back, and soon. The clicks and clacks of the one who had spoken to her back at the caverns echoed in her mind. The importance was not what had been said, but how it had been said. She couldn't stop thinking about that complex language of the mazag now that they were so close.

But a new threat loomed on the horizon. Clouds the color of coal lined the south-western sky, the direction they were headed. Nature itself was trying to keep them from the Rivellis Peninsula, warning them that the chamber was not to be disturbed. Lucan did not heed such warnings. Now the skiff was jolting along on the wind, a wind that seemed dangerously strong to Janir, but she had never been to sea before. Perhaps this was normal? Lightning bolts in the dark clouds. Those were not normal, even she knew that. In spite of foul weather in the direction they were traveling, Lucan seemed not to notice. Two more sailors had rebelled against him since the captain, and they had both been swiftly done away with. The remainder had learned from the mistakes of their compatriots, and deemed it best for their health not to question this temperamental Argetallam.

Lucan stared at the stormy horizon with a set jaw and a stubborn outlook. He would keep going until he succeeded or it killed him.

As they drew nearer to the storm, the sea became quieter, and quieter. Janir could sense that it was not a good sign. Janir twisted around and stared over the prow of the ship. She could see that wind coming at them, closer, ever closer, whooshing upon them like a host of furious warriors. The oarsmen had stopped rowing. Lucan had stopped shouting. No one moved. No one breathed. The water was still, hardly moving. Those few heart beats seemed to last forever, dragging out. Even Karile said nothing. Dimly, in the distance, there was a sharp wailing, the screaming of the wind as it drew nearer. Thunder rumbled like the stomach of a hungry beast; lightning split the sky. The pitch black clouds masked the sun, and swept in for the kill.

The wall of rain, wind and thunder hit them like a wave of bricks. The wind snapped the mast in two as if it were fashioned of twigs, the rain seemed to weight Janir down on the deck. Lucan was shouting commands that she couldn't hear; the sailors were shouting and two of them were swept overboard. Exactly what happened to them next, she couldn't tell because she stopped watching them shortly thereafter. She could hardly breathe without taking in water, so she coughed and sputtered as if she were caught near a fire.

"Hold onto each other!" Saoven yelled.

Karile clung to her arm in the near darkness and Saoven was somewhere to her left, with one arm behind her back, gripping Karile. A wave swept over the deck, and Janir was suddenly grateful that she was chained to the prow. The strong pull as the wave washed over seemed to be dragging her to the other side. She thought her wrists would snap off, but surprisingly, they didn't. As the wave receded back into the sea, Janir and the other two coughed and spat out sea water that tasted as bad as the sand in the Staspin Waste, fishy, salty and slimy, all at the same time. And cold, icy cold. The ship was heaving up and down, rising up on a wave and then smashing down with a splash on the water. It was terrible. As the ship went into the air, Janir felt herself lift above the ship, connected to it only by the chains on her wrists. As it went down, she felt herself slamming down on the hardened wood. Her head hurt, and her backside did too, from crashing down on the deck. Rain pelted her eyes, clouding her vision. She tried to bat the water out of them, but no sooner had she done that when more water poured from the sky to replace it.

"I hate this place!" Karile screamed, and she only heard that because during all the bouncing around, her ear had ended up in front of his mouth.

She jerked away from his loud shrieking and slammed into Saoven's lip with the back of her head. "Sorry!" she shouted.

There was a muffled sound of acknowledgement from the elf and then another wave hit. Again it seemed to be dragging her into the sea, trying to claim her as its own. Karile was whining about something, but she didn't care. There was something wet and slimy on her neck, probably seaweed, but whatever it was, at that moment she loathed it with as much fury as she did Lucan.

Between waves, the air cleared for a split second, and she realized that the oars had been abandoned. No one was in sight. Lucan had been washed over board, she thought with a strange sense of sadness. But then she spotted the tiny door to below deck move, and she nearly screamed in disgust. How dare he leave her here, to be drowned!

Up the skiff heaved again, jumbling them all in a frantic pile before smashing down in the water. Janir thought perhaps she had landed with her head on Saoven's chest, but she could no longer tell the difference between people and wood anymore. The cold water had numbed her wrists so they didn't hurt, but she hated not being able to feel Karile clenching her arm. That meant she had to open her eyes in the downpour and look for him. Of course he was still there, a blurry pile of robe and legs hunched beside her. They kept clinging to each other, just trying not to fall overboard. They battled to stay linked together.

How long had this been going on? A few minutes? An hour? Days? She lost track of time as they fought to keep a grip on one another in the violent storm. Suddenly, a loud creaking, scraping, tearing sound met her ears.

"That can't be good!" Karile shouted.

The skiff was flung like rubble out of a catapult into the pouring rain. Higher, higher and higher. It rose on top of a massive wave. This was going to be very painful when they came down, Janir gauged.

SMASH!

It was very painful. Apparently their chains had

broken sometime during the storm, because Janir was being thrown from the ship, into the tossing sea, being sucked down. She struggled against the current and felt Saoven thrashing beside her. She didn't feel Karile. Blindly, Janir groped in the wet darkness for him, but she couldn't find him. Saoven and she managed to get their heads above water, but something pulled them back into a wave. In spite of her struggling, the salt water was over her head, choking her very existence. Now she was drowning, and it was horrible. Oddly, the idea that she would never get to see Kalbo again crossed her mind. Drowning in the sea and thinking of a horse!

She felt the current pulling on the wrist Karile had been chained to. She struggled, trying to get him out of the current. What was that? Were her feet touching something? With a start, Janir realized that her feet were touching rocks. The rain gradually began to thin, and between waves Janir saw that she was stumbling after a short figure in a wildly flapping robe. Karile had dragged them into the waves to get them to shore. As if an invisible hand had just shoved back a curtain, they were out of the more brutal rain, but still overshadowed by the massive dark clouds. As if the sea couldn't bear to relinquish them, one last huge wave rose out of the water, and charged toward them like a host of thundering warriors. Janir felt it strike her back, driving her down and forward onto a sandy beach. She slammed into sand and felt the individual grains grinding into her sunburned cheek. A soft, comforting rain trickled down from the sky, caressing instead of striking. Like the tongues of a thousand cats, the waves still licked her toes, as if to remind her that it was because of their mercy she was still breathing. Saoven crashed onto the sand beside her, gasping for air just as she was. To her right lay Karile, breathing hard as well. Thunder crackled in the distance, and then the world went black.

Softly, a breeze holding the scent of salt blew across her face. Sleepy sea birds cawed overhead, a few lizards were crawling under nearby logs. Scuttling sideways, a crab scooted past her eyes on his way to the water. The tan sand was sticking to her face as she forced herself to lift her head with what seemed to be an incredible amount of effort. A crimson sun was setting behind them, sinking slowly into the water. They were on a beach, at dusk, she gathered. Where?

Still as stone, Saoven was lying beside her, and to her relief, he was breathing. Karile was lying on his stomach, propped up on his elbows, staring down at the sand. No, not at the sand, she realized. He was staring at his wrists, bound by shackles. The enchanter was muttering incomprehensible words, staring at his chains intently, as if he were trying to melt them with his gaze. Suddenly, they popped open and released him.

"Ahh," Karile sighed, rubbing his wrists.

"Mine next," Janir piped up.

Karile's head snapped around to her. "In a minute." He scrambled to his feet and disappeared into the line of cedar trees and marsh grass.

"Do you really need to do that now?" Janir shouted, shaking her chains.

"Yes!" Karile called back from the trees.

Janir sighed and glanced at Saoven. Deliberately, his eyes were beginning to open and blink in the fading light. He had bled where she accidentally rammed him with the back of her skull, and sand covered his face. Still, even with all that he was rather…

"Much better," Karile happily announced, trotting back across the sand.

"Good," Janir snapped, turning from Saoven to glower up at the enchanter, "now get me out of these."

"Pushy, pushy, pushy," Karile chided.

"Now!" Janir shouted.

"Alright, alright." The enchanter knelt down and began repeating the incantations over her shackles. After what seemed to be a very long time, the wrist irons snapped open.

"Do you know where we are?" Janir wondered, surveying the beach, the sparse marsh grass and the cedar trees.

Karile seemed about to giggle. "The Rivellis Peninsula."

"But that was supposed to be still a day off," Janir countered.

"Interesting things, storms," Karile mused, "they move you in the water a lot faster than you expect." Taking on an imitative air, Karile made his voice go much deeper. "Ride the worst storm in history, half drown, and save a day on travel, it's that easy!"

"How cute," Janir dismissively acknowledged. "Now take off Saoven's," she commanded, rubbing the raw skin where the irons had chafed red rings around her wrists. Karile seemed about to protest, but a harsh glare silenced him and sent him back to work.

Saoven dreamily shook his head and massaged his wrists. "What happened?" the elf wondered, blinking in rapid succession.

"Just a little incantation I learned in *My Big Black Book of Spells*, how to find and get to the shore in a storm," Karile proudly announced.

"From a forbidden library, no doubt," Janir mumbled.

"Enchanter," Saoven murmured, rising to his feet and pulling Janir up after him. "I may very well choke before completing this sentence, however," Saoven appeared to be bracing himself as if for an extremely unpleasant task, "you saved us, thank you." Saoven blurted out the words as if they had caused him great pain.

Janir stared down at her toes. Unfortunately, her boots had been ripped off in the storm and now she was barefoot. Not that it was a total loss; they had become damaged and full of holes back in the Staspin Waste. A glance at her dress and leggings confirmed her suspicions. The skirt was in tatters and hung down in strips. As for the leggings, they had gaping holes all over. Her long sleeves were in ribbons, her bodice was clinging to her skin with damage here and there, just like the rest of her clothes. Nothing she could do about any of that, so she wriggled her toes in the sand. How that feeling brought back memories. Saoven and Karile seemed to have faired no better. They reminded her of something in one of the stories Armandius used to tell her about pirates. Only Karile's shapeless, grungy garment was unscathed. Even though that it had been very violently washed in the sea, Janir could still not distinguish whether the huge piece of clothing was a dirty gray or a faded brown.

"Why, you're welcome, Goblin. You are much more appreciative than *some people*," Karile glanced suggestively at Janir.

"Thanks Karile," she amended.

The young enchanter rolled his eyes in disgust. "What is the world coming to?" he sighed, spreading his stick-like arms and taking a few steps backward for dramatic effect.

"Karile, be careful!" Janir shrieked.

The enchanter jumped several inches in the air and Janir dove toward him. Encircling her arms around a spot in the sand to keep Karile or the elf from stepping on it. She hit the sand with a thump, but it was soft and she didn't care. After a few seconds, Janir found herself staring into a pair of tiny black eyes.

"What is it?" Karile gasped with terror. "Sea snakes? Man-eating crabs? Poisonous clams? There are poisonous clams, aren't there?" But even as he recoiled in fear, he was still Karile. The enchanter leaned over her at an awkward angle to behold the creatures Janir had saved him from stepping on.

"Turtles?" Karile incredulously sought to

confirm. "You screamed and dove at me, for *turtles?*"

"You were going to step on them!" Janir countered, intently watching the small hatchlings push their way through the sand.

Saoven knelt down and picked up one of the small hatchlings that had worked its way through the sand and inquisitively murmured something in a language Janir couldn't comprehend. The tiny green turtle sneezed, made a clumsy and seemingly meaningless motion with its head, and Saoven laughed as if something very funny had been said. His laugh was a musical, sweet sound. The Argetallam liked it.

Janir and Karile glanced at one another to seek explanation, then shrugged. Who knew what the turtle had said?

More and more baby turtles forced their way through the sand into the fading light of the evening, until more than twenty-six small green babies were scuttling over the beach.

Janir began watching for them like a hawk. She knew that they would be coming and yes, there they were. With a vicious toss, she sent a hungry eekle crab flying off like a ball into the fading light.

"Baby turtles are not for eating!" she angrily exclaimed, snatching up several more of the purple eekle crabs and flinging them with a practiced accuracy. They seemed to appear out of nowhere when there was food around.

"What are you doing?" Karile wondered.

"Saving baby turtles!" Janir snapped back, renewing her assault on the crabs.

Karile stared with a confused expression as Janir

tossed crabs like dirty socks and Saoven laughed at some inaudible conversation.

"I am on a desolate beach with the Crab Tosser and the Turtle Whisperer," he mumbled. "I take it you have a thing for baby turtles," he nodded with resolution as Janir maliciously cursed an eekle crab that came too close.

Slowly, all the baby turtles shoved their way up through the sand and scuttled along the beach toward the lapping waves. Janir crawled along beside them on her hands and knees, snatching up all the eekle crabs that came within reach.

"I'm on to you!" Janir snapped at a large crab. With a swift motion, she sent that crab sailing through the air.

"Just out of curiosity Janir, how did you learn to pick up crabs and throw them without getting pinched?" Karile wondered, leaning over one, debating how to best toss it.

"My father taught me," she dismissively replied.

"You mean Lord Caersynn?"

"No. My father."

"Oh, really? Is crab tossing an Argetallam sport?"

"No," Janir snapped back, picking up a turtle and gently placing it in a receding wave. Then she whipped a fierce gaze on Karile to signal the end of their conversation. She had tried for years to keep from remembering. The white sand beaches near Adasha, the waving palm trees, the sparkling blue sea. The one day she could recall when she hadn't been afraid of her father, her one pleasant memory of him. Something slid down her cheek. No, she would not cry. She had resolved years before that she would never weep over her Argetallam family.

She assisted the last of the turtles into the waves and stayed there. Her legs tucked under her, hands at the water's brink with the waves gently licking the tips of her fingers, staring across the water. Why couldn't her memories of him be all bad?

"We should be going," Saoven interrupted.

"Why?" Karile wondered.

Janir followed Saoven's gaze back out across the water. At first she spotted nothing, then as she looked closer…several red shapes bobbing on the horizon.

She glanced at Saoven and sprang to her feet. They each grabbed an arm and dragged Karile with them into the trees. The enchanter protested and complained the entire way, which his friends completely ignored. How had the beasts gotten through the storm? Janir wondered. Perhaps they had swum around it or maybe they had just swum through it. As the trees thickened behind them, Janir glanced back at the monsters. To her alarm, one was rising out of the waves not a hundred sword lengths offshore, clacking and hissing its disgust. Its speech was barely audible above the sound of the splashing waves and thudding feet, but still she managed to make out three very distinct words in the jumble of noise.

"*Come back, fleshlings!*" it snapped.

Why did people always shout that when they were chasing someone? Did they actually think that the prey would just turn around and go running back to the predator? *Here I am, eat me!* Not likely.

Keep running, keep running.

Cedar boughs whipped her face and snagged her dress, but she refused to slow. Thorns, stones and sharp grasses tormented her bare feet with each step, but she pressed on.

Saoven was leading the way, gripping one of Karile's arms and dragging him through the dense brush. The elf seemed to be lamenting how if he had been alone, he could have melted into the trees without a sound and barely a motion. With these two he had to charge through the forest like a warhorse, bending branches and leaving footprints. Janir had noticed that their path would be rather clear to the trained eyes and noses of the mazag, so they had best flee as quickly as possible.

A loud crashing met her ears as heavy limbs forced their way through the trees. Roaring and hissing echoed in her ears. Karile realized why they had grabbed him, and now he was running on his own, struggling to keep pace behind Saoven. Janir galloped behind the enchanter and glanced over her shoulder in time to glimpse a red foreleg tearing aside a strong-looking cedar. With a shudder, she again set herself to running after Karile. Saoven halted mid-stride and called back to make sure she was still following. Shouting that she still was, Janir struggled to follow the fleet elf. Her skirt tore on some stray branch and another scratched her face. The forest seemed to be holding her back, trying to catch her for the mazag.

Ahead, Saoven seemed to have found some-thing to peak his interest. He had halted where the trees seemed to stop, and was surveying the sunken ground below. Could there have been a draw at any worse place? Janir slowed behind Karile, but then the loud clacking of the mazag behind her won over her reason. She bolted straight toward Saoven, her flight instincts taking over completely. The wizard, the elf and the Argetallam collided with angry shouting and screams of terror as Janir realized how far down it was. The trio tumbled down the steep and rocky slope. Karile said something that sounded similar to a last rites prayer. Saoven angrily shouted that in the future she should watch where she was going. Janir was preoccupied trying to keep the loose rocks away from her head. At the bottom, they just lay there for awhile. The world was spinning and doing cartwheels around her. Up was down and down was up.

Then Janir realized the loud clacking of the beast was directly overhead, that the huge creature had already descended to their level and was glowering above. It drew its head back, calculating. It sniffed the air contemplatively, then clacked a loud and clear message.

"*You do not have the Key, so I shall feast on your flesh!*"

The beast traced invisible patterns in the air with its whip-tail, considering which one of them to eat first.

Why wasn't Saoven doing something besides just lying there, staring at the beast? But what else could he do?

The monster flicked its tongue at Karile, then Janir, then Saoven. As if sampling the air around them to determine which one to eat first.

Following Saoven's lead, Janir concentrated on remaining as still as she possibly could. The beast sniffed the air, experimentally. For several agonizing moments, the only sounds were the sinuous swishing of the mazag's tail and the thudding of Janir's heart in her ears. Interrupting the agonizing stretch of relative silence, the faint hum of a flying insect wafted toward Janir from the general direction of Karile. It buzzed around the enchanter's head several times and then landed casually on his arm. Every fiber of Janir's being felt tangled in that one insect's movement. Karile jumped suddenly, and swatted the fly as it bit him.

With a hiss and a final clack, the mazag eagerly snapped up Karile.

"No!" Janir cried, but it was too late. The mazag was already stuffing Karile head-first between its four mandibles.

Janir couldn't bear to watch. She scrambled over to Saoven. Reassuringly, he gripped her hand and whispered. "There's nothing we can do."

Janir felt tears coursing down her cheeks, but nodded. Over the past few weeks Karile had become very dear to her, and now he was being eaten alive by a mazag. Saoven scrambled to his feet and turned to half-lead, half-drag her to the other side and out of the draw, but another huge mazag blocked the way with its massive hulk. Then another and another. They were surrounded on all four sides by the huge beasts. No escape. Saoven positioned Janir behind him, which was sweet but wouldn't do much good considering that there was one on each side. Sensing that their victory was nigh, the mazag clacked and clicked triumphantly.

"*We have won, fleshlings, and you are about to die!*"

Janir was considering starting a last rites prayer herself, when there came a suffocated wheezing from behind them. Janir glanced back at the mazag with Karile's flailing legs still visible from between its mandibles. The beast's yellow eyes were bulging from its head, the inside flesh on its mandibles was purple.

"*What is awry, Mazag Skeris?*" one of the beasts clacked.

A straggled wheezing was the only response.

"*The enchanter's second skin seems to be blocking her throat!*" clicked another.

The three mazag rushed to the side of their compatriot. Saoven gripped Janir's hand again and lead her quickly out of the draw into the line of trees. There they crouched side-by-side behind a spiny bush to see if Karile might still live.

"*Spit it out, Mazag Skeris!*"

"*Use your tongue!*"

"*Breathe through your nostrils!*"

The mazag, the one called Skeris, toppled sideways, and began convulsing uncontrollably.

"*I shall rip it out!*" decreed one, leaning toward Karile's kicking legs with open jaws.

"*No! If you tear its legs off, we shall never remove it!*" protested another.

"*Then what shall I do?*" demanded the rebuked

mazag.

"*Hit him!*"

Obediently, the mazag who had been just standing there during this conversation, raised a webbed claw and struck Karile with the side of its paw, driving him deeper into Mazag Skeris' throat. Mazag Skeris' eyes bulged even wider and its twitching became more rapid.

"*Stupid one!*"

"*You said to hit him!*" the by-stander protested.

"*I meant Mazag Skeris, you imbecilic reptile! Hit her!*" the leader-like one clacked.

"*Very well,*" the third, the one who had threatened to rip off Karile's legs, acknowledged. It raised its claw above Mazag Skeris' twitching head, formed it into the mazag equivalent of a fist and slammed down as hard as it could. By now Janir had begun to pity Mazag Skeris, who seemed to freeze up like a set of cogs not oiled often enough, right before it went stiff, with its legs sticking out at odd angles in every which direction.

"*Were both your eggs dropped down a waterfall?*" the leader-like mazag demanded.

"*Well, there was this one time...when I was still in my egg and....*"

"*Shut up! Hit him on the back!*" the leader-like mazag clacked, pounding on Mazag Skeris with a vigor that could easily break bones and shatter skulls. Even as she cringed at the sheer force of their poundings, Janir was thoroughly confused, was Mazag Skeris a he or a she? Not even his...her...its kind, seemed to have made up their minds.

Mazag Skeris desperately gasped for air with a pitiful wheezing sound. The other mazag fussed over their compatriot with concern, clicking and clacking in a crooning way.

Karile shot out of Mazag Skeris' throat like... there wasn't anything Janir could think to compare the image to. The enchanter came back into the fading light of day with yellow slime coating his face and arms. He landed in a moderately large collection of gorse shrubs. Hastily, Janir and Saoven ran to the shrubs just as Karile landed with a thunk onto the ground and lay motionless as a dead rat.

"Karile!" Janir hissed, shaking the enchanter's shoulders desperately.

"Being digested...being digested..." moaned the wizard.

"He's still alive," Saoven tersely announced, slinging the enchanter over one shoulder like the load of mostly useless luggage that he was.

With the beasts brooding over the other, the elf and Argetallam made their way through the forest as quickly as is possible when toting a limp wizard.

Janir didn't know how long they ran. Soon all the forest looked the same; the scratches on her arms and face hardly felt any different. Rocks and sharp twigs stopped bothering her feet so much. The sound of the mazag faded into the distance, and all she could hear was her own thudding heart and rapid breathing. When Saoven told her to turn, she did, but besides that she might just as well have been alone. This forest felt lonely, like it was trying to isolate her from everyone else. Divide and conquer. Still, she glanced back at Saoven, to make sure she hadn't run too far ahead of him.

He was motioning frantically for her to watch where she was headed. Janir pivoted her head to straight in front of her, just in the nick of time to collide with a black figure in chain mail. Lucan shoved her in the chest, sending her flat on her back on the coarse marsh grass.

"Did you actually think that you could escape me?" Lucan had several cuts and a black eye, and his tunic was ripped in places, but he still held that air of authority and command. Only eight of the warrior-slaves were still with him, and it seemed that the unfortunate crew had been done away with. The warrior-slaves also showed signs of wear and tear, but as always they said nothing in complaint.

"Well, I admit I had my hopes," Janir confessed.

"Frankly, I am surprised you survived that," Lucan remarked. "I lost all the crew and one of my converts. But still," he stooped down to stare dauntingly into her eyes. "*I* survived."

One of the warrior-slaves had hoisted Karile onto his shoulder, while two others stood on either side of Saoven.

"Is the wizard alive?" Lucan demanded.

"Yes, milord," the warrior-slaves confirmed.

"Good, I shall need him," Lucan glanced down at Janir with an evil look she was all too familiar with. "Now," Lucan had an eager glint in his eyes, "let's go treasure hunting!"

CHAPTER 9

Back into the Bowels of the Earth

"I'm telling you, I'm not going down there! I'd rather be mazag fodder!" Karile shrieked.

"That can be arranged," Lucan impatiently snapped, urging his warrior-slaves to hurry. Karile was lying on the ground, his arms wrapped in a death grip around a slender, flawless square pillar, his body stretched out with two warrior-slaves tugging on each of his feet.

It had taken a few hours, but Lucan and his warrior-slaves had discovered the Temple of Amatahns. Personally, Janir was beginning to think this Amatahns character rather pompous. Who names both a key to nearly limitless power, and a temple holding the power, after himself? Tucked away amid the cedar and spruce, they had come to a large square structure. The temple was a large square, with smaller square levels receding up to the top. Fascinatingly, they had not spotted the top of the massive temple from the beach. But then, she reminded herself, it had been dusk.

The mazag had caught their scent again, and they had been pursued into the perfectly square temple doors. Just when Janir thought that they were all dead, the beasts had reached the doorway and an interesting thing had happened. They halted, nervously sniffed the threshold, eyed it up and down, and then refused to enter. It was as if the door had been constructed to keep the monsters out, ban them from entering. The four of them just remained there, clacking and growling their displeasure.

The mortals and elf wandered for hours within the walls. The wizard had awakened after a half hour, and Lucan kept on demanding information of him. Karile would tell Lucan whatever it was the Argetallam wanted to know after a bit of prompting. As they passed a curious mosaic of a flaxen-haired girl with blood on her face and two black rods in her hands for the third time, Lucan had become suspicious and threatened to use the karkaton on Karile if he didn't stop stalling.

One of Lucan's warrior-slaves shoved Janir forward as Lucan again commanded them to press on. On into the temple they went. Greenish-white lights glowed from between the cracks in the stone. It was a sickly green, like the color of a filthy pond's floor. Lucan would not be deterred now. Into the greenish-white unknown they plunged, toward whatever horrid things might be awaiting them here.

Janir remembered all too well what had been inside the last cavern she had blundered into, and now she trudged on only out of fear of Lucan. Maybe there was nothing bad in this cave, she told herself. Perhaps she had just been unlucky that day and entered the only cave in all of Brevia that had monsters in it. Today might be luckier. It was possible that today the fickle creature Fortune would smile on them, and they would encounter no more beasts.

Then she glanced toward the front of their little column and viewed her brother rigidly holding a karkaton inches away from Karile's ear. On second thought, the luckiest thing that could happen right then and there would have been for a huge monster with big teeth to spring up from the stone and gobble down Lucan.

As they rounded yet another bend, they came to a place where the ground dropped down at a right angle into a broad and shallow staircase. No lights glowed in the staircase, and even Lucan hesitated a half moment before commanding that torches be lit, then striding down into the shadows with Karile still in his grasp. The stairs were so long that Janir had to take several steps before she arrived at the next drop. The warrior-slaves marched wordlessly behind her and Saoven's eyes were unreadable.

"What's wrong? I mean, besides the obvious," Janir whispered in an undertone.

"I know what this place is," Saoven somberly replied. His sober nature was sending shivers of dread down her spine.

She remained silent, waiting for a more detailed explanation and nearly tripped on one of the steps. Saoven graciously caught her and dragged her upright again.

"It is a fortress," Saoven whispered as their heads

came closer together.

Janir glanced around in bewilderment. "Then where are the guards?"

Lucan had stopped abruptly, and now Janir plowed into him. Angrily, he shoved her backwards onto the hard stone, jarring her head and bruising backside, but she scrambled up as quickly as she could without remark. Because, truth be told, she was embarrassed at how often Saoven kept helping her up.

Lucan stood as still as the stone walls around them, staring straight ahead like a forest animal that has spotted something and doesn't know whether to flee or fight. The warrior-slaves followed their leader's cue and stood perfectly still, hardly breathing. With the caution of a forest rabbit, Janir carefully peered around Lucan's shoulder.

They had reached a place where those broad and shallow stairs finally stopped and gave way to a flat surface of stone. Before them, a shaft of white light had penetrated the darkness and was shining down on the most alarming sight Janir had seen since entering the temple. Standing just behind a lovely rounded arch without moving, it was a knight, fully armored. He might have actually been half the size of his silhouette, if someone were to take all those heavy steel plates off him. Where there weren't steel plates, well-oiled chain mailed showed. Not even the slightest trace of normal cloth or leather was to be seen. Just steel and iron.

As if to shield him from the sight of the intruders, his visor was sealed shut like a gate to forbidden realm. Looking closely, Janir couldn't discern even the slightest trace of air or even eye slits on the helm. That wasn't probable, she must have just missed spotting them. A lone sentinel, the knight stood with his legs spread apart in battle position, and a huge halberd clenched in both his chain-mail gauntlets. The axe was nearly the same size as its wielder and styled a wicked spike on the back that reminded Janir of a giant steel thorn. Like the knight's armor, it glittered with polishing, as if waiting thirstily for its next victim's blood.

Having narrowly escaped the executioner's axe back in Green Haven, Janir felt a certain queasy feeling at the sight of one so massive and ready-looking. She could almost hear it saying: *Thought that you could escape me? Ha!* Janir shook her head, now her imagination was giving axes words.

Lucan stared at the knight with as much bewilderment as she did. "Who are you?" Lucan demanded in his haughtiest tone.

No answer, just the stillness.

"I am Lucan Vanmar Argetallam, stand down and I may let you live," he jeered.

Silence.

With a practiced eloquence, Lucan released a river of some rather coarse remarks, using words she shouldn't have been so surprised to hear him use, and some words she pondered the meaning of for sometime afterward. Janir could see how such a tirade could be infuriating. Lucan never once increased the speed of the insults, never once faltered but recited the imaginary facts as if God himself had told him.

With a flawless efficiency, Lucan insulted every maternal member of the knight's immediate family, even made the wild guess that the knight had two sisters who were prostitutes in the local shipyard. He had doubtless used these methods to induce blind fury in men before. But this one didn't move a muscle. Not even the slightest twitch.

"Do you challenge me to a duel? What will you do?" Lucan scoffed at length.

Not a word; even the slight draft that had been in the stairway seemed to have frozen.

Seeming to have run out of other offensive lines, Lucan finished with an ultimatum: "Then prepare to die screaming like a woman in childbirth!"

That eerie quiet.

Lucan had apparently never been ignored on this one, because he balked for a second and then curiously leaned from side to side to get a better view of the knight. "Did you hear me?" Lucan shouted. "I said, 'prepare to die screaming like a woman in childbirth!'"

No response.

"I insulted your mother, several times! Hello!" her brother cried. "I called her floozy, and I called you worse, hello?" Lucan was still clutching the enchanter's arm with a claw-like grip, but now he was leaning closer to the knight and surveying him more carefully.

"Floozy?" Karile repeated with confusion, "what does that even mean?"

Viciously, Lucan jerked Karile's arm to remind the enchanter of his place, and then shoved him in the direction of one of the warrior-slaves. The faithful convert caught Karile in an iron grasp and stood absolutely still.

"I heard lots of words at my father's garrison, but *floozy*? It must be a particularly bad word," Karile reasoned, with apparent glee at having just learned a new seemingly taboo term.

No one was paying attention to Karile now as Lucan carefully picked his way toward the motionless knight. Flicking out the other karkaton from his belt, her brother cautiously stepped closer to the lone sentinel. Janir felt an alien feeling of what seemed to be concern for her brother, but she tried to quell it before she started thinking about it too much. The knight didn't move as Lucan eased up to the knight's right side, the side opposite the huge axe blade.

Standing so close that he could have heard the knight breathing, Lucan gingerly raised one of the karkaton and tapped softly on the helmet.

The ringing was hollow, empty. Just a suit of armor with no knight inside.

Lucan malignantly kicked one of the massive greaves, and the whole suit went crashing to the ground like a house of toy blocks. Smaller pieces clattered away, and the larger ones just lay there in a small cloud of dust, still as they had been before, merely in a different position.

Lucan suddenly seemed quite silly, having used all his excellent swear and curse words on an empty suit of armor. At his flustered expression alone, Janir would have smiled, maybe even laughed, had it been anyone besides Lucan, that is.

They eased past the heap of armor, into the passage that the empty-armor knight had been so faithfully guarding. Down they went into the stuffy shadows. Further and further into wherever it was that they were entering. A mountain? Under the sea by now?

Being in no position to question their heading, Saoven, Janir and Karile held their tongues.

We're lost. There was no doubt about it. Lucan hadn't cursed for the space of several minutes and was glancing around each part in the tunnels with a restricted desperation.

Finally, Lucan noticed everyone else's dragging feet. Or maybe he felt that his point was made and he could let them rest. Whatever the case, he announced that they would stay in this place where the tunnels became abruptly wider. It was rather convenient, Janir thought, that such a nice place should be fixed. As if the builders had anticipated their arrival...

They lit a fire in the middle of the oval-shaped segment of the tunnels. It seemed that the warrior-slaves even carried the stuff to make bright, slow-burning fires with them. Lighting a fire that far underground might not have been Lucan's most brilliant idea, but no one questioned him. The warrior-slaves held their tongues because they couldn't have protested his commands even if they had wanted to, and the others, because they were afraid of losing theirs.

Janir was curled on the stone, leaning against the smooth wall, with Karile on one side and Saoven on the other. The usual arrangement. The fire danced and played with shadows on the walls, as if these walls hadn't seen such light for ages and planned to make the most of it. Lucan posted a sentinel at each end of the oval, one to guard each opening into the tunnels.

For the first time, Lucan seemed confused and lost from his place on the other side of the fire. Like things weren't going quite as planned.

Clank! Clank! Clank!

It was faint, but steady. Something clattering, like when Lucan had knocked over that suit of armor. Then it stopped somewhere in the corridors.

"It's nothing," Lucan snapped, when he spotted the warrior-slaves uneasy expressions. "It's just air pockets rattling iron deposits." It was a creative story, a complete farce, and the slaves believed it without a blink. Sometimes it seemed that obedience could amount to imbecility. But Janir of course, knew it wasn't air pockets or iron deposits.

But as it stopped, she felt her body relax in relief, even though she didn't remember tensing it. She stared down into the soothing fire. Out of the corner of her eye she saw the patterns of the fire glinting off Lucan's wicked dagger which was actually quite pretty in the firelight. The light also glinted off several odds and ends lying about, the buckles on Lucan's boots, the knives at the belt of a warrior-slave, the armor of one of the sentinels.

But…the sentinels hadn't been wearing armor.

Janir wanted to scream as she spotted the knight, or rather the supposedly empty suit of armor, standing there before them where the guard had been only two seconds ago. Now the loyal convert lay in a red heap, soundlessly murdered. The evil axe was bloody, and the knight or whatever it was, seemed to be staring at Lucan.

"Son of a…" Lucan sprang to his feet like a startled wolf, and the still-living converts leapt to attention.

Before the maiden and wizard could jump up, Saoven caught them and pulled them back down, making an unmistakable silencing gesture with his hands. Somehow, without Janir meaning to do it, her hands clutched Saoven's shoulder and her eyes were on the verge of bugging out of her head.

Now she fully understood the phrase "frozen in terror." She couldn't move. Couldn't even squeak in fear. Noiseless suits of armor that go around chopping people up: that was nearly beyond Janir's mental capacity. Lucan jutted out his jaw with a defiant air.

"Clever," he clapped his hands together. "How clever you are. Leaving your armor set up like that, now claiming it to come, and kill us, who by now will be thinking that you are an invincible spirit or the like, and be shaking in our boots." Lucan seemed to think this was all just a very good plan. "Utterly brilliant, I shall have to try it out myself someday." He laughed and clapped his hands for a space, then paused and stared at the knight with a dangerous glint in his eyes.

"Well, my cunning foe," Lucan was almost smiling with delight. "'Tis a shameful pity to destroy such talent, but I must admit, I am going to take immense pleasure in killing you," he smirked, flicking out the karkaton. A voice emitted from the helmet. A low, tortured voice, a voice of ages, a voice of war, of pain, of suffering.

"Unfortunately for you," the deep, masculine tone stated levelly. "I died eons ago."

"Wh..." Lucan never got to finish his question, because just then the spirit, or demon, was laying about with the wicked axe, hacking apart several of Lucan's men.

"Many have entered, none shall leave!" that horrible voice passionately shouted. Blood and screams seemed to be everywhere. Janir brought her hands to her eyes and buried her face in Saoven's shoulder. Karile was behind her, doing much the same thing against her shoulder. Janir didn't see any of it, so she was uncertain what happened. She didn't know what had transpired until it was finished. After what seemed like an eternity of smashing, and crushing, it was over.

Lucan had managed somehow to cram one of the karkaton between the knight's visor and helmet. As the knight died or whatever, there was no screaming, no flash of light, no pulse of ear-splitting sound. The suit of armor simply crumpled to the ground and fell apart as it had before, with a soft golden glow emitting from the scattered parts.

The golden glow grew brighter and seemed to waft up from the heap of armor like smoke rising from a fire. Expecting something horrible to happen, Janir braced herself for the inevitable. She was expecting it to possess all of them and turn them into suits of armor like itself, or something along those lines.

But no, it just drifted into the air and dissipated like smoke.

Lucan checked his remaining warrior-slaves, six in all. Two had just been slaughtered by the empty suit of armor, and lay in two piles of arms, legs and torsos. Janir threw her gaze away from the gore; she couldn't bring herself to look back even though she tried. For some reason she felt that she needed to overcome her revulsion at the sight, even though she really didn't want to. She didn't want to become like Lucan.

Even Lucan was unnerved by the empty suit of armor incident and so commanded them to get up and march on. Invigorated by fear, Janir no longer felt weary. Karile had taken to whipping his head around to stare at anything even the least bit incongruous. While Lucan now walked with both karkaton in his hands, and his every motion was made cautiously.

The tunnels seemed to go on forever, twisting and snapping this way and that. Janir felt a certain pang of sadness for the warrior-slaves. She wondered if they kept their own thoughts while they wore the silver collars. If they really had their own course of action they wanted to follow, but couldn't. She didn't bother to ask Lucan; he wouldn't care either way. But still she wondered---had those men and all the warrior-slaves Lucan had already lost, and all the ones Arge-tallams had been getting killed for centuries, been fighting against the magic in a desperate attempt to save their lives? Were their poor souls free now that their trammeled bodies were destroyed? Briefly, Janir tried to imagine having someone command her to do something she absolutely had to. Something that was definite suicide, but she had to do. Even though every fiber of her being was screaming out in defiance.

The idea was too horrible for her to imagine. But then, would she want to be a total slave? Would she want to keep her own thoughts if it came down to that, even though every second would be utter torture? Would it be better to sacrifice freedom of actions for freedom of thought, or would it be better to submit completely to another's will? She shoved the thought to the back of her mind, not wanting to dwell on such a subject at such a time.

No one afterward could say how far they trudged through the shadows. None could remember how many times Karile stubbed his toe on slightly elevated slabs of stone. They might have marched through the empty stone halls for hours or minutes. Several times, Lucan halted their party and listened intently, then deciding that it had been nothing, continued on. It hardly mattered. If there were anymore of those things about, if there was an army.....Janir preferred not to think of it. But she was soon forced to.

The tunnels gave way to a simple arch, but since she was behind Lucan, she didn't realize what they were entering. Light was coming from the other side of the arch, like starlight. Well-lit, but not bright.

Janir stumbled out of the tunnels into the largest room she had ever imagined possible. The tunnels led out on to a kind of bridge that spanned across the colossus. Straight ahead, on the other side of the bridge, Janir spotted the distant opening of another tunnel leading off somewhere else.

Knights, or suits of armor, just like the one Lucan had supposedly killed, legions upon legions of them, lined the inside of the huge room. They stood on shelf-like crevices that were staggered back from the ceiling, miles above them and to the stone floor, miles below. All around them, these scores of silent sentinels stood staring off into space. Their weapons held at the ready, their helmets facing straight ahead. Some of them were so far away that Janir could barely make out their shapes. Like leaves in an iron forest, they covered the walls of the gigantic room. Glancing about made Janir dizzy. Made her feel her own sheer *smallness.*

"You asked where the guards were, Janir," Saoven reminded the maiden. "I think we just found the barracks."

It did appear to be a barracks of sorts, one in which each soldier took up no more space than he did while standing. Again, she was swept away by the sheer *number* of them, there must have been at *least* tens of thousands!

"Do you think they're going to attack?" Janir nervously inquired.

"No. Not likely. They probably have not moved for thousands of years," Saoven assured her, as his eyes browsed over the seemingly endless number of knights.

"There was that one who just tried to kill us,"

Karile indignantly pointed out. "How long since he last moved? Better yet, how long since someone escaped from here?"

"Stop talking!" Lucan hissed, marching on toward the end of the bridge and the next tunnel. "According to you, wizard, the chamber is somewhere around here, and we are going to find it!"

It seemed to take forever to reach the other end of the bridge. It never seemed to be getting any closer. About half way out, Janir happened to glance behind her, past the four warrior-slaves who were tailing them.

"Lucan?" she hesitantly ventured.

"What?!" her brother angrily snapped, infuriated that his sister dare speak to him.

"Were those knights there before?"

Lucan stopped and whirled around to behold three of the suits of armor, or what ever they were, standing with swords, and a spear by the mouth of the last tunnel. For the first time since they had been eight years old, Janir saw fear, unmistakable fear, in Lucan's eyes.

Lucan seemed to be contemplating his options. He didn't contemplate long. "Take this," he shoved one of the karkaton toward her.

"Why?" Janir wondered, completely bewildered.

"I offer you a weapon, and you question me?" Lucan was nearly shouting.

Obediently, Janir took the karkaton. Like before, she felt that strange feeling of balance and peace when her fingers closed around the sleek black rod.

"Come with me," he commanded, striding back

toward the motionless warriors.

"What are we doing?" Janir was thoroughly confused. Surely Lucan couldn't be thinking what he seemed to be.

"You're coming with me to kill them!" Lucan furiously shouted. His motions were stiff and rigid as the karkaton in his clenched fist burned him with resentment.

"Why can't one of your warrior-slaves do it?" Janir tried to evade this course of action.

"Because the magic in the karkaton only serves our kind and it would wound or kill anyone else who tried to wield it, Stupid!" Lucan was fairly shrieking.

"No!" someone protested. It was Saoven. "I shan't let you take her back there," he resolved.

"Yes." Lucan turned a steely gaze to the elf. "Oh yes, you shall."

"You will not take her back to fight those things!" Saoven repeated. "This is your doing, undo it yourself."

"Saoven..." Janir began. But she really didn't know what to say. What could she say? Their eyes met for a moment, one moment in which the rest of the world seemed to fade away. He truly didn't want her to go, he was afraid for her, terrified even. That was comforting somehow, but at the same time it made her feel...odd. She couldn't describe the feeling inside her chest. Surprise? Had she expected him to want her dead? No, she just hadn't expected him to want her alive with that kind of *intensity*.

"Would you keep her here against her will?" Lucan coldly hissed, ice in his voice and eyes.

"What do you mean?" Saoven demanded.

"She will come willingly and freely, because if she does not, my loyal converts shall kill you and the enchanter," Lucan glanced at his warrior-slaves to confirm that it was an order, then to Janir.

It seemed to require superhuman strength, but she managed to unlock her fear-stricken neck muscles and stiffly nod.

"Excellent," Lucan icily stated and whirled around to march on toward the empty-armor knights.

Janir trotted after him, then cast a sad glance back at Saoven and Karile. The enchanter was telling the convert who was clenching his arm to, "Put the knife away! She hasn't done anything yet!" So he didn't see her look back. The elf ignored the blade that was hovering behind his neck, he just stared after her with blank, unreadable eyes.

Janir felt as if her execution awaited with the suits of armor, her impending doom held in their weapons. It was made worse by the everlasting trek back to the knights. They must have walked nearly a mile.

Finally, they were standing not twenty paces away. It took an extreme effort of will for Janir to keep herself upright and silent.

Lucan edged up sideways toward one of the knights, and commanded her to do the same. She was nearly dumbfounded that she actually did it, and before she realized, she was standing not two feet away from the huge steel knight. Her heart was pounding like the Zebulun River; every single thing she saw was in vivid detail, her senses sharpened by the intense fear she felt.

Lucan conveyed through motions and angry glares what she was supposed to be doing. Obediently, Janir angled herself around the giant sword held in the suit's gleaming fist, never once taking her eyes off the sparkling blade. Following Lucan's cue, she drove her karkaton into the neck of the armor in a gap where the neck joint would normally be. It was difficult; she had to cram it several different ways, but finally she did manage to wedge it between the metal plates. If the armor hadn't been standing stationary, she never could have done it.

Like before, there was no bang or flash of light. The armor simply crumpled to the ground; the magic that had held it together dispersed. The golden smoke rose from the dismantled armor and wafted away before dissipating into thin air. The one Lucan had attacked clattered to pieces about the same moment. Now her brother stood over the strewn remains of their former foe with triumph.

Turning to the third knight Lucan sneered. "Stupid, utterly stupid. Your compatriot could have fought and killed my sister easily but instead he let her…"

Like a river restrained by a broken dam, the third knight swung his sword at Lucan and completed a full sweep in less than the blink of an eye.

Lucan dodged to the side, throwing himself on the ground with razor-sharp reflexes. Janir evaded the sweeping sword, only to be met by a massive elbow.

She did several turns in the air then sprawled on

the ground, disorientated. Which way was up? The karkaton lay out of reach, too far away for her to grab in time.

It was just as she had dreamt in her nightmares, the executioner raising his blade high above her head. His massive hulk blocked the sun or whatever light it was that illuminated the barracks. All she saw was his frightening silhouette. Saoven or Karile, quite possibly both, shouted something, but she couldn't hear from so far away.

Rolling to one side, Janir heard the clang of the sword striking the stone as she flipped out of its path. A moment later, the blade was embedded a good two inches in the stone beside her. The blade was so polished that she could see her own wide eyes and flared nostrils reflected as if by a mirror.

Lucan struck from behind, struggling to cram the karkaton between the tight plates. Like a slow-motion warrior, the knight jerked his axe free, and began to whirl around to slice Lucan in two. Thinking with that instantaneous brilliance that Janir envied so much, her brother clung to the shoulder plates of the armor and hauled himself onto the knight's back. The knight spun around in circles with her brother clinging to his back like a wicked monkey. The evil sword swept behind the knight's head in a futile attempt to reach him. Armor only lets the wearer extend so far, and that limit had been reached. Lucan bashed the armor, denting it with the karkaton in an attempt to bend the plates out of shape enough to fit the karkaton in. It sounded like a dance accompaniment, Lucan banging the plates in an almost rhythmic pattern, like drums, and the knight's steel shoes providing the refrain.

Janir nudged a piece of armor that looked like a breast plate with her toe and placed it in the path of the twirling knight. The effect was as desired. The plate slid under the knight's massive weight, sending him toppling to the ground. But unlike the time Lucan had kicked the one in the tunnels, this one didn't fall apart. He just rolled sideways, crushing Lucan under his massive hulk. Lucan went into an uncontrollable spasm of cursing and sputtered insults. As much as she loathed her brother, Janir decided that she didn't want him to die. She snatched up her dropped karkaton and dove at the knight's visor, which was facing up since he had rolled to squish her bother. The knight didn't raise his sword, which had fallen out of his hand and was inaccessible to his fists; he had to let her jab her karkaton between his visor plates.

The armor fell apart as if it were made of leaves, like the other three had before it. The soft golden glow wafted away from the pile of armor, swirling in the air before disappearing completely.

Lucan uttered several more coarse oaths as he shoved the armor off himself. "Bloody nuisance, that's what they are!" he furiously shouted to her.

Janir ignored him. She was still watching the golden glow dissolve into the elements.

As if she had stolen it from him, Lucan snatched back the karkaton she held, grabbed her arm, and proceeded to drag her back to the middle of the bridge. Saoven heaved a sigh of relief when she was tossed like a dead rat at him and Karile. But there was no time for happy sentiments, as Lucan was already pressing them on again.

These empty-armor-knight creatures were terrifying, but also strange. They always waited until after you spoke to attack. Why would that be? But then, she reminded herself, that one convert hadn't spoken at all. Still, the other knights had stood motionless as they were killed, waiting for someone to speak.

"Lucan..." Janir hesitantly ventured.

"What!" Lucan screamed, whirling on her with the pent-up fury of five whole minutes.

"I don't think you should talk to the empty-armor-knights anymore," she tried to sound as placating as she could.

Telling him what to do? That caught his attention like a knife in the eye. "Why not?" His voice was defiant and cruel at once.

"Because," Janir felt her heart fluttering, "they don't attack until you challenge them."

"What about that other one? It killed my converts even though they never spoke," Lucan snapped.

"No, but you did," Janir humbly reminded him.

"Speak the common tongue, girl!" Lucan shouted.

"If they are magical beings or whatever, would they be able to tell, magically speaking, between you and your converts?" Janir validated. "I mean, you use Argetallam powers, *your* powers, to make them like.....that."

Lucan was silent for two entire heart beats. "No."

"Then, maybe it was killing you instead of the convert."

"What kind of magic would cause that? I've never heard of it. Besides, magically, they wouldn't be able to tell you and me apart," Lucan snapped.

"True, but I was a little out of reach that one time and just now it did try to kill me," Janir pointed out.

Karile stared at the ground thoughtfully during this conversation, and he concocted the answer. "A word spell!" he gleefully shouted.

"Shut up!" Lucan shrieked. "Shut up! I will not take orders or advice from *you* of all people!" he screamed, jabbing a finger in the air, in Janir's general direction.

"What did I ever...?"

"You were born!" Lucan hissed.

"Yes Lucan, we all know that Janir is your elder by a trifling three..."

"Silence, Wizard!" Lucan's eyes were blazing with a fury that even Janir hadn't seen in him before.

Like a prisoner, wrongly convicted, Lucan leaned toward her with a pained fury, so close, Janir could make out the individual pores on his skin. His teeth were locked in an iron clamp, his fists clenched as if he were squeezing the life out of her just by tightening his grip.

"Do you have any idea what happened after you left?" Lucan demanded.

Hit with one of those rare bursts of audacity, (probably left over from the empty-armor knight duel) she gave a snapped retort. "No, I don't know. As you'll recall, I left."

"A messenger told us what had happened. My mother could hardly contain her delight," Lucan grimly began.

The other eight seemed to fade into the background; it was just her and her brother, arguing it out in the middle of a magical temple with possessed suits of armor all around them.

"I should think that would be a happy part of your childhood," Janir sarcastically remarked.

"Master went into a state of depression that lasted for two entire months!" Lucan screamed. "He thought you and your whore of a mother were both dead! More's the pity that you survived!"

"I can't help that I..." she began.

"He said he wished it had been my mother and me!" Lucan screamed, his voice cracking.

At first, Janir didn't believe this. But then she considered the fact that Lucan had kept her alive for this long. Logically, one would kill the person they felt jealousy toward, not spare them in near-mint condition for weeks. On second thought, if Lucan's mind operated the way it appeared, he might see returning her as a means of gaining favor with their father.

"I find that hard to believe," Janir countered. "Eight years living with him, he never once told me he loved me. He never once hinted that he *liked* me. If he really did go into depression after I was reported dead, I find it hard to believe."

"The sea turtles."

"What?" Janir stared at Lucan harder.

"What about, the sea turtles?" Lucan's voice had become cold again, his shield from the world again raised.

"How did you know…?"

"I watched from the palm trees, with my mother," Lucan bitterly replied. "Not only that, but the seashell? You do remember? The dappled brown one with the spiral shape? He has never done anything like that for *me*." His original anger vented, Lucan continued. "Mother said after that I needed to show I was stronger than you, and show it by putting you in your proper place."

Janir considered that for a moment. Now that she thought back to her Argetallam life, the day with the sea turtles was about the time Lucan had started bullying her with intensity. "Why would your mother think that would make a difference? Doesn't she know how strict the rules are?"

"She is a Stlavish aristocrat! She thinks that our rules of succession are the same as theirs," Lucan cried with flaring anger.

Bringing up his mother had been a bad idea. Apparently, she was as much a sore spot as their father was.

"That is why!" he surmised. "That is why I shall not take orders from anyone, least of all…*you!*"

To show her his utter defiance, he glared at her, took a deep breath and before any of the not-warrior-slaves could stop him, he yelled at the top of his lungs. "I ANNOUNCE THE ONCOMING DESTRUCTION OF ALL THE INHABITANTS OF THIS TEMPLE!!!"

His voice echoed like the wailing of a war trumpet. Nothing happened. The powerful announcement receded and became fainter with each repetition off the stone. Janir held her breath and waited. Karile was beside her, looking like someone had just clubbed him over the head.

Then, like the shuffling of ten thousand metal leaves, there came a clanking, as all of the knights that lined the walls in their little shelf-like crevices came to life.

"What's happening?" Janir gasped.

The knights were turning sideways, and beginning to march. The deafening noise of ten thousand pairs of metal feet clanging on stone rang in her ears. All of them filed toward a large doorway in the wall that Janir hadn't noticed before. They marched in segregated units, perfectly together. Not a word or sound whispered among them, just dutiful marching.

"What's happening?" Janir repeated, now scared out of her wits.

"I think," Karile shouted above the clamor, barely audible. "I think that your brother just declared war on ten thousand empty suits of armor. Should we be running?"

CHAPTER 10
Amatahns' Chamber

L ucan and his remaining warrior slaves closed
the door at the entrance. 'Closed' might not
have been the right word, they more dragged
and fought with it. It was strange that Amatahns, or
who ever had designed the temple, had decided to
include a huge iron door and the wooden braces to
hold it closed.

They were at the other end of the bridge, with the
ten-thousand or so empty suits of armor marching
along, heading straight for them. Lucan was down to
a trio of warrior-slaves now, as the other three had
been used to "slow down" the empty-armor knights.
The worst part was that those seemingly fearless
converts hadn't even made the empty-armor knights
miss a step, they were merely trod under like dirt
beneath the plough.

As the nearest line of empty-armor knights
neared, the heavy iron door began to close. Janir
joined the others in shoving it along as quickly as
they could. It had to have been at least a sword-
length of solid iron fixed on massive hinges the size

of saddles.

"Slab of Dwarven scrap!" Saoven grunted and shoved as hard as he could against the slick iron.

So dwarves had made the huge slab of metal that was their only hope, the girl considered with mild interest. Perhaps that meant that it would hold against the oncoming horde.

Janir drove her shoulder into it, straining with every fiber of her body to move it. She braced her bare feet on the stone floor and leaned against the door, staring up at the top of it towering so far above her, just to be sure it was moving. She wasn't sure it was. With all six of them fighting to close the enormous hulk, it swung shut at an agonizingly deliberate pace. Karile was standing to the side, encouraging them like a spectator at a tournament.

"You're moving! You're moving! Just three more sword-lengths to go before it's shut!" he cheered. Perhaps this had been installed as a cruel joke, a way for adventurers (or idiots, as Janir was beginning to call them) to save themselves if they could close the huge door that was impossible to close.

They shut it just as the first axe struck it. The pounding of dozens of axes and swords on the massive iron doors thudded like the drums before an execution. From this side, Janir could still hear the sound of iron hitting iron. It was a very thick door, Janir reminded herself. It would take them days to dent their way through, or so she fervently hoped. Karile sat astride one of the braces, pounding on it with his fists, trying to get it down, while Saoven was shoving bolts in place. As for Janir, she mostly just got in the way.

They were all panting from the run across the bridge, which had seemed like it would never end. Even the warrior-slaves stood with their mouths open. Lucan stood bent over, leaning against the door which was already being pounded to bits on the other side. The room was large and crafted of limestone. Lights seemed to come from under the cracks in the stone and around the pillars. The pillars went on for about six rows and then a rectangular doorway led into what appeared to be a room just like this place. Strange markings decorated the pillars and walls. The tiny pictures must have had meaning, but Janir had no time to ponder them.

"Come," Lucan snapped, straightening his back, "we must move on."

As a warrior-slave grabbed each of them and followed after Lucan, he marched without any apparent fears or qualms.

On they went, past the rows of pillars and toward the next doorway. It was not at all far to the next room, and soon they were stationed behind Lucan. He was standing absolutely still, gawking at the spectacle before them.

Low pillars lined the inside of the rounded room, supporting the bottom edges of the dome that rose above them. The smaller, lower ring around the outskirts of the ceiling was lined with drawings and small columns of pictures. In the center of the dome, on a slightly raised terrace, it stood.

The chamber, constructed of the purest, clearest crystal, stood about the height of a man and just big enough for one to stand inside. It sparkled like a lake in the moonlight, glistened like the sea under stars. Inside the thin walls, the pale outline of delicate crystal cogs was visible on this side. Lucan stared at the perfect rectangular solid that the chamber formed. It was flawlessly and seamlessly crafted from a single piece of quartz to contain the greatest controllable power known to the Earth. On the side that faced them, there was an empty space in the center, just the right size for the Key of Amatahns to fit.

Instead of stepping up the terrace and inserting the Key where it was meant to fit, Lucan barked a quick command to his warrior-slaves. They scattered to opposite ends of the circular chamber, and reported back to him with exactly the same words, "No way out, my lord."

Now what were they going to do? Locked in a room with only one way out, and empty-armor knights there, what could they do?

Lucan seemed to consider it a minor obstacle. He glanced past the doorway they had come through, at the one they had sealed. Then he shrugged and sat casually on the edge of the crystal chamber's terrace. Drawing out his dagger, he began running a smooth stone over the edge to sharpen the blade.

Janir decided not to question him, as she doubted that she wanted to know why he was doing that, and so skirted off to Karile and Saoven who were discussing something behind the pillars.

"What are you doing?" Janir asked, as Karile was tracing his fingers over the small pictures and Saoven was doing the same to a section several columns away.

"Reading them," Karile dismissively replied.

"Learning what the empty suits of armor are," Saoven murmured absently.

Janir was silent for several seconds. Neither the enchanter nor the elf offered the explanation she awaited, so she interrupted them again. "What are they?"

"It's complicated," Karile weakly replied, after a space of hesitation.

"Exceedingly complicated," Saoven agreed.

Both of them went back to reading.

"We have time," Janir remarked.

Karile shrugged. "They're ghosts. Does that answer your question?" the wizard indignantly snapped.

"No."

"It's like this," Karile began, making it appear that he was doing her a huge favor and that she should be able to read ancient wall art as well as he could. Then he went into an explanation that he often got wrong, and Saoven often corrected him.

As far as Janir could discern, the empty suits of armor had once been real knights, they were an entire army in fact. The soldiers who fought in the wars against the mazag all those years ago ("Four thousand and thirty-eight," Saoven interjected). The mazag had been wiser then, great philosophers and scholars. They had kinds of magic that have been lost since their collapse, for their entire existence relied on magic. They had inhabited most of what is now

Brevia and Stlaven, built huge cities and temples, and lived with the other three races in peace for eons. They were the Father Creator's chosen race. It was their duty to be spiritual and moral authorities, to lead and guide the less gifted races. Then came the Shadow Wars. No one is certain anymore why, but the mazag and most the other three chief races ("Dwarves, mortals and elves," Saoven remarked) fought for supremacy over the lands. An ancient race of men now extinct had declared war on the other peoples of the world and the mazag had sided with them in the bloodshed.

During the times of peace, the mazag had taught much of their arts to a young mortal named Amatahns. Amatahns naturally sided with his people when the war broke out, a series of conflicts that lasted for a decade before *it* happened. With his former teachers and their allies inflicting great damages against them in battle, the enchanter feared for the lives of his race.

So Amatahns and several enchanters from all three races, took a child, a nine-year-old farm boy from Brevia by the name of Drell. Amatahns tortured him, used instruments of torture now destroyed ("The Creon," Saoven naturally supplied) to change him. For over five years the wizard relentlessly tortured him until the process was completed. He used the magic of all three allied races to create a being that would be invincible against magic, what they called "the Invulnerable." Or in their ancient tongue, "Argetallam." Brought into existence to be the savior to a mostly defeated army comprised of the three races. Using Drell's memories of intense torture and pain, they constructed weapons for him, the karkaton. Inflicting fatal, stunning, or excruciating pain; depending on which Drell wanted, and keeping any wound he might sustain from growing worse until it could be treated, these they called the "perfect weapons" (or karkaton). They taught Drell to make these weapons, using his own blood, the scales of a werewarg and the tears of a griffin.

When they finally released Drell from the agony they had inflicted on him, they expected him to obey them because of the fear of it happening again. But they had done their work too well and created a completely invulnerable mortal. Once the mazag were defeated, he rebelled and refused to fight for the enchanters any longer.

"There is so much about the first Argetallam on these walls, because Amatahns was fascinated with the magic used," Saoven gauged.

Dismayed at the mazag's behavior toward those they were supposed to protect, the Father Creator allowed Drell and Amatahns to take away the mazag's knowledge and wisdom, and seal their magic in the chamber. After that, the mazag were chased out of Brevia and into the caves and mountains to live as beasts. Knowing that they had once had knowledge, knowing that it had been taken from them and remembering that their own student's creation had been their downfall…they were to live in regret and shame for eternity.

Realizing that someone would need to protect the chamber, Amatahns imprisoned the souls of the ten-thousand or so knights who had fought in the Shadow Wars into their suits of armor and set them up in a grand temple, where they would stay bound to protect it until the end of time, when the stars rained from the heavens.

As for the mortal allies of the mazag, they were wiped out in the ensuing bloodbath that followed the mazag's downfall. Amatahns then sailed across the sea where he felt that he was needed and never returned.

"Then what happened?" Janir demanded.

"What do you mean? I've told you," Karile defensively replied.

"What happened to Drell!" Janir screamed.

"That is rather simple," Saoven interjected. "He returned to the farmlands of Brevia, raised an impressive family of thirteen children and died a pauper on his two acre farm."

"You mean...everyone just forgot him?" Janir sadly ventured.

"Until two or three generations later, when it was discovered that all his children, grandchildren, and great-grand children had his same abilities, yes," Saoven confirmed.

"Why did that happen? Did Amatahns intend for the gift, or curse, to be hereditary?" Janir demanded.

"I believe it was just a quirk in the magic, and that he didn't even consider it," Saoven replied. "Drell's children seem to have simply gained an evolution of his powers that was more potent and powerful than anything mankind had caused prior."

Lucan and his warrior-slaves ate something indescribable, the color of dirt with black flecks. Must have been bread. None of the other three were offered any, and none of them asked. They slept on the floor around the crystal chamber that night. The stone was dusty with thousands of years of residue, and Karile sneezed like a cat in a flour mill.

Saoven was across from her, sound asleep by appearances. But she suspected that he was just pretending to make her and Karile feel better. He looked more peaceful when he was truly asleep. The wizard was undoubtedly deep in slumber, his usual hog-like sounds caused Lucan to glare groggily at him from his place up on the terrace steps.

Janir couldn't close her eyes even though they were heavy as bricks. She couldn't sleep. The sound of the empty-suit knights, pounding on the doors kept her sharply awake. No fire had been lit here. Light the color of the stars seemed to bathe the crystal chamber in a gentle glow, as if it were trying to lull them all to sleep.

A piercing, sharp noise rattled the air and shook the ground. Janir bolted upright along with everyone else, to behold in terror an axe blade sticking through the iron door. Soon dozens of axes and swords were shoving their way through, making the hole in the door bigger, and bigger.

They all remained motionless as the hole was widened enough to let a knight through. The knight clattered to the ground, lay still for a moment, rose forebodingly to his feet and began marching toward them deliberately.

"Come, Janir," Lucan snapped, shoving a karkaton in her direction again. Saoven didn't protest this time, and Janir didn't look back. As he always did, Lucan strode swiftly and with conviction. Ironically, his stride seemed to become more confident the more frightened he was. Janir had to scramble to keep up with him.

"Don't speak to him, and he can't kill you," Lucan announced as if it had been his own conclusion. But Lucan had already issued a challenge and he was fair game.

The knight seemed to have his eyes locked on her brother, holding a giant spear expertly with both hands. Lucan feinted to the right to draw the knight's attention. It worked. The huge hulk veered to the left to jab in Lucan's direction.

Janir dove at the knight, aiming for the back of his neck with her karkaton. It took one swipe sideways with his spear and she was lying on the ground gasping for air. It was ridiculous, he hadn't even hit her with the head of the spear and she was helpless!

A disgusted sound escaped her brother as he dodged the spear head again. Holding her side with her left hand, Janir staggered to her feet with the karkaton clenched in the other.

Like a harpoon toward a fish, the spear stabbed in Lucan's direction again. He knocked it off course with his karkaton and it embedded its tip in the stone. The knight spun around faster than he should have, and jabbed Janir in the middle of her chest with the butt of the spear. Sprawled on the ground gasping, Janir watched Lucan repeatedly feint from side to side, dodging the evil head of the spear with a practiced precision. As she lay there, her body and every last one of her bruises, cuts and scratches begged her to remain on the ground.

But if she gave up, it would all be over. Struggling to her feet again, Janir dove at the knight this time to be met with a heavily armored elbow in the face. She lay on her back for a space, staring up at the vaulted ceiling of the temple, and seeing stars with the eye that wasn't blinking with pain. Her head hurt now too, from slamming into the stone.

I am pathetic, she thought to herself, forcing her body to stand for a third time.

She rose in time to see Lucan make a slight error and stumble to his left. Frantically, he tried to rise but was too late. The spear found its mark this time and buried itself in Lucan's right side.

Lucan cried out and clenched the shaft, while the knight ruthlessly rammed him against the pillar, driving the spear deeper.

Resolving not to fail this time, Janir dove at the knight's neck again. With his back exposed, she made short work of cramming the tip of her karkaton deep between the neck plates of his armor. He shuddered, and crumpled to the ground in shambles, various pieces clattering this way and that.

With the knight at last defeated, Janir knelt beside Lucan. His face was contorted into an expression of agony and he gripped the part of the spear that was still outside of him, with a helpless light in his eyes. Janir wondered if that was what Drell had looked like, all those years ago, when he had been undergoing the transformation from a normal mortal to an Argetallam, like a small child in huge pain.

"Pull it out, Janir," he pleaded, sounding for the first time desperate and weak.

"Lucan, if I do you'll bleed out," Janir spoke in a calm voice, and caught his other hand.

"No, I won't," he groaned. "Give me the karkaton and pull it out."

Obediently, she handed her brother both the karkaton. Lucan gripped her shoulder with his other hand and again commanded her to jerk the spear out. For a moment she saw the white bones of his ribs before blood welled over the wound. Lucan gasped and cried out, his hand tightening like a vice on her shoulder. He squeezed her so hard Janir wanted to scream herself, but did not. Pausing for half a breath, Lucan fumblingly staggered to his feet. Another knight was already fitting through the opening in the door and Lucan was scrambling not to be near when it came through.

Although he instinctively tried to shove her away, Lucan had to submit to letting Janir support him as he slowly trudged back to the other end of the crystal chamber. About halfway there, the warrior-slaves came and half-carried Lucan back to the steps of the crystal chamber's terrace. With the attentiveness of mothers to a sick child, they laid him out gently on the step. Janir looked back at the empty-armor knights. Six of them had broken through now, and they were marching uniformly toward the others.

"Lucan!" Janir whispered. "What do we do?"

"I have failed," Lucan moaned, dropping the

karkaton. "I failed Master. I failed my people."

"What are we going to do?" Janir repeated.

"I failed," Lucan murmured.

Janir glanced again to the increasing number of empty-armor knights nearing them at a steady pace. "What are we to do?" Janir demanded, leaning over Lucan, seizing his tunic and pulling him up closer to her face.

"I failed," he whispered again. Then a hard, icy light came into his eyes. A cruel light. "But I will not fail completely."

Fighting to stand, Lucan commanded one of the warrior-slaves by name, to bring him his pack. His rummaged through it for a moment and pulled out the Key of Amatahns, which Janir had not seen since the Staspin Waste.

With the help of Janir and his converts, Lucan staggered up the terrace steps to the crystal chamber. As he brought the Key closer to its place in the chamber's side, an excited silvery light shone from the chamber and there was a faint whirring sound as the chamber sensed that its missing part was close. Lucan unceremoniously crammed the Key into the slot.

There was a flurry of light activity inside the chamber, and a thrill of sound.

After several seconds, one side of the chamber swung open, and a foggy mist swirled and seeped out the bottom. Struck by the beauty of the sight, Janir stood as a child seeing stars for the first time. The crystal glistened like a lake in the moonlight or fog of the early dawn. Forgetting that the power inside could kill her, she just stood there wordlessly staring.

She was jerked back to reality when Lucan seized her arm. "I may have failed to bring back the magic contained herein, but I will not fail to see to it that no one will ever be able to use it. And I will not fail to make certain that *you* do not live," he coldly glared into her eyes.

Before Janir realized what happened, Lucan had shoved her into the chamber, slammed the crystal door shut and removed the Key. To make sure that neither Saoven nor Karile could rescue her, Lucan tossed the Key at the oncoming horde, where it was trampled under foot.

Defenseless against what was coming, Janir screamed and pounded on the door. She kicked all four of the clear sides of the chamber, looking for a way out.

Saoven and Karile were at the door a moment later, trying to pry it open. They couldn't. Janir laid a hand on her side of the chamber, Saoven stared at her from the other side with a mournful, tortured gaze. He rested his hand on the outside of the glass with an agonized motion and she saw him shout the name: "Janir!" He mouthed something else too, but she couldn't hear through the chamber.

Then the pain started.

CHAPTER 11
What Death Feels Like

Pain. Agony. Torture.

Those three words rang through her head as the wisps of pink mist came down from the top of the chamber and seemed to pierce through her body. Intensely, she could feel something hard and sharp being driven through her ears, through her eyes, her belly, neck, and back. Rods being forced through her head down to her legs. From above and sideways they seemed to be ramming their way into her flesh like sharp, iron worms.

Janir screamed, but no sound came, or if it did it was drowned out by that horrible ringing noise that stabbed at her ears. A malicious entity was in her chest, like a hand or a claw, and it was crushing... not her heart but something else. Agony weakening her, Janir doubled over and leaned pressed against the glass. In a vain attempt to shut out that terrible ringing, she clamped her hands over her ears, with no success to stop the sound. The ringing continued, and she pressed harder in vain. Light flooded her vision, she clenched her eye lids shut, but still the bright white lights were everywhere.

There was a wetness on her face. Tears. She was sobbing as the magic tore her apart, slowly. Perhaps she screamed again, but like before, she couldn't be sure. Her head throbbed with every beat of her heart, shooting pain throughout her whole body. That which was keeping her alive was being used as an instrument of torture against her.

Thrashing from side to side, Janir tried to shake off the rods of magic that were being driven through her, the claws, the ringing and the lights. There was a slight sensation of her head hitting both sides of the chamber, but those new bruises and all her old ones were nothing compared to the relentless agony that afflicted her now. Her hands groped over her body. There were no rods sticking through her; those were all just the magic piercing into her, punishing her for her stupidity to enter.

Janir only knew that she had crumbled to her knees because there was a slight increase of pain there. In desperation, she slammed her body into the sides of the chamber, trying to break the crystal walls.

Death. She wanted to die. She begged the magic to let her die. Nothing could be worse than this. It hurt more than she had ever imagined anything to hurt. Not much longer now, she didn't think she could survive this for more than a few moments. Although she was longing for an end as the agony shot through her, she understood why people feared it if this was what it felt like. But death is often as cruel in his asceticism as he is in his greed.

The pain continued and Janir didn't think she could bear it any longer. It was too much, she wasn't strong enough for this distilled agony. Every kind of pain imaginable, tearing, slicing, burning, freezing, stabbing...purified and condensed.

With a mounting sense of futility, she curled into a ball at the bottom of the chamber, screaming and struggling against the pain, trying to make it leave her alone. The magic stabbed down at her from above like an evil bird pecking at a helplessly stranded fish.

Struggling to get the lights away and the ringing to silence itself, she crammed her knees up to her eyes and pressed her hands as hard as she could over her ears. She rocked from side to side, willing to attempt anything, if only the excruciation would stop.

Then it was over. There was no other way to put it. The pain ended. She just lay there for a moment as the cruel ringing subsided and the lights dimmed.

The power of Amatahns had been unable to kill her by that method and like a living thing, reasoned another. It settled over her in a thick, impenetrable cloud. She couldn't breathe. Fighting to draw breath, she tried desperately to rid herself of the thick cloud of magic. Her efforts were futile.

Shudders racked her body. The uncontrollable convulsions she had felt before only once. A viridescent sheen went over her eyes. Something was taking over her, forcing its mastery over her and assuming command of her actions. It hurt, and normally she would have been screaming in pain. But after the chamber, this felt like a pinprick. Fighting against the magic, she flipped sideways and writhed on the ground as something more powerful than she had ever felt before took possession of her. Groaning, Janir arched her back, and just as quickly curled in a ball. Frozen.

Riangar.

She was incapable of feeling. Not fear, love or compassion. Only rage and anger. Just fire. There was a screaming sound as the power of the chamber was confronted with the fury of the Riangar. An agonized screeching shook the air and sent a tremor through the Earth.

Out of the corner of her eye, she saw Saoven and Karile doubling over with their hands pressed over their ears. Lucan rolled off the steps with his hands held in the same position. The empty-armor knights stopped abruptly.

The heavy covering of invisible ash that she felt, shook and trembled against the Riangar. But this Riangar was even more powerful than when she had killed Duke Ronan. There was something coming alive in her, manifesting itself to its full power, like a dragon who only flicks his tail at a mouse, but rises and uses his full capabilities to fight another dragon.

Janir felt a snapping and cracking inside her, as if a cage had been containing her full magic and was now crumbling to release the beast within.

Quickly, almost as if it were escaping, the heavy aura that had settled about her tried to flee out of the chamber. The crystal chamber trembled precariously, cracked and shattered into countless shards. Rushing away as a river does, the power of Amatahns whooshed toward the empty-armor knights.

The wave of magic slowly peeled their armor into pieces. Each individual plate of metal was severed from the rest. As the wind swept back toward them, each line of empty-armor knights it touched crumpled to the ground motionless. They fell like houses of cards, as if they had never been upright in the first place. They scattered like chaff in the wind.

The green glow that the world had become, dimmed until it was seen in natural light again. Janir felt drained, like a doll deprived of its stuffing, a scarecrow robbed of its pole. Strong hands gathered her up from the stone floor and crystal shards.

Someone was speaking, and it sounded far away. "Janir!"

"Saoven?" she coughed. Sweat beaded her forehead and she was finding it hard to hold her eyes open. She leaned against Saoven's shoulder for support. Karile was explaining something at ninety words a minute that she didn't understand, or want to. Gently, Saoven brushed stray strands of hair behind her ear, and put an arm around her shoulders. Janir didn't want to move, she didn't want to speak. Exhausted, she only wished to curl up and sleep. Resigning to the drained feeling, she let her eyelids slide shut.

"Impossible!" Lucan shouted.

"It's obviously not impossible, because it's happening, you idiot," Karile insulted. "What's impossible?" he added as an afterthought, realizing that he didn't know what Lucan was talking about.

"You..." Lucan pointed at Janir and tried to

scramble backwards as if she were a poisonous snake, but his wound kept him from moving more than a few inches. "You...defeated it!" Lucan gasped. "You defeated the power of Amatahns, of an entire race!"

Following this thought to its logical reasoning seemed to require a supernatural effort on her part, but Janir managed to process the statement. "What is your point?" Janir forced her lips to move.

Lucan now seemed to be speaking to himself more than to anyone else. "Of course," he growled, "you over-powered it. The same magic we were created to combat, and it seems that it was therefore unable to compete with you."

Swinging his head from side to side as if reading the thoughts on a page, he continued speaking to himself. Speaking so fast that Janir's weary mind could barely keep track of the words. "It seems that the Power of Amatahns was not such a threat to us after all," Lucan glanced up at her.

Even though Janir was fighting to understand her brother's words, she was quite certain that even an Argetallam should not have been able to survive that.

"But still, by all accounts, even Master's.....you should be dead. Which means..."

Fighting against the restraints of her body, Janir had made herself open her eyes and stare at her brother with a blank expression; it was all she could manage.

"Which means..."

Since their misadventures coming here, the maiden had seen fear in her brother's eyes. But never once had that fear been directed at her. Now it was, pure and simple terror. Unmasked and unhidden.

"Kill her," Lucan commanded his converts. "Kill her now."

As for the maiden herself, being this tired had taken away the emotion of fear for the time being. All she felt was irritation at the converts for drawing those sharp daggers.

"Stop it," she commanded, before Saoven or Karile could do anything.

Like horses galloping toward a wall, they stopped. This new development caught her attention. They had never obeyed her over her brother before.

"Put your weapons away," she experimentally added.

They did.

Then another very strange thing happened. Like puppets suddenly picked up by the puppeteer, the warrior-slaves gained expression and extra-necessary motions. Simple things such as a twitch at the corner of one's mouth, the spontaneous blink out of rhythm.

"Have you any other commands, mistress?" one asked.

It was difficult to know then who was more surprised at this spontaneous display of speech. Not once had the converts spoken, except to reply to a direct question. In all the weeks they had traveled together, not once had one of them spoken before being spoken to, saving, of course, Camak who Lucan had killed back in the Staspin Waste. Suddenly, Janir noticed that the warrior-slaves were different. They didn't all seem mono-visual to her, although her eyes were cloudy and she couldn't tell what they looked like.

"No!" Lucan shouted. "This can't be happening!" he screamed.

"Shut up, Lucan," Janir mumbled. How pleasant it was to finally say it.

"Shall we silence him for you, mistress?" another inquired.

When they called her "mistress," it reminded her too much of her father's chosen name. She didn't like it, but she felt that these poor souls would take it as rage if she told them that.

"Why can they now speak, Lucan?" Saoven demanded.

Lucan glared evil thoughts at the elf for a moment before replying, but he seemed to think that his enemies would learn the truth either way and he had nothing to lose.

"Janir is now by some means more powerful than I am; she has *blunderingly*," he added the word with scorn to show that it had been completely accidental on Janir's part, "taken mastery of the power that controls them. And they're adapting to fit what they believe would please her most. I prefer them to be silent, but they know Janir doesn't," Lucan snapped. Adapting? How would they know what Janir wanted in the first place?

"What would you have us do, my lady?" the one who had first spoken inquired.

So it was true, they had somehow sensed her seemingly undisplayed displeasure at the initial title of respect.

A tremor shook the temple around them. A golden mist was rising from the thousands of empty-armor suits now destroyed.

"We need to get out of here," Janir reasoned, scrambling to her feet. She felt much better than just a few seconds ago. Perhaps it had something to do with the converts, but it just as likely wasn't and didn't matter. All three of the converts rushed to help Janir stand.

"I'm fine!" she shouted, shoving them away. Then spotting their downcast faces, hastily added: "I'm not angry at you; grab Lucan and let's go."

Perhaps they took her command too literally, because then all three of them were trying to pick up Lucan at once, pulling him in opposite directions and making him swear with the pain.

"No, no, no!" she screeched, then checked her temper again. "You, take Lucan. You two, follow."

"Stay close behind; do not become separated," Saoven calmly ordered. After checking Janir, he skirted off with the convert holding Lucan beside him.

Snatching up both her karkaton, Janir beckoned for the other two warrior-slaves to follow after her. Yes, she felt much better, revitalized even.

After stopping again to see that she was following, Saoven lead the way, Janir and the warrior-slaves trotting behind, with Karile…..where was that little anomaly? Janir glanced back to see Karile gingerly sifting through the plates of armor.

"Come on!" Janir shouted, bounding back to

snatch him by the collar and dragged him along.

"What were you thinking!" she angrily demanded.

He shouted something inaudible.

Rolling her eyes, Janir handed Karile to one of the warrior-slaves who had run back after her, and continued belting out of the crystal room beside him. A large portion of stone slammed down where they had been moments before.

It was hazardous crossing the great stone bridge a second time. Countless metal plates lay as thick as autumn leaves on a forest floor and were treacherous footing. The earth was groaning, shifting and changing itself. Trying to seal in the power that had been taken.

"My lady!" one of the warrior-slaves cried her new title and began dragging her along. "We must hurry, my lady. The cavern collapses!"

Leaping into a run, Janir raced after the others whom she had fallen behind. The other converts had pressed on while this one had come back for her. Making a mental note that she must learn all their names, Janir sped on, the convert pacing at her side.

It was a long run back through the maze of tunnels, especially with all the rubble and stray rock collapsing. Confusion and chaos reigned in the green-lit labyrinth like cruel kings. Dirt and dust that had been settled for eons was floating through the air as if to taste flight one last time before the whole temple sank into the earth for eternity. Shaking like a trembling leaf, the massive stone colossus, which had seemed so strong and solid before, was surrendering to the earth from whence it came, as if all its determination and will to exist had been lost with the theft of its prize. Stumbling through the rubble and trying to find her way back, Janir was certain that she was going to die more than once. In the smog of dust, so thick it made her choke, Saoven's voice called out several times to guide her and the last convert. The grit of the temple was in her eyes, making them water; her teeth were coated in the grime. Once she tripped on a stray brick that had fallen out of the ceiling and fell to the ground. Her head struck something in the viridescent dust cloud, and a quick feel with her finger tips confirmed that blood was trickling down the side of her head. Dirt caked around the wound, drawn like moths to light at dusk. She had no idea how the loyal convert knew where she was in that smoky redundancy; nonetheless, she felt his iron fists catching her collar and hauling her upright.

Just when Janir was beginning to wonder if they would be able to get out, the light of early dawn, not the sickly lights of the temple, shone ahead. The light being only a faint dot, Janir didn't realize that the others were halted at the doorway.

Saoven stood in front with Karile, the warrior-slave holding Lucan, and the third warrior-slave. The others cowering behind the elf. With admiration, Janir noted how Saoven always tried to place himself between others and danger when faced with it.

Janir stepped past the others gingerly to stand

beside the elf, and face the four clacking mazag.

"Key, Key. Give us the Key. It is ours, we want it. Give, give it now."

A quick evaluation of her circumstances revealed that she could not fight four angry hissing mazag with her karkaton. Fighting their way out of this was not an option. The temple was collapsing behind them and the only way out was solidly blocked.

"We need to get out," Janir calmly stated. "Please let us pass."

"Give us the Key."

"Please," Janir pleaded with mounting desperation. "If you don't let us out...we'll die."

It sounded a ridiculously weak argument once she said it. But it was true, and she could think of no negative outcome for the mazag. Saoven and Karile stared at her sideways.

"Talking to beasts, are you now?" Saoven half jokingly teased. But the gravity in his undertone, countered the playful expression on his face.

"You can't hear them?" Janir inquired.

"No. I cannot. It is simple hissing and clacking to me," Saoven replied.

"They were the original enemies of our kind," Lucan gasped, becoming weaker as his blood was lost. A concerned glance at her brother's wound showed that dirt and grime had stuck to his bloodied side. "Understanding comes with pain..."

"What do they want?" Karile asked, cutting to the chase as he usually did when death was on the line.

"Key. Key. We must have it. Our race depends on it."

"They want the Key of Amatahns," Janir replied. Which happened to be buried under thousands upon thousands of tons of stone and earth at that moment.

Behind her, Karile raised a tentative hand like a schoolboy in class. "I...er...have it," Karile sheepishly admitted. At a sharp look from Saoven, he continued. "That's what I was grabbing, you see. When I was shoveling through all that armor."

Lucan rolled his eyes as if the wizard had claimed that fireflies eat stars to shine.

"What possessed you to bring the cursed thing?" Janir demanded. "It has brought about nothing but trouble and misfortune."

"Never mind," Saoven interrupted. "If the Key is what they want, then we have no choice but to give it to them."

"Must we?"

"Enchanter, the temple is literally collapsing about our ears, there is one way out, that way is guarded by mazag. We have a potential way of being rid of them, and you ask if we must try it? Yes!" Saoven shouted the last word with unrestrained irritance.

Karile gave a reluctant sigh, and deliberately drew the shining silver egg out of his robe.

"What is the point of stealing, if you're just going to give it back?" he muttered. Cradling the egg in both hands, the enchanter knelt by the threshold of the doorway where the beasts still refused to enter.

Carefully placing it on the very edge of the threshold, Karile gently tapped the egg, letting it roll half a rotation to the mazag's side of the doorway.

Eagerly, the mazag who seemed to be the leader,

snatched it up in its jaws and swallowed it.

"All that, just to eat it!" Karile indignantly screamed. "Too bad I don't have a frying pan, or else I could have cooked it for you!"

"*'Tis the safest way to transport the Queen,*" another mazag replied. Janir relayed the sentence.

"Oh, I get it. So the Key is just a cover around the egg that contains your next ruler, or whatever?" Karile sought to affirm.

"*In the egg is the mother of the next generation,*" the first mazag stated. "*For protecting her, we are eternally in your debt.*"

"But we're the ones who stole it in the first place!" Janir instinctively protested.

"*That matters not; you kept her safe and now we owe you a boon; name it and it shall be yours, Fledgling!*"

"Wait," Janir caught the name. "What did you call me?"

"*Fledgling. That is what you are, is it not?*"

Strangely, the mazag turned out to be delightful companions. Janir hesitantly leaned against the warm sides of one as the large fire started with mazag breath roared center of their circle. The beasts lay curled like lizards on the soft beach, basking in its glow. Essentially, they were lizards, Janir reminded herself. The beasts had not only allowed them to exit the temple before it collapsed, but they had been kind enough to give them a ride to the beach. Odd, how old animosities were forgotten with the return of their Queen's egg. Now it was as if the mazag and the fleshlings had been lifelong friends. The fire pranced and leaped in the night air, as if dancing to the beat of the waves on the surf.

Karile was a shapeless mass of snoring robe, while the three warrior-slaves slumped against the tails and side of two mazag. Now the warrior-slaves were obsessive about Janir. Incessantly asking her if there was anything that they could do for her, if she would prefer if they stood or sat. Finally she had commanded them to relax, and they had practically dropped where they stood. Now they lay asleep as the dead.

Saoven was staring at her gravely from across the fire. Both he and she were thinking the same thing. What to do with the third figure who sat cowering to the side.

Bitterly, Lucan glared at his sister. Elves have an earned reputation for being skilled in the ways of healing, and although Saoven was a warrior and not a healer, he had patched Lucan together rather nicely. Lucan had been sullen about being tended, but realized that he needed help and so submitted resentfully to the elf's treatments. Now the young Argetallam had a clean white bandage wrapped about his ribs and wild ribwort plantain leaves pressed against the wound.

At length, Saoven rose to his feet and motioned for Janir to follow him. They threaded between the sleeping lizards' tails and carefully stepped past Karile onto the moonlit beach. They walked side by side away from the others, and when they were no more than a quarter of a mile away, Janir could no longer hear Karile's hog-like nocturnal vocalizations. A half-moon hung over them like a blinking, but ever watchful eye. Wiggling her bare toes in the soft sand, Janir strolled beside the elf at a leisurely pace. When they were out of an earshot of the others, Saoven turned to her and held her gaze for a very long moment. Several times, he seemed about to say something, then stopped.

"What are we going to do with Lucan?" Janir wondered, glancing back furtively at the slumbering shapes of the mazag encircling the others.

"We should kill him," Saoven unenthusiastically replied, but with an untempered honesty.

Janir swallowed. "Must we?"

"He has been abusing you for weeks and you still wish to spare him?" Saoven incredulously surmised.

"I know he's evil and all that but," Janir hesitated as she contemplated how to best put words to her thoughts. "I hope you don't take this wrong...but I pity him."

"Why?"

"Because...he's...it's hard to explain but I feel as if he never had the chance to be any different. I remember what you said about regretting showing mercy to the Argetallams before, however, can we show compassion again? Just once more? Please?" Janir pleaded, beseechingly gazing up at Saoven.

Saoven was quiet. "You feel compassion for the one who would have killed you?"

"Well, when you put it that way it sounds rather

moronic, doesn't it? But yes," Janir replied.

The elf stared at her. Janir wondered what he was thinking, his expression held no interpretable emotion.

"I have never met anyone like you, Argetallam or otherwise," Saoven deliberately and cautiously remarked with a wrinkled brow.

Feeling a sudden desire to change the subject, Janir shook her head. "Can you believe that Karile and I were stupid enough to crawl into the mazag's cavern and steal the most valuable object on Earth; all with the intent of keeping it from my family?"

"Stupid, yes. Slightly naïve as well," Saoven gravely assented.

Janir glanced sharply at him.

"People were killed as a result of your actions. And a world could have been lost as well," Saoven had taken on the tone of rebuking parent. The Argetallam hung her head. She knew his words to be true. Still the cold, motionless face of Florete could be seen in her mind's eye.

"I know," Janir softly replied, "and I sincerely regret it."

"All the same," Saoven took on a lighter, less accusing air. "What you did was brave, though misguided. And lives would have been lost in any event."

Lifting her eyes from the sand, the maiden stared up at him.

"In the end, you probably saved the world. But remember the price, dear one," Saoven added with a sympathetic tone.

Janir lowered her eyes again. "I doubt I will be able to forget it."

"Do not be overly troubled. Foolishness may beget priceless offspring. Let us pray that yours shall," Saoven let those words sink into her soul before he continued.

"There is something that I have been waiting to tell you," he began.

"What?" she curiously leaned closer.

"I was in Avenport to return you to Saaradan; Armandius wants you back, but you must be there by midsummer's eve or you are banished under pain of death from Brevia by the High King," Saoven announced.

"How far off is midsummer's eve?"

"Three weeks," Saoven replied, seemingly unconcerned with the fact.

"But it will take at least four weeks to get from here to Saaradan!" Janir screamed, plopping to the ground and striking her fist on the sand in exasperation.

"By land," Saoven nodded.

"What do you mean, 'by land'?" Janir glanced at him sideways.

"The mazag said they owed you a favor," Saoven reminded her. "Perhaps that would include a ride to Saaradan."

"But how do you think people along the countryside will react to mazag swimming up to the capital?" Janir pointed out.

"Stop concerning yourself with bridges that as of yet need not be crossed," Saoven placated.

Janir was silent for awhile, then remembered the thing she had been waiting to ask him all this time. Scrambling to her feet, she made her query.

"I was told to ask you, what was that about, in the Vermilion Market, when that elf tried to get the Key from me?"

"What?" Saoven's eyes snapped around to her. "The Vermilion Market exists?"

"Yes I was there, but who was the elf? He's called Malkalar...or something beginning with an 'm'," Janir explained.

Saoven was quiet.

"He's dark, with brilliant blue eyes; oh, and he's an enchanter," Janir described her assailant.

"Searching for the Key of Amatahns? Are you certain?" Saoven demanded, spontaneously concerned.

"Yes," Janir replied.

Saoven seemed suddenly very worried and distressed. "No, no, no, no," he murmured, adding something else in Elvish that she didn't understand.

"Who is he?" Janir renewed her inquiry.

"You mortals are not even meant to be aware of his existence; he is supposed to be a secret," Saoven's hands had flown to his face, and he covered his eyes with them in a tired gesture that Janir's master sometimes used.

"Not anymore, apparently," Janir remarked. "So who is he?"

"I cannot reveal that," Saoven stiffly replied, obviously unhappy with the fact, but determined to be loyal to it. His hands dropped to his sides again.

"You know that I'm an Argetallam!" Janir protested, irritated that he was so openly keeping secrets from her.

"So does the entire Brevian elite, by now," the elf curtly announced, but then seemed to consider something. "Janir," Saoven grew very grave. "I will tell you, but you must pledge that you will repeat this knowledge to none without the consent of Velaskas or myself."

"If it's so secretive, why are you bothering to tell me at all?" Janir asked, as the question occurred to her.

"Would you prefer that I not?" Saoven retorted.

"Fair enough. I agree to tell no one." Then another thought occurred to her. "But my master already knows, correct?"

Saoven stared at her blankly for several seconds before replying. "This secret is kept by my entire race; I am not supposed to tell anyone, even a king, least of all beings an Argetallam."

Realizing the gravity of this issue, Janir solemnly nodded, while wondering; why would he tell her?

With a sigh, Saoven elaborated. "There has never been a more powerful enchanter among elves, mortals, or any of the other races, than Malkalar."

"So why keep him a secret?" Janir wondered.

"Because he is the son of our king," Saoven's voice dropped to a whisper.

Janir was quiet. How did that one detail merit all this secrecy? "Oh, I see. The evil offspring of the most noble king; there's one in every story, isn't there?" Janir flippantly remarked.

"Janir!" Saoven snapped. "Do not mock my king! Nor my prince, though he be what he is."

She paused, considering a counter-remark. Then realized that she had been out of line with that phrase. "Forgive me, but what is he that is so significant?"

Saoven sighed and glanced about the beach furtively, checking for spying eyes. "It was his will that none of the other races know of his existence. For some reason, he refuses to allow anyone outside of the elves know that he is," Saoven explained in a low tone.

"Why?" she was baffled.

"If no one knows he exists, none can learn his name."

Janir's expression of total confusion prompted more elaboration.

"There is power in a name, Janir," the elf whispered, "a power that can both create and destroy. A name can be used to raise mountains and cast down kings."

When another blank stare was her only acknowledgement, he continued.

"A name gives a title to who we are, it gives us an identity. We cannot be ourselves without them. To know a person's name is the first step to seeing what is in their soul."

"But I met a seeress who knows his name," Janir countered.

"Seers and seeresses know most of what goes on in the world, and they are not generous with their information in any event. You are the only one outside my race and the Seers, who knows of him,

Janir. I implore that you take that burden responsibly," Saoven concluded. "My people must not learn that I revealed such knowledge to an Argetallam."

Janir nodded, but her mind was still wondering after several things. Why had Malkalar needed a seeress? Had he simply been rescuing Zeerla? Not likely. While dwelling on unanswered questions, who had hired the Argetallams to obtain the Key and the power in the first place? Perhaps she would never know. What about Bricen trying to have Armandius killed? Janir had to warn her master as soon as possible.

Suddenly, there was a commotion from the small encampment; the hiss of a mazag and a scream of pain from a mortal mouth.

Janir and Saoven glanced at each other and then charged back across the sand. They had wandered much further than Janir had thought, and it was a decent run back to the mazag and the other fleshlings.

Saoven was faster than Janir, and arrived some hundred paces ahead of her. The maiden arrived on the scene to find the mazag called Mazag Teris, whimpering because of a slice on its upper forearm, two of the warrior-slaves lying seriously wounded, the third with a minor wound on his shoulder.

"*The wretched scion of the Staspin Waste!*" shrieked Mazag Teris, fussing over the torn flesh.

"Forgive us, my lady. We tried to stop him!" the less-damaged convert rushed to Janir's feet and groveled before her with remorse.

"Who?" Janir demanded.

"Your brother, he has escaped!"

EPILOGUE

The reflected light from the cheerfully shining sun danced on the white stone walls of the fountain house. In Brevia they would be experiencing the first gusts of cold, but here it was just as warm as in a Brevian summer. The water splashed and played blissfully, seemingly unaware of the horrors that went on around it.

Standing by the brink of the water, staring absently into the ripples, stood a middle-aged man with a dark countenance to match his dark beard and tanned skin. His large leather boots were coated in a film of dust from the surrounding outposts, though the rest of his clothes were fresh. His black tunic was gathered at the waist by a broad leather belt, to which a collection of torture blades and daggers were neatly secured. Half-consciously, one hand rested on the hilt of his favorite weapon, a sleek black rod, while the other fingered a spiral seashell hanging about his neck on a snug leather string.

At a sound behind him, he spun around with the swiftness of a mountain cat. Within a heartbeat, he had struck the newcomer with the speed and accuracy of a viper. Groveling on the tile and clutching the blistering welt where the karkaton had struck, the second party silently struggled against the bite of the rod for a space before speaking.

"Did I startle you, Master?" The trespasser humbly backed out of reach and bowed to the ground.

"You should know better, than to approach me in such a manner, Ernic," the first man icily stated and replaced his weapon at his side.

"Forgive me, Master," the servant rose to his feet slowly, but kept his head bowed to show respect for several moments before submissively looking into his lord's eyes. "I often forget that as the Lord Argetallam, you must always be wary of assassins."

"No," the Lord Argetallam emotionlessly corrected, "they should be wary of me." There was no hint of arrogance, nor of boastful vanity in the statement, merely one man stating a fact he believed to be true.

"Indeed, they should be," Ernic agreed with a smile. Ernic was young, barely in his twenties, with a youthful, almost annoying, energy to match. The brand of two parallel black bars on his left palm, marked him as lower than an Argetallam, but the leather garb he wore, marked him as loftier than any other slave in the Staspin Waste. At age six, after watching the slaughter of his family, Ernic had been taken from his home in Brevia, and made to serve the Argetallams. When he had come of age and began thinking treacherous thoughts, they had been purged from his mind. Now he was the most relied-upon servant of the Lord Argetallam, trusted with tasks and secrets that anyone else might be slain for overhearing.

"I must know, Ernic," the Lord Argetallam coldly stated, distractedly pacing along the edge of the fountain. "I must know if the rumors are true."

Ernic nodded attentively.

"I must know if she is still alive," the Lord Argetallam turned away from Ernic and stared off into space. "In the six months since my son's return from his failed mission, the rumors have grown more frequent. They say that she was taken in by the Lord Armandius Caersynn, and from there on the story varies. Some say that she was killed around six months ago; others claim that she still lives." The Lord Argetallam whirled on Ernic suddenly and commanded, "Go, find this Armandius Caersynn and learn if he knows anything about my daughter."

"I would go to hell, if you so wished it, Master," Ernic bowed slightly. "I still wonder, do you not know? I mean, she is your daughter. Would you not have felt it if she died?"

The Lord Argetallam cocked his head threateningly. "Are you implying that I had an emotional attachment to my child?" he demanded.

"Not at all, Master," Ernic placated.

"I gave her a pair of karkaton for that very reason. There is always a chance that she was able to use them and that someone may have dressed whatever wounds she sustained."

"Her powers were the weakest of any Argetallam ever born, Master. I doubt that she could have suspended her wounds for long," Ernic remarked.

"True. But there has been a presence, or spirit

following me at times when none can be seen. If she is alive it could be her," the Lord Argetallam coldly explained.

"How could she be a spirit and alive?" Ernic inquired.

"There is no stronger bond in all the world than that between a parent and a child, with the combined effects of our bloodline's weak connection, it could be causing her mind to be transported through her dreams to here."

"Would it not work both ways then?"

The Lord Argetallam would have killed anyone else who dared to question him this far. However, with Ernic he simply glared with hostility at the youth and moved on. "Find her. My other spies cannot be trusted with this."

"Master?"

"I had five children living here, two years ago, Ernic," the Lord Argetallam coldly stated.

"That many?"

"Now only Lucan, Kestrell, and if she lives, Janir, survive. Someone is purging my offspring. I know not who else I can trust with this."

Ernic nodded. "No one, not even your niece Emilla could torture your commands from my lips," Ernic fervently assured his lord.

The Lord Argetallam scoffed at the idea. "She broke your mind once," he remarked.

"But only to make sure that I would never betray Argetallam-kind. The thought she placed in my mind is still strong, and I will do anything to obey it," Ernic sincerely and heartily assured his master.

With satisfaction, the Lord Argetallam saw that his niece's hold over Ernic was unweakened after all these years. Under her uncle's tutelage, Emilla had never tortured a man she could not break.

"But I must say," Ernic added, "that it is unlikely she survived the massacre at the Norwin Pass. Even if she did, the Brevians likely killed her as soon as she was discovered."

"Of that I am aware," the Lord Argetallam coldly replied. "But if I understand Armandius as I believe I do, he has a reason for keeping my daughter alive. That and her mother never lied to me."

"Forgive me Master, but what reason could a Brevian possibly have?" Ernic ventured, then ducked his head, realizing that it may have been too probing a question.

The Lord Argetallam glared at him. "My daughter is not mine alone," he icily replied.

"Master?"

"She had a mother, you know," the Lord Argetallam carelessly pointed out. "'Caersynn' was Aryana's name. Fascinating, do you not agree, that a man with the same name is rumored to be aiding an Argetallam?"

"Aryana?" Ernic's brow wrinkled.

"Yes. That was the name of my daughter's mother."

"I know, Milord," Ernic bowed. "But if you'll forgive me for saying so, you seldom use the names of any of your other courtesans…"

"Your point is?" the Lord Argetallam demanded.

"I was wondering why, Master," Ernic knelt to his knees and touched his forehead to the stone, sensing that this conversation was entering dangerous territory. But knowing that now he had asked, the query must be followed through.

"It is no concern of yours," the Lord Argetallam snapped, clubbing Ernic in the back of the head.

"True, true. I ask your forgiveness, Master," Ernic remorsefully groveled.

"Your apology is noted, if you wish forgiveness, journey to Brevia and learn if this rumored maiden is indeed my daughter. Go!"

ACKNOWLEDGMENTS

I would like to thank all the people involved in the editing, design, and publication of this book. I never could have achieved what I have without your help. Special thanks to: Sam L. Pfiester, for giving me my big break; Suzanne O'Bryan and Walt Herbert, for their insightful editorial work; and Lynn Rohm, for so beautifully designing and formatting my manuscript.

8682469R0

Made in the USA
Charleston, SC
03 July 2011